Praise for *Bad News of the Heart*:

"Douglas Glover is a writer of the greatest and most variegated gifts. The dozen stories in *Bad News of the Heart* seem to have been written by twelve distinct, extraordinary talents. Sharp and clear in tone, it is a funny book and sad, poetic and gritty by turns, and always magnificent. Glover is that rarest of artists, a true master in an age that needs masters desperately."—Darin Strauss

"Douglas Glover's stories are bizarre, wild, and Byzantine in their telling, excursions into the intricate worlds of exploded love, erotic insanity, brutal lunatic despair. He casts a benevolent eye on his lonely and often paranoid souls, finding corners that shine through the madness with slapstick logic and undefeated laughter. Douglas Glover is a gifted writer, a provocateur of the language."—William Kennedy

"*Bad News of the Heart* is good news for those of us who love fine original fiction. Douglas Glover is a writer who has not only mastered the art of the page turning narrative but has done so with intimacy and humor, no easy task. This is a collection that will not only surely please discerning readers everywhere but will hold an appeal to all fans of popular fiction. Give this book a try—you will be rewarded."—Oscar Hijuelos

"Douglas Glover's stories are extraordinarily rich and multi-faceted—full of dark humor, ingenuity, and passion."—Madison Smartt Bell

"Douglas Glover seduces you with prose that is clever, sarcastic, lecherous, original and precise, and then—just when you think you have his number—he turns you upside down, slays you with an unexpected phrase, and makes you realize you were a fool to think you could categorize him. In the confines of a sentence, he can stagger your mind with insight, flush your face with outrage, double you over with amusement, or, quite simply and sharply, break your heart. Anyone who cares about storytelling, desire, or language—hell, anyone who *reads*—should be reading Douglas Glover."—Lisa Carey

Bad News of the Heart

DOUGLAS GLOVER

Dalkey Archive Press

"La Corriveau," "My Romance," "Iglaf and Swan," "The Indonesian Client," "Bad News of the Heart," "State of the Nation," and "A Piece of the True Cross" originally appeared in *16 Categories of Desire*. Copyright © 2000 by Douglas Glover. Published in this edition by arrangement with the originating publisher, Goose Lane Editions.

"Why I Decide to Kill Myself and Other Jokes," "The Obituary Writer," "A Man in a Box," and "A Guide to Animal Behaviour" originally appeared in *A Guide to Animal Behaviour*. Copyright © 1991 by Douglas Glover. Published in this edition by arrangement with the originating publisher, Goose Lane Editions.

"Dog Attempts to Drown Man in Saskatoon" originally appeared in *Dog Attempts to Drown Man in Saskatoon*. Copyright © 1985 by Douglas Glover. Published in this edition by arrangement with the originating publisher, Talonbooks.

Cover art copyright © 2002 by Andrzej Michael Karwacki at 1217studios.com

Library of Congress Cataloging-in-Publication Data

Glover, Douglas H., 1948–
    Bad news of the heart / Douglas Glover.— 1st ed.
        p. cm.
    ISBN 1-56478-286-7 (pbk. : alk. paper)
    1. United States—Social life and customs—Fiction. I. Title.

PR9199.3.G584B3 2003
813'.54—dc21

                                                          2002041510

Partially funded by grants from the Lannan Foundation and the Illinois Arts Council, a state agency.

Dalkey Archive Press books are published by the Center for Book Culture, a nonprofit organization.

www.centerforbookculture.org

Printed on permanent/durable acid-free paper and bound in the United States of America.

Contents

BAD NEWS OF THE HEART

Iglaf and Swan

THIS IS HOW IT GOES: a boy named Iglaf, whose parents had immigrated from Estonia in the 1940s after much trouble in their native land, met a girl named Swan at a potluck supper and open mike poetry reading in the basement of the Estonian Church on Broadview the summer of 1969. They became lovers that night, burnt a hole in his mattress with an overturned candle, drank wine from peanut butter jars and read their poems aloud between embraces. Near dawn they fell asleep in each other's arms, but then Swan woke up, wrapped a sheet around her breasts, sniffed the smell of burnt ticking in her hair, and stared at him. What was she trying to make out? What had disturbed her sleep?

The fierceness of her regard woke Iglaf from a dream—as he remembered it later, something about a book he had read or written. He rubbed his eyes, then met her gaze. Something in her face turned his heart to stone. He knew that he loved her. He knew that she loved him. But he knew Swan would never stay. His life was over in that moment. All hope abandoned. The future a nightmare of cajolery, recrimination, begging and jealousy. In that moment, he knew he would lose himself trying to keep her, and, having made that sacrifice, fail. But also in that moment he decided that a year, a month, even a day of Swan's love was worth any sacrifice. He even convinced himself that his was a romantic gesture, that there was some glory in a life of misery, some salvation in throwing himself away for those breasts, those eyes. In any case, it was already too late, and he knew it. Later it occurred to him that maybe he had never really had the courage to be himself—a poet, an adventurer, anyway—that he had needed a way out of that terrible struggle, that he found the lesser vision comfortably definite.

Swan, an insightful and intelligent girl, comprehended all this in an instant. The light of love guttered in her heart, a flash of loathing exploded in her head, though she was careful to disguise it with a rueful smile and a knowing twinkle in her eye. Iglaf interpreted this knowing twinkle as the kindling of desire for him. With a rush of gratitude, he took her in his arms, and they began to make love again, slowly, despairingly. She wept this time. It hurt when he moved inside her, though she whispered "I love you" over and over as his passion rose. When it was over, she loathed herself as well.

It took Iglaf and Swan ten years to separate. He was teaching high school English in Forest Hill, she spent mornings looking after their daughter Lily and afternoons working at a futon store on St. Clair, where she made love to the owner in a dusty storage room. The owner's name was Kreuzen. He was her father's age, a Czech émigré, also bitter, lost. He made love violently, briskly, without any preamble or pretence of emotion. His face was a rigid mask of anger when he came. He would tell her nothing about his past. The mask was all she had. But this suited Swan. Kreuzen's wife had left him years before. He had a grown son about Swan's age, who, once a month, would stand at the shop door, shouting, "You fucking pig! You fucking pig!" "He's an actor," said Kreuzen. "He can't get work. You have to hate your father if you're an actor and can't work."

Kreuzen would sit in the storeroom behind the futon shop for hours during the day or talk in his own language to a steady stream of shabby visitors. Swan would read him her poetry, to which he would respond with a tired shrug. Sometimes she would meet one or another of the Czech men who came to visit Kreuzen. Each time she would tell Iglaf and the brief spasms of emotion which followed seemed to sustain them, feed their love.

Iglaf put on weight, wore vests and threadbare secondhand tweed jackets, smoked a pipe and affected a world-weary wisdom which he used to seduce a series of female students. These affairs followed a hair-raising pattern of infatuation, obsession and then disengagement which involved public scenes, hysterical tears on the girl's part, bitter recrimination. Twice he nearly got fired from his job, but each time Swan saved him by sitting through the internal inquiries holding his hand (the first time she actually breast-fed Lily during the proceedings), facing down angry parents, testifying about his goodness, his professionalism, the wonder of their marriage. Always, Iglaf managed to shift the blame onto the girl. But, without saying anything, Iglaf and Swan both knew they wouldn't be able to save him a third time.

One summer in the late seventies, Swan enrolled in an evening writing course. She did this because, she told herself, some outside structure—a regular class, an instructor—would get her writing poetry again. "I lost myself in my marriage," she told Iglaf, who said nothing, but winced. It was a subtle gesture he had perfected over the years, a slight lowering of the shoulders, a shadowing of the eyes, a turning away. Swan and Lily reacted to the wince with guilt, a stab of pain. Swan would rage inwardly about the wince, but Lily spent her days trying to keep her father from wincing. She thought that when he didn't wince it was love.

Of them all, Kreuzen was the most truthful. He said, "You never stopped writing poetry. You're just not very good at it. You're like my son. You use art and your lives as excuses for each other." Swan spent the afternoon weeping on Kreuzen's cot, then dragged all her notebooks, drafts, diaries—everything she kept at the futon shop—to the dumpster. She knew she was finished, that she had failed at her whole life. But oddly that realization made her feel cleaned out and powerful. Kreuzen watched dispassionately. He said, "Now you'll leave us. You're making a dramatic exit. I've done my job." When she tried to kiss him, he told her to get out.

A week later she was sleeping with her writing teacher and trying not to remember what Kreuzen had said, that she had ever been in the back of the futon store. The writing instructor had published one book of poems years before and showed no promise any longer of writing another. He was married but made a practice of sleeping with at least one of his students each term, in fact had come to think of this as one of the requirements of his profession. At first he had seen his student lovers as the bright new stars who would rouse him from his artistic slumber. He had believed himself in love—several times. But now he resented Swan for her naïve hopes, her sentimental and self-serving little poems and her lovely body. Rather than giving him new energy, she seemed almost to be sucking the energy out of him, though he could not fathom how. Everything he did he did out of anger.

Swan, for her part, saw him as a great soul—she mistook his fatigued restraint for a species of spiritual tranquility. She called him her poetry guru and was, briefly, cheerful and optimistic. While she was sleeping with the poetry teacher, she was also beginning to hope she might rebuild her marriage. Her new sexual energy radiated throughout the house. Even Lily noticed, and the little girl began to imitate her mother's hip-rolling walk, her casual way of strolling through rooms half-clothed, her habit of singing to herself the current pop tunes that were already a little too young for her.

Iglaf noticed, too, and took advantage of the new warmth. Their sex had never been better: nights, they smoked dope and experimented with each other's bodies, fantasizing together, playing roles, pushing each other to new ecstasies. But this new sex was also strangely empty, and one day Lily woke up and caught her parents in bed with another woman, one of Swan's poetry friends, a pretty blond girl with a tattoo on her belly and a knowing eye.

A year later, Swan and her tattooed friend were hitchhiking through Europe and North Africa. She had borrowed money from Iglaf and Kreuzen. Swan already felt too old for this, spent her days in a confusion of anxiety, moodiness and self-reproach until she found a new boy to fuck. She wrote long, witty, self-ironic letters to Lily and Kreuzen—sometimes the same letter to both—describing her tour as a series of comic-erotic misadventures. The letters made her feel creative again. They were easier to write than poetry. She ended each with a request for Kreuzen or Lily to keep the letter safe for the book she was going to make out of them when she came home.

Lily stayed with Iglaf. At first, after her parents separated, there had been an attempt to share custody. They had shuttled her back and forth between them in taxis with a little duffel full of clothes, stuffed toys and homework. They had argued endlessly over child support, clothing allowances, gym fees, drop-off times, sick days. Swan had brought home lovers. Lily could hear them making love in the bedroom from the daybed where she slept. Iglaf had grown weepy, depressed. He blamed himself for everything, especially blamed himself for falling in love with Swan and wasting his talent. Lily tried to comfort him. She kept his apartment clean, did the washing, cooked small meals or ordered out. Iglaf watched television while Lily bustled around, trying to be cheerful. Years later, he would say he had had a nervous breakdown.

Now, Lily was ten. She hid her mother's letters from Iglaf. He had gone cold to her, rarely spoke, dressed with elaborate punctilio for work and wore a series of flamboyant hats to cover his thinning hair. Everything he said and did around Lily was a rebuke, as if to say, "All this is because of you." He talked to women on the phone long into the night, his voice dropping to a stage whisper, then bursting into loud peals of laughter. He bought pornographic magazines by mail and took to sunbathing naked in a hidden corner up on the roof of their building. But he never saw anyone, never went out. He would sit in front of the TV with an unread mystery novel in his lap and a can of beer in his hand, spend hours like that.

Once, Lily overheard Iglaf telling one of his telephone women that he was writing again, that he had gotten through mourning his marriage and had found his voice. She was briefly hopeful. He had always said writing was the only thing that made him happy. But then she realized it was just a story he was telling, that all his art went into those late night phone conversations. What she remembered most from that period were Iglaf's maniacal smile, his lips stretched taut over his gums, his teeth shining big and too white against the tan of his face, and the heavy sag of his genitals in the bikini briefs he wore when he came slipping back from his tanning sessions.

Lily began to write, first poems, then stories, sweet little girl stories full of elves and fairies and made up words. She had a fantasy, a vision of her own death, and her father coming upon her writings in an old trunk under her bed, weeping at the beauty of her words. Pale, dressed in black, she roamed the city, nervous, fearful, always looking down but conscious of the way lone men and boys stared at her, vaguely excited by this. On her eleventh birthday, she got a letter from her mother—the first in a month—with an amusing account of how Swan had caught herpes from a man she met in a Venice disco.

Swan was still sick when she came back from Europe. She had stopped eating, grown gaunt. Her breath was bad, her sores refused to clear up. She imagined she had cancer. She told Lily, "I'm scared. I can't stop myself from doing anything but eat." At first, because she had no money and nowhere to go, she stayed with Iglaf, sleeping on a cot in Lily's room. She slept through the mornings, went to yoga classes, drank herbal remedies she bought from a Chinese apothecary off Spadina Avenue. In the night she would dream the same dream over and over: she was on a stage under a fierce spotlight, naked. The audience, men and women, jeered and pelted her with garbage. She would begin to touch herself, almost fainting from the shame and dark excitement, while the shouts and laughter grew louder and louder. In her sleep, she would roll over on her belly and begin to masturbate, sometimes waking Lily with her sighs, waking herself when she came, hating herself.

Iglaf was thirty-three, looked years older with his thinning hair, sun-hardened skin and salt-and-pepper beard. He frightened Lily and Swan with his manic cheerfulness, his too-wide smile that seemed to conceal a violent threat. He would play the gracious host around Swan, then lose control of himself and try to paw her, begging her to make love. Once Lily woke up to find her father naked in her bedroom, sobbing noisily, trying to pull the blankets off Swan, Swan's sleepy, petulant voice whispering, "No, no, no." This frigid, hysterical travesty of a family mystified Lily. She thought the forced cheerfulness of her parents, seated across from each other at the dinner table, was love, but love made her feel as if there were an iron belt around her belly, cinched tighter and tighter each day. Love made her want to die.

She had a boyfriend now, a pale, skinny kid who called himself Captain Nemo, which he said was the Latin word for nobody. He was four years older than Lily, but somehow naïve and unworldly, which appealed to her. He wore his hair in a pink Mohawk and carved up his hands and arms with ballpoint pen tattoos. They would wander the city together, day and night, Nemo declaiming his rebellious philosophy of life in hoarse, fearful whispers while Lily listened, barely uttering a word. They would go into the ravines to smoke dope when Lily had money or sometimes sniff glue when she didn't. They drank cheap wine once and vomited over each other. Sometimes they would try to make love, but they were nervous and inexperienced and had no notion of tenderness. Nemo mostly came before he could enter her. Lily hated sex, but she was deeply attached to Nemo, would do anything for him.

It was a strange, narrow world Lily had entered. She cut school, had no friends besides Nemo. She had been betrayed in so many ways that she could not imagine a world of constancy and trust. As she closed herself off more and more from the outside just to keep safe, she even began to feel that she had betrayed herself. Her confusion and loathing turned inward. She seemed to walk among the dead. Even Nemo noticed how quiet she had become, how she seemed to soak up words and energy without reacting, how everything sank into Lily, seemed to tremble on the surface a moment, and then eerily slip out of sight. Her deadness frightened him.

Lily was still writing. She no longer knew why. She filled notebook after notebook with rambling fantasy romances, tales of gentle knights in armour and princesses under spells or trapped in towers, goblins, ogres, dwarves, elves and sorcerers. When she wrote, she remembered her father's agonized attempts to drive himself at his desk or her mother's voice mumbling poems to herself while Lily drifted off to sleep in her crib—her very own Madonna of the Poems. She remembered all her parents' brave dreams and their disappointments. She was in love with the sad drama of their lives. But when Captain Nemo finally blushed and stuttered out the words "I love you," she fled from him as if wounded.

This is a dark story, growing darker still: before she turned fifteen, Lily was dead. At the end, she had come to think of herself as a mistake, a misprint, an unintended result. It seemed a simple thing to fix with Valium from Swan's medicine cabinet and a plastic garbage bag from under the sink. Lily had learned to adore unconsciousness, blackouts and altered states—ecstasy was in becoming nothing. Nothingness had a voluptuousness she found nowhere else in life. She became greedy for it the way others become greedy for sex. Nemo noticed when no one else did. He noticed the way her eyes worked, the way she stopped looking at him and, instead, stared greedily and nervously at the drugs he brought. Unconsciousness became her companion. Nothingness became her lover. It wiped out her childish fantasies, which she had come to despise. She stopped writing when she knew no one would ever read what she wrote.

Briefly, on the night of Lily's death, Iglaf and Swan were together again. Swan was incoherent, bereft; Iglaf put his heart into arranging things for Lily and thought about nothing else. His grief and his quiet competence gave Iglaf a dignity Swan had never noticed before. To Iglaf his woundedness was a sign that had no meaning until his daughter died, and when she died, he was suddenly whole. Her death gave him a role he had been practicing for all his life. But the way he bore his suffering comforted Swan. They had lost everything; no one else knew how much, and how much they had subconsciously depended on Lily to make up their losses, to be their audience and interlocutor. Now Swan wanted his dignity to be a model for her own.

When Iglaf dropped Swan at her apartment, she asked him to stay.

At first, he only held her; she brewed tea; they reminded each other of the night Lily was born and made each other weep. Momentarily, Iglaf lost his composure; in Swan's arms, he moaned, "What have we done?" and she said, "Shh, my darling" and kissed him. They both knew there was some trickery involved; they had acted so long, they no longer yearned for an end to the acting but for clear and simple parts, as close as most of us come to honesty. Swan lit candles and read Lily's poems aloud, while Iglaf slouched in her bedroom easy chair, his waistcoat unbuttoned, his arms hanging down, looking like a Victorian illustration. When they made love, finally, they wept and said Lily's name. They had never before felt so close, and the closeness aroused them. Without saying anything, they both knew they wanted to make another child, to call back the girl who had died, the family they had never been. They made love that way, as though they were in love, their soft, pathetic voices whispering to each other desperately of love and promises.

For a moment, they both forgot they had other lovers, that their lives had become petty, shallow and tawdry. Iglaf poured himself into Swan again and again with an abandonment he had never felt. He caught himself gloating over his prowess but pushed the thought from his mind. Swan submitted—to everything. She had never been so open to a man, but, thinking that, comparing this moment to others, she felt the edge of self-consciousness rising and pictured Lily's body to drive her back into the ecstasy of loss. With Lily gone, they both thought, there is no one else and no tomorrow. They only wished that the moment could go on and on, that they could exist forever on the cusp of someone else's death, that they could always feel this important, tragic and redeemed.

The next day, they lingered in bed as long as they could, alternating fits of weeping with laughter and a kind of childish, gleeful lust. But they were exhausted, and the pure orgasms of the night before escaped them. A different kind of sadness grew in them, a sense of emptiness and failure, as Iglaf made the necessary phone calls, trying moment by moment to keep the world at bay. Swan made breakfast; they looked at photo albums and read the poems again. Then Iglaf left to get changed, and Swan's latest boyfriend came by to comfort her. But through the funeral and the wake, they had a kind of intensity together. And they both knew they would never feel this close to love again.

Soon Swan was living with a painter on Beverley Street, a man with a studio loft in the old clothing district on Spadina, a gruff, silent man who painted lucrative, if old-fashioned, abstract expressionist works on large canvasses for corporate clients and loathed himself. Swan realized she fell for men who hated themselves and hated her and called it love. She had figured this out from her therapist, who also hated himself and had seduced her. She did not think the therapist was either wise or a guru. Sex had become a plumbing issue for Swan. When she watched her painter, she wondered what he thought, painstakingly but mechanically applying the colour. She thought how hopeless it all must seem. "It's not about hope," he said. "I get paid to be a cliché, which is better than being a cliché and not getting paid for it."

Iglaf was in therapy, too, trying to fix himself, rid himself of the self-pity that dogged his life. He was living with a plain, depressed woman he called Rubenesque but whom he was not so secretly ashamed of. "She does things for him in bed no one else will," said Swan, who had lost the anxious restraint that had once attracted men and become, suddenly, crude. Iglaf told everyone how his marriage had destroyed his writing and how no one in Canada could write anyway because it was a debased and barren culture. He invoked Lily and the names of other poetic suicides and somehow managed to imply that he was one of them, only not quite dead yet. He was always saying, "We must get together and talk about writing." He founded writers' groups at the school where he taught, groups mostly for serious girls and introverted boys. He loved to inspire in others the dream of his own noble failure, the mountains he had barely failed to climb, and a sense of their own mediocrity and doom within the context of Canada. He loved making the children feel bad about themselves while, on the surface, appearing to nurture them.

Swan herself was making a small splash in the Toronto poetry world as Lily's mother, as the guardian of her words. Swan carefully collected, organized and rewrote Lily's poems and diaries. It did not seem to bother her that the poems and diaries damned her, and, of course, she cut the most direct references, telling herself that occasionally Lily's thinking had been reductive and maladroit (we all blame our mothers and fathers). It seemed to Swan that Lily had been born sad, that she had been doomed from the beginning, and she presented herself as heroic and self-sacrificing in the face of her daughter's depression. Lily's poems came out, first in small magazines, then as a book. The critics compared her with Sylvia Plath and Anne Sexton and the boy poet Chatterton. And when she read them in public, Swan briefly forgot that they weren't her poems. She felt like herself, beautiful and poetic, the centre of attention, with the lights shining down and her strong, unfaltering voice declaiming the words of the one person she had truly loved (who, in those moments, did not seem distinguishable from herself).

For Iglaf, who once or twice came to Swan's readings, these moments spawned a strange dementia. He saw himself and Swan reading their poetry nearly twenty years before in the church basement on Broadview, remembered making love, the smell of burnt ticking, the sultry resonance of Swan's voice and the long, shameful years that followed, and making love again the night Lily died. He remembered Lily, though he could not remember her well, just as he could no longer remember who he was himself. That he was partly aware of this only made matters worse. As a test, he tried to remember the last poem he had read and loved. He shuddered. Paradoxically, he found a certain erotic pleasure in his shame, in submitting to the deep humiliation of each new moment. He tried to remember what Lily looked like. He tried to concentrate on the poems Swan was reading, but couldn't. His face wore that toothy grin, tears splashed down his cheeks. His eyes were fixed on Swan, but he saw nothing. He knew that it was all an act, that all he had was his shame, and that, even so, everything that had happened had happened for love.

All the rest is twilight, bits of life manufactured without hope. Iglaf and Swan are not old; there are no dramatic exits available. Swan marries the painter. She learns to cook and mounts elegant dinner parties at which she drinks too much and talks too loudly. She has a shrewd eye for human foible and makes an art of insidious seating arrangements. She loves to revive old feuds, or encourage lushes to backslide, or provoke jealous arguments between young lovers. Swan herself grows nervous and rancorous as these evenings wear on and often ends up being ushered to bed in tears before the party is over. She gets away with this because the painter is powerful and despises everyone and enjoys watching his wife make a fool of herself and his friends.

Iglaf marries the Rubenesque woman, who promptly becomes obese. He drags her around, embarrassment incarnate, though secretly his voluptuary tastes run to masochism, and she suits his darker fantasies. The Rubenesque woman, whipsawed between Iglaf's desires and his coldness, grows ever more depressed, tearful and needy. He adores young women, the younger the better, but, paradoxically, is quite safe now because he is so obvious and repulsive. He still corners earnest girls after class and exclaims, through that toothy grin, "We must talk about writing." Perversely, he seems to enjoy the discomfort he causes. For Iglaf affection is corruption, and any effect is better than no effect.

From time to time, Swan and Iglaf meet, for they both still haunt the fringes of the Toronto literary scene. They cannot conceal their envy of youth and passion and, of course, writers who manage to write. They are fading, but desire never ends—only, after a time, it twists into some reduced caricature of itself. Iglaf and Swan have become the kind of readers who confuse criticism with discrimination.

But the harsh lights always reveal a harsher reality. Swan is not well. A new sore is beginning to appear on her lip, concealed with foundation and lipstick. Her nose is pinched, her hair brittle and not quite the right colour for her skin. Iglaf sees this and pities her, though in pitying her he pities himself. And seeing her straining for a sense of triumph against the weight of despair in her heart makes him love her again, or makes him think, at least, that they are alike, harbour the same paradoxes and aborted dreams.

He will hang about Swan, on these occasions, emitting guffaws of laughter, looking quite mad but full of a certain proprietary solicitude which does not escape her. Swan will feel Iglaf beside her in a way, she thinks, she has not felt him for years. He is overweight, too tanned, affects the same tweed jacket and the cap to hide his baldness. That smile is chiselled into his face, his manner is enthusiastic and unctuous. But she, too, all at once, feels a vast pity for his brave front. Swan suddenly remembers the boy Iglaf, how his naiveté, his abashed sweetness and embarrassed stoop once charmed her. And she thinks briefly that we fall in love with each other's failings, with our own vulnerabilities mirrored in the other.

She sees his sadness. Something too difficult to untangle comes into her heart. Everything is ruined, she thinks. The thought wars with her hardened facade, the contradictions rip through her. She too remembers the smell of burnt ticking, the feel of the bed sheet wrapped around her. Words like fate and history and love slip through her head but find no place to catch and hold. More and more, she has noticed, the words all seem spoken by someone else. Beyond the words, there exists only a mysterious emptiness. The feelings she recognizes as her own—shame, boredom, embarrassment, regret, resentment—remind her only that she once believed there was a message, but she has gotten it wrong. She suddenly feels panicky, lost in an endless regress of negation: she has gotten it wrong, but what if she is wrong about getting it wrong?

In her confusion, Swan reaches for Iglaf and touches his wrist protectively. Iglaf feels her touch and falls silent. The warmth of her hand seems a balm for all his wounds. The phrase "aborted dreams" sticks in his mind, and he remembers a dream from long ago, something about a book he had read or written. There is a thought, just on the tip of his tongue, he would like to tell Lily. But it is gone.

State of the Nation

WE IN THE REPUBLIC are exhausted.

Our enemies have lain down their arms, leaving us suddenly without a national purpose.

Brown people are pouring over the border to take up work we heedlessly relinquish in our pursuit of leisure and sexual gratification.

Nights, I drive down the coast road to the marshes at the mouth of the Tijuana River and park and watch them crawling across the border like insects.

The country is awash in brown people and perverts of all kinds.

The fat woman across the street (we are four storeys up) has pushed her bed to the window and lolls there naked, exposing herself, masturbating shamelessly with an assortment of household objects: salamis, broom handles, cat brushes, vacuum cleaner attachments, bits of broken furniture, aerosol cans, stereo albums, pizza cutters and cork screws.

Sometimes she simply lies with her head thrown back in ecstasy, holding the lips of her vulva open.

This is an electrifying development, let me tell you.

All of a sudden, I have an attention span again.

Prior to this, I often couldn't think of a reason to go out or stay in (except at night when the sewagy, rotting smell of the Tijuana wafted me southwards along the coast road). Occasionally, I have stood before the door for hours on end, trying to decide what to do.

Now I race to get up before she does, shower and comb my hair, then dash down the stairs for a box of week-old raspberry Danish pastries, five pounds of salted peanuts and a dozen Mexican beers. Usually I am in position, stretched on my Naugahyde recliner in front of the window, before she stirs, before she thrusts the first dainty foot from beneath her soiled pink sheets.

Sometimes she waves.

On one hand, I keep a cooler for the beer, a carton of Marlboros, a slab of Irish butter, my pastries and peanuts. On the other, I have a large steel garbage can (I am a firm believer in design efficiency).

I throw the trash—bottles, rinds, husks, butts, packaging, spent matches—into the garbage can, which occasionally leads to minor fires that annoy the neighbours, but cause no more harm than a little localized air pollution and a mark like a storm cloud on my ceiling.

Once I woke up to find the hair on the left side of my head blazing like a fatwood torch.

One day we meet accidentally in the greeting card shop at the corner (I go there to read—I can't get through a whole book anymore).

I'm abashed. I have nothing to say.

She says, Are you the guy with the telescope?

I nod. I am wearing a leather World War I aviator's helmet with goggles, a white silk scarf, yellow shorts printed with nodding palm fronds and Birkenstocks.

I don't want to fuck you, she says. I want things to go on just as they are. You understand? Only I want to see you too. Everything. I have binoculars. I'll watch.

A purulent musk assails my nostrils. Sweat pools in deltas under her arms, slides down the side of her nose like translucent snails.

Her eyes roll up in terror.

She flails the air with her arms, then tilts backward into an array of comic wedding anniversary cards and crashes to the floor.

I can see what effort this terse communication has cost her. This access of vulnerability has its own peculiar allure.

And I rush away in a panic, fearing nothing so much as love and the loss of love, worried above all else that, having revealed herself, she will now retreat into the shell of anonymity by which we all protect ourselves from hurt.

But things go on just as before.

Except that now I strip off and parade myself in front of the window from time to time and wave.

She no longer waves back. Engrossed as she is in her pleasure, she rarely has a hand to spare.

Then she tries to kill herself. She lets me watch the whole thing, ripping up sheets to tie off her arms, slicing her wrists vertically instead of horizontally in order to avoid severing the tendons, then letting the blood spurt in a decreasing trajectory over her thighs and sheets.

After a while, I call 911 and save her life.

One of the EMS guys vomits when he enters her apartment. From what I can see, she is not much of a neatness freak.

In the hospital, she mistakes me for someone else, someone named Buddy.

From internal evidence, I conclude that Buddy is her brother, that he disappeared twenty-two years ago after accidentally shooting a boy named Natrone Hales to death in the family garage. The boys were twelve at the time.

I have brought her a spring posy from a gift shop downstairs operated by a blind person who reads the money with his fingers. I got eighty-two dollars in change from a ten-dollar bill.

Presently, she begins to yell at me for going off like that, for never sending a postcard.

I say I called twice, both times on her birthday, and both times I hung up when she answered.

She looks at me. Her features soften. She says I called more than twice like that.

I say, Yeah.

You look about the same, she says.

I tell her about the man who held me in a closet for eight years against my will, the time in the hospital, the girl I loved who died of anthrax, the accident with the car when I had no insurance and had to pay off the kid's medical bills holding down three jobs and how he used to come around in that custom wheelchair and taunt me, about my time in 'Nam, my self-esteem problems, the hole in my nose from drugs, my bladder spasms.

What happened to your hair?

A fire, I say.

I say, I don't think you really know me.

Oh, Buddy, Buddy, Buddy, she says.

I try to lie down beside her on the bed, but there is no beside her. I end up on the floor.

Why did you do that? she asks. You haven't changed.

Who will you want me to be tomorrow? I think, as I leave, realizing that there is a mystery here, a truth about the nature of love, that we are always falling in love with some picture, that the real person eludes us, though he is always jumping up and down in the background, waving his arms and shouting for attention—someone has turned off the sound.

Mostly, I am afraid that with my luck the real Buddy will walk through the door any minute now.

In *Time* magazine, I read that the Buddhists call this place the hungry-ghost world.

On the way out of the hospital, I ask the blind guy at the gift shop for change for a twenty. I give him a five and get forty-nine dollars back.

You made a mistake, I say.

He gives me another ten.

I don't get down to the hospital for a week because I can't figure out who I think she is, maybe just one of those multiple-personality sluts you meet in the bars these days, women who give you five percent of their souls and take no responsibility.

When I do go, she is sitting up in bed with a food tray. She has combed her hair, she's wearing a pink nightgown, she's lost weight.

Ominously, they have untied her hands.

She smiles and says, I'm glad you stopped by.

The voice of total insanity, I think.

I got something for you, she says, handing me a gift-wrapped parcel.

It's a new universal remote for my TV and entertainment centre.

I nearly weep with gratitude. No one has ever given me a present before.

Then I recall that I'm not sure who I am supposed to be today.

She says, A year ago I was a nurse in Arizona. One day, an old prospector drove down out of the Two Heads mountains to drop off a ten-year-old Apache girl he'd bought and got pregnant.

He said we could do what we wanted with her. He just couldn't use her now that she was pregnant. He'd have to go and get another.

The Apache girl didn't even know she was pregnant. The doctors delivered her, then put both of them up for adoption—without ever telling the girl what had really happened to her.

I kept thinking about her, that this important thing had occurred without her knowing it, that somewhere there was another person closer to her than life, without either of them being aware of it. I imagined she must have been haunted by a feeling of something just out of reach, a mystery without a name.

I asked myself, What if, later on, she were to meet her child in the street? Would she just pass by? Or would she feel tugged toward him?

She stops talking for a moment, looks a little frightened.

I say, That's exactly the relationship I have with reality most days.

She smiles again and says, I guess I cracked up. I believe drugs and alcohol were involved. They are most of the time.

You mean you're normal now? I ask.

You're not Buddy, are you?

I am out of there, a crushing weight on my chest—heartburn or love, I can't tell which.

The blind guy at the gift shop is watching the local news on TV with the volume on high torque. A band of Yuma Indians on the border near Nogales has just sold its tribal land to the city of San Diego for a landfill and plans to use the money to start a casino.

We should put 'em on a boat and send 'em back where they came from, he says.

I ask for a Snickers bar and give him a five.

He gives me back four Jacksons and change.

I say, I can't take this. You counted wrong.

Oh boy, he says. Just checking. I got burned twice last week. Called the cops. Eight of them got the place staked out right now, waiting for my signal.

Don't die, I think, suddenly fearful.

I click back to CNN and catch the news from the Republic of Paranoia, where only victims are citizens with rights.

Hell, our army won't even consider fighting a country where the people can afford shoes anymore.

I knew a woman once who said love is nothing but a mechanism for heat exchange.

She said, We are just roadkill on the highway to nowhere.

I click the remote and see myself as a slim young man with a future. I see my country, violent and innocent again, like a flash of sheet lightning in history. I see her cradling a child to her breast, the child feeling absolutely safe and unafraid.

I think, Sadness, sadness, sadness.

Dog Attempts to Drown Man in Saskatoon

My wife and I decide to separate, and then suddenly we are almost happy together. The pathos of our situation, our private and unique tragedy, lends romance to each small act. We see everything in the round, the facets as opposed to the flat banality that was wedging us apart. When she asks me to go to the Mendel Art Gallery Sunday afternoon, I do not say no with the usual mounting irritation that drives me into myself. I say yes and some hardness within me seems to melt into a pleasant sadness. We look into each other's eyes and realize with a start that we are looking for the first time because it is the last. We are both thinking, "Who is this person to whom I have been married? What has been the meaning of our relationship?" These are questions we have never asked ourselves; we have been a blind couple groping with each other in the dark. Instead of saying to myself, "Not the art gallery again! What does she care about art? She has no education. She's merely bored and on Sunday afternoon in Saskatoon the only place you can go is the old sausage-maker's mausoleum of art!" Instead of putting up arguments, I think, "Poor Lucy, pursued by the assassins of her past, unable to be still. Perhaps if I had her memories I also would be unable to stay in on a Sunday afternoon." Somewhere that cretin Pascal says that all our problems stem from not being able to sit quietly in a room alone. If Pascal had had Lucy's mother, he would never have written anything so foolish. Also, at the age of nine, she saw her younger brother run over and killed by a highway roller. Faced with that, would Pascal have written anything? (Now I am defending my wife against Pascal! A month ago I would have used the same passage to bludgeon her.)

Note. Already this is not the story I wanted to tell. That is buried, gone, lost—its action fragmented and distorted by inexact recollection. Directly it was completed, it had disappeared, gone with the past into that strange realm of suspended animation, that coatrack of despair, wherein all our completed acts await, gathering dust, until we come for them again. I am trying to give you the truth, though I could try harder, and only refrain because I know that that way leads to madness. So I offer an approximation, a shadow play, such as would excite children, full of blind spots and irrelevant adumbrations, too little in parts; elsewhere too much. Alternately I will frustrate you and lead you astray. I can only say that, at the outset, my intention was otherwise; I sought only clarity and simple conclusions. Now I know the worst—that reasons are out of joint with actions, that my best explanation will be obscure, subtle and unsatisfying, and that the human mind is a tangle of unexplored pathways.

"My wife and I decide to separate, and then suddenly we are almost happy together." This is a sentence full of ironies and lies. For example, I call her my wife. Technically this is true. But now that I am leaving, the thought is in both our hearts: "Can a marriage of eleven months really be called a marriage?" Moreover, it was only a civil ceremony, a ten-minute formality performed at the City Hall by a man who, one could tell, had been drinking heavily over lunch. Perhaps if we had done it in a cathedral surrounded by robed priests intoning Latin benedictions we would not now be falling apart. As we put on our coats to go to the art gallery, I mention this idea to Lucy. "A year," she says. "With Latin we might have lasted a year." We laugh. This is the most courageous statement she has made since we became aware of our defeat, better than all her sour tears. Usually she is too self-conscious to make jokes. Seeing me smile, she blushes and becomes confused, happy to have pleased me, happy to be happy, in the final analysis, happy to be sad because the sadness frees her to be what she could never be before. Like many people, we are both masters of beginnings and endings, but founder in the middle of things. It takes a wise and mature individual to manage that which intervenes, the duration which is a necessary part of life and marriage. So there is a sense in which we are not married, though something is ending. And therein lies the greater irony. For in ending, in separating, we are finally and ineluctably together, locked as it were in a ritual recantation. We are going to the art gallery (I am guilty of over-determining the symbol) together.

It is winter in Saskatoon, to my mind the best of seasons because it is the most inimical to human existence. The weather forecaster gives the temperature, the wind chill factor and the number of seconds it takes to freeze exposed skin. Driving between towns one remembers to pack a winter survival kit (matches, candle, chocolate, flares, down sleeping bag) in case of a breakdown. Earlier in the week just outside the city limits a man disappeared after setting out to walk a quarter of a mile from one farmhouse to another, swallowed up by the cold prairie night. (This is, I believe, a not unpleasant way to die once the initial period of discomfort has been passed.) Summer in Saskatoon is a collection of minor irritants: heat and dust, blackflies and tent caterpillars, the nighttime electrical storms that leave the unpaved concession roads impassable troughs of gumbo mud. But winter has the beauty of a plausible finality. I drive out to the airport early in the morning to watch jets land in a pink haze of ice crystals. During the long nights the *aurora borealis* seems to touch the rooftops. But best of all is the city itself which takes on a kind of ghostliness, a dreamlike quality that combines emptiness (there seem to be so few people) and the mists rising from the heated buildings to produce a mystery. Daily I tramp the paths along the riverbank, crossing and re-crossing the bridges, watching the way the city changes in the pale winter light. Beneath me the unfrozen parts of the river smoke and boil, raging to become still. Winter in Saskatoon is a time of anxious waiting and endurance; all that beauty is alien, a constant threat. Many things do not endure. Our marriage, for example, was vernal, a product of the brief, sweet prairie spring.

Neither Lucy nor I was born here; Mendel came from Russia. In fact there is a feeling of the camp about Saskatoon, the temporary abode. At the university there are photographs of the town—in 1905 there were three frame buildings and a tent. In a bar I nearly came to blows with a man campaigning to preserve a movie theatre built in 1934. In Saskatoon that is ancient history, that is the cave painting at Lascaux. Lucy hails from an even newer settlement in the wild Peace River country where her father went to raise cattle and ended up a truck mechanic. Seven years ago she came to Saskatoon to work in a garment factory (her left hand bears a burn scar from a clothes press). Next fall she begins law school. Despite this evidence of intelligence, determination and ability, Lucy has no confidence in herself. In her mother's eyes she will never measure up, and that is all that is important. I myself am a proud man and a gutter snob. I wear a ring in my left ear and my hair long. My parents migrated from a farm in Wisconsin to a farm in Saskatchewan in 1952 and still drive back every year to see the trees. I am two courses short of a degree in philosophy which I will never receive. I make my living at what comes to hand, house painting when I am wandering; since I settled with Lucy, I've worked as the lone overnight editor at the local newspaper. Against the bosses, I am a union man; against the union, I am an independent. When the publisher asked me to work days, I quit. That was a month ago. That was when Lucy knew I was leaving. Deep down she understands my nature. Mendel is another case: he was a butcher and a man who left traces. Now on the north bank of the river there are giant meat-packing plants spilling forth the odours of death, guts and excrement. Across the street are the holding pens for the cattle and the rail lines that bring them to slaughter. Before building his art gallery Mendel actually kept his paintings in this sprawling complex of buildings, inside the slaughterhouse. If you went to his office, you would sit in a waiting room with a Picasso or a Rouault on the wall. Perhaps even a van Gogh. The gallery is downriver at the opposite end of the city, very clean and modern. But whenever I go there I hear the panicky bellowing of the death-driven steers and see the streams of blood and the carcasses and smell the stench and imagine the poor beasts rolling their eyes at Gauguin's green and luscious leaves as the bolt enters their brains.

We have decided to separate. It is a wintry Sunday afternoon. We are going to the Mendel Art Gallery. Watching Lucy shake her hair out and tuck it into her knitted hat, I suddenly feel close to tears. Behind her are the framed photographs of weathered prairie farmhouses, the vigorous spider plants, the scarred child's school desk where she does her studying, the brick-and-board bookshelf with her meagre library. (After eleven months there is still nothing of me that will remain.) This is an old song; there is no gesture of Lucy's that does not fill me instantly with pity, the child's hand held up to deflect the blow, her desperate attempts to conceal unworthiness. For her part she naturally sees me as the father who, in that earlier existence, proved so practised in evasion and flight. The fact that I am now leaving her only reinforces her intuition—it is as if she has expected it all along, almost as if she has been working toward it. This goes to show the force of initial impressions. For example, I will never forget the first time I saw Lucy. She was limping across Broadway, her feet swathed in bandages and jammed into her pumps, her face alternately distorted with agony and composed in dignity. I followed her for blocks—she was beautiful and wounded, the kind of woman I am always looking for to redeem me. Similarly, what she will always remember is that first night we spent together when all I did was hold her while she slept because, taking the bus home, she had seen a naked man masturbating in a window. Thus she had arrived at my door, laughing hysterically, afraid to stay at her own place alone, completely undone. At first she had played the temptress because she thought that was what I wanted. She kissed me hungrily and unfastened my shirt buttons. Then she ran into the bathroom and came out crying because she had dropped and broken the soap dish. That was when I put my arms around her and comforted her, which was what she had wanted from the beginning.

An apology for my style: I am not so much apologizing as invoking a tradition. Heraclitus whose philosophy may not have been written in fragments but certainly comes to us in that form. Kierkegaard who mocked Hegel's system-building by writing everything as if it were an afterthought, *The Unscientific Postscript.* Nietzsche who wrote in aphorisms or what he called "attempts," dry runs at the subject matter, even arguing contradictory points of view in order to see all sides. Wittgenstein's *Investigations,* his fragmentary response to the architectonic of the earlier *Tractatus.* Traditional story writers compose a beginning, a middle and an end, stringing these together in continuity as if there were some whole which they represented. Whereas I am writing fragments and discursive circumlocutions about an object that may not be complete or may be infinite. "Dog Attempts to Drown Man in Saskatoon" is my title, cribbed from a facetious newspaper head-line. Lucy and I were married because of her feet and because she glimpsed a man masturbating in a window as her bus took her home from work. I feel that in discussing these occurrences, these facts (our separation, the dog, the city, the weather, a trip to the art gallery) as constitutive of a non-system, I am peeling away some of the mystery of human life. I am also of the opinion that Mendel should have left the paintings in the slaughterhouse.

The discerning reader will by now have trapped me in a number of inconsistencies and doubtful statements. For example, we are not separating—I am leaving my wife and she has accepted that fact because it reaffirms her sense of herself as a person worthy of being left. Moreover it was wrong of me to pity her. Lucy is a quietly capable woman about to embark on what will inevitably be a successful career. She is not a waif nor could she ever redeem me with her suffering. Likewise she was wrong to view me as forever gentle and forbearing in the sexual department. And finally I suspect that there was more than coincidence in the fact that she spotted the man in his window on my night off from the newspaper. I do not doubt that she saw the man; he is a recurring nightmare of Lucy's. But whether she saw him that particular night, or some night in the past, or whether she made him up out of whole cloth and came to believe in him, I cannot say. About her feet, however, I have been truthful. That day she had just come from her doctor after having the stitches removed.

Lucy's clumsiness. Her clumsiness stems from the fact that she was born with six toes on each foot. This defect, I'm sure, had something to do with the way her mother mistreated her. Among uneducated folk there is often a feeling that physical anomalies reflect mental flaws. And as a kind of punishment for being born (and afterwards because her brother had died), Lucy's feet were never looked at by a competent doctor. It wasn't until she was twenty-six and beginning to enjoy a new life that she underwent a painful operation to have the vestigial digits excised. This surgery left her big toes all but powerless; now they flop like stubby, white worms at the ends of her feet. Where she had been a schoolgirl athlete with six toes, she became awkward and ungainly with five.

Her mother, Celeste, is one of those women who make feminism a *cause célèbre*—no, that is being glib. Truthfully, she was never any man's slave. I have the impression that after the first realization, the first inkling that she had married the wrong man, she entered into the role of submissive female with a strange, destructive gusto. She seems to have had an immoderate amount of hate in her, enough to spread its poison among the many people who touched her in a kind of negative of the parable of loaves and fishes. And the man, the father, was not so far as I can tell cruel, merely ineffectual, just the wrong man. Once, years later, Lucy and Celeste were riding on a bus together when Celeste pointed to a man sitting a few seats ahead and said, "That is the one I loved." That was all she ever said on the topic and the man himself was a balding, petty functionary type, completely uninteresting except in terms of the exaggerated passion Celeste had invested in him over the years. Soon after Lucy's father married Celeste he realized he would never be able to live with her—he absconded for the army, abandoning her with the first child in a drover's shack on a cattle baron's estate. (From time to time Lucy attempts to write about her childhood—her stories always seem unbelievable—a world of infanticide, blood feuds and brutality. I can barely credit these tales, seeing her so prim and composed, not prim but you know how she sits very straight in her chair and her hair is always in place and her clothes are expensive if not quite stylish and her manners are correct without being at all natural; Lucy is composed in the sense of being made up or put together out of pieces, not in the sense of being tranquil. But nevertheless she carries these *cauchemars* in her head: the dead babies found beneath the fence row, blood on sheets, shotgun blasts in the night, her brother going under the highway roller, her mother's cruel silence.) The father fled as I say. He sent them money orders, three-quarters of his pay, to that point he was responsible. Celeste never spoke of him and his infrequent visits home were always a surprise to the children; his visits and the locked bedroom door and the hot, breathy silence of what went on behind the door, Celeste's rising vexation and hysteria; the new pregnancy; the postmarks on the money orders. Then the boy died. Perhaps he was Celeste's favourite, a perfect one to hold over the tall, already beautiful, monster with six toes and (I conjecture again) her father's look. The boy died and the house went silent—Celeste had forbidden a word to be spoken—and this was the worst for Lucy, the cold parlour circumspection of Protestant mourning. They did not utter a redeeming sound, only replayed the image of the boy running, laughing, racing the machine, then tripping and going under, being sucked under—

Lucy did not even see the body, and in an access of delayed grief almost two decades later she would tell me she had always assumed he just flattened out like a cartoon character. Celeste refused to weep; only her hatred grew like a heavy weight against her children. And in that vacuum, that terrible silence accorded all feeling and especially the mysteries of sex and death, the locked door of the bedroom and the shut coffin lid, the absent father and the absent brother, somehow became inextricably entwined in Lucy's mind; she was only nine, a most beautiful monster, surrounded by absent gods and a bitter worship. So that when she saw the naked man calmly masturbating in the upper storey window from her bus, framed as it were under the cornice of a Saskatoon rooming house, it was for her like a vision of the centre of the mystery, the scene behind the locked door, the corpse in its coffin, God, and she immediately imagined her mother waiting irritably in the shadow just out of sight with a towel to wipe the sperm from the windowpane, aroused, yet almost fainting at the grotesque denial of her female passion.

Do not, if you wish, believe any of the above. It is psychological jazz written *en marge;* I am a poet of marginalia. Some of what I write is utter crap and wishful thinking. Lucy is not "happy to be sad"; she is seething inside because I am betraying her. Her anger gives her the courage to make jokes; she blushes when I laugh because she still hopes that I will stay. Of course my willingness to accompany her to the art gallery is inspired by guilt. She is completely aware of this fact. Her invitation is premeditated, manipulative. No gesture is lost; all our acts are linked and repeated. She is, after all, Celeste's daughter. Also do not believe for a moment that I hate that woman for what she was. That instant on the bus in a distant town when she pointed out the man she truly loved, she somehow redeemed herself for Lucy and for me, showing herself receptive of forgiveness and pity. Nor do I hate Lucy though I am leaving her.

My wife and I decide to separate, and then suddenly we are almost happy together. I repeat this crucial opening sentence for the purpose of reminding myself of my general intention. In a separate notebook next to me (vodka on ice sweating onto and blurring the ruled pages) I have a list of subjects to cover: 1) blindness (the man the dog led into the river was blind); 2) a man I know who was gored by a bison (real name to be withheld); 3) Susan the weaver and her little girl and the plan for us to live in Pelican Narrows; 4) the wolves at the city zoo; 5) the battlefields of Batoche and Duck Lake; 6) bridge symbolism; 7) a fuller description of the death of Lucy's brother; 8) three photographs of Lucy in my possession; 9) my wish to have met Mendel (he is dead) and be his friend; 10) the story of the story of how the dog tried to drown the man in Saskatoon.

Call this a play. Call me Orestes. Call her mother Clytemnestra. Her father, the wandering warrior king. (When he died accidentally a year ago, they sent Lucy his diary. Every day of his life he had recorded the weather; that was all.) Like everyone else, we married because we thought we could change one another. I was the brother-friend come to slay the tyrant Celeste; Lucy was to teach me the meaning of suffering. But there is no meaning and in the labyrinth of Lucy's mind the spirit of her past eluded me. Take sex for instance. She is taller than I am; people sometimes think she must be a model. She is without a doubt the most beautiful woman I have been to bed with. Yet there is no passion, no arousal. Between the legs she is as dry as a prairie summer. I am tender, but tenderness is no substitute for biology. Penetration is always painful. She gasps, winces. She will not perform oral sex though sometimes she likes having it done to her, providing she can overcome her embarrassment. What she does love is for me to wrestle her to the living-room carpet and strip her clothes off in a mock rape. She squeals and protests and then scampers naked to the bedroom where she waits impatiently while I get undressed. Only once have I detected her orgasm— this while she sat on my lap fully clothed and I manipulated her with my fingers. It goes without saying she will not talk about these things. She protects herself from herself and there is never any feeling that we are together. When Lucy's periods began, Celeste told her she had cancer. More than once she was forced to eat garbage from a dog's dish. Sometimes her mother would simply lock her out of the house for the night. These stories are shocking; Celeste was undoubtedly mad. By hatred, mother and daughter are manacled together for eternity. "You can change," I say with all my heart. "A woman who only sees herself as a victim never gets wise to herself." "No," she says, touching my hand sadly. "Ah! Ah!" I think, between weeping and words. Nostalgia is form; hope is content. Lucy is an empty building, a frenzy of restlessness, a soul without a future. And I fling out in desperation, Orestes-like, seeking my own Athens and release.

More bunk! I'll let you know now that we are not going to the art gallery as I write this. Everything happened some time ago and I am living far away in another country. (Structuralists would characterize my style as "robbing the signifier of the signified." My opening sentence, my premise, is now practically destitute of meaning, or it means everything. Really, this is what happens when you try to tell the truth about something; you end up like the snake biting its own tail. There are a hundred reasons why I left Lucy. I don't want to seem shallow. I don't want to say, well, I was a meat-and-potatoes person and she was a vegetarian, or that I sometimes believe she simply orchestrated the whole fiasco, seduced me, married me, and then refused to be a wife— yes, I would prefer to think that I was guiltless, that I didn't just wander off fecklessly like her father. To explain this, or for that matter to explain why the dog led the man into the river, you have to explain the world, even God—if we accept Gödel's theorem regarding the unjustifiability of systems from within. Everything is a symbol of everything else. Or everything is a symbol of death as Levi-Strauss says. In other words, there is no signified and life is nothing but a long haunting. Perhaps that is all that I am trying to say. . . .) However, we *did* visit the art gallery one winter Sunday near the end of our eleven-month marriage. There were two temporary exhibitions and all of Mendel's slaughterhouse pictures had been stored in the basement. One wing was devoted to photographs of grain elevators, very phallic with their little overhanging roofs. We laughed about this together; Lucy was kittenish, pretending to be shocked. Then she walked across the hall alone to contemplate the acrylic prairie-scapes by local artists. I descended the stairs to drink coffee and watch the frozen river. This was downstream from the Idylwyld Bridge where the fellow went in (there is an open stretch of two or three hundred yards where a hot water outlet prevents the river from freezing over completely) and it occurred to me that if he had actually drowned, if the current had dragged him under the ice, they wouldn't have found his body until the spring breakup. And probably they would have discovered it hung up on the weir which I could see from the gallery window.

Forget it. A bad picture: Lucy upstairs "appreciating" art, me downstairs thinking of bodies under the ice. Any moment now she will come skipping towards me flushed with excitement after a successful cultural adventure. That is not what I meant to show you. That Lucy is not a person, she is a caricature. When legends are born, people die. Rather let us look at the place where all reasons converge. No. Let me tell you how Lucy is redeemed: preamble and anecdote. Her greatest fear is that she will turn into Celeste. Naturally, without noticing it, she is becoming more and more like her mother every day. She has the financial independence Celeste no doubt craved, and she has been disappointed in love. Three times. The first man made himself into a wandering rage with drugs. The second was an adulterer. Now me. Already she is acquiring an edge of bitterness, of why-me-ness. But, and this is an Everest of a but, the woman can dance! I don't mean at the disco or in the ballroom; I don't mean she studied ballet. We were strolling in Diefenbaker Park one summer day shortly after our wedding (this is on the bluffs overlooking Mendel's meat-packing plant) when we came upon a puppet show. It was some sort of children's fair: there were petting zoos, pony rides, candy stands, bicycles being given away as prizes, all that kind of thing in addition to the puppets. It was a famous troupe which had started in the sixties as part of the counter-culture movement—I need not mention the name. The climax of the performance was a stately dance by two giant puppets perhaps thirty feet tall, a man and a woman, backwoods types. We arrived just in time to see the woman rise from the ground, supported by three puppeteers. She rises from the grass stiffly then spreads her massive arms towards the man and an orchestra begins a reel. It is an astounding sight. I notice that the children in the audience are rapt. And suddenly I am aware of Lucy, her face aflame, this crazy grin and her eyes dazzled. She is looking straight up at the giant woman. The music, as I say, begins and the puppet sways and opens her arms towards her partner (they are both very stern, very grave) and Lucy begins to sway and spread her arms. She lifts her feet gently, one after the other, begins to turn, then swings back. She doesn't know what she is doing; this is completely unselfconscious. There is only Lucy and the puppets and the dance. She is a child again and I am in awe of her innocence. It is a scene that brings a lump to my throat: the high, hot, summer sun, the children's faces like flowers in a sea of grass, the towering, swaying puppets, and Lucy lost in herself. Lucy, dancing. Probably she no longer remembers this incident. At the time, or shortly after, she said, "Oh no! Did I really? Tell me I didn't do that!" She was laughing, not really embarrassed. "Did anyone see me?" And when the puppeteers passed the hat at the end of the show, I turned out my pockets, I gave them everything I had.

I smoke Gitanes. I like to drink in an Indian bar on 20th Street near Eaton's. My nose was broken in a car accident when I was eighteen; it grew back crooked. I speak softly; sometimes I stutter. I don't like crowds. In my spare time, I paint large pictures of the city. Photographic realism is my style. I work on a pencil grid using egg tempera because it's better for detail. I do shopping centres, old movie theatres that are about to be torn down, slaughterhouses. While everyone else is looking out at the prairie, I peer inward and record what is merely transitory, what is human. Artifice. Nature defeats me. I cannot paint ripples on a lake, or the movement of leaves, or a woman's face. Like most people, I suppose, my heart is broken because I cannot be what I wish to be. On the day in question, one of the coldest of the year, I hike down from the university along Saskatchewan Drive overlooking the old railway hotel, the modest office blocks, and the ice-shrouded gardens of the city. I carry a camera, snapping end-of-the-world photos for a future canvas. At the Third Avenue Bridge I pause to admire the lattice of I-beams, black against the frozen mist swirling up from the river and the translucent exhaust plumes of the ghostly cars shuttling to and fro. Crossing the street, I descend the wooden steps into Rotary Park, taking two more shots of the bridge at a close angle before the film breaks from the cold. I swing round, focussing on the squat ugliness of the Idylwyld Bridge with its fat concrete piers obscuring the view upriver, and then suddenly an icy finger seems to touch my heart: out on the river, on the very edge of the snowy crust where the turbid waters from the outlet pipe churn and steam, a black dog is playing. I refocus. The dog scampers in a tight circle, races toward the brink, skids to a stop, barks furiously at something in the grey water. I stumble forward a step or two. Then I see the man, swept downstream, bobbing in the current, his arms flailing stiffly. In another instant, the dog leaps after him, disappears, almost as if I had dreamed it. I don't quite know what I am doing, you understand. The river is no man's land. First I am plunging through the knee-deep snow of the park. Then I lose my footing on the bank and find myself sliding on my seat onto the river ice. Before I have time to think, "There is a man in the river," I am sprinting to intercept him, struggling to untangle the camera from around my neck, stripping off my coat. I have forgotten momentarily how long it takes exposed skin to freeze and am lost in a frenzy of speculation upon the impossibility of existence in the river, the horror of the current dragging you under the ice at the end of the open water, the creeping numbness, again the impossibility, the alienness of the idea itself, the dog and the man immersed. I feel the ice rolling under me, throw myself flat, wrapped in a gentle terror, then inch forward again, spread-eagled, throwing my coat by a sleeve, screaming, "Catch it! Catch it!" to the man whirling toward me, scrabbling with bloody hands at the crumbling ledge. All this occupies less time than it takes to tell. He is a strange bearlike creature, huge in an old duffel coat with its hood up, steam rising around him, his face bloated and purple, his red hands clawing at the ice shelf, an inhuman "awing" sound emanating from his throat, his eyes rolling upwards. He makes no effort to reach the coat sleeve trailed before him as the current carries him by. Then the dog appears, paddling towards the man, straining to keep its head above the choppy surface. The dog barks, rests a paw on the man's shoulder, seems to drag him under a little, and then the man is striking out wildly, fighting the dog off, being twisted out into the open water by the eddies. I see the leather hand harness flapping from the dog's neck and suddenly the full horror of the situation assails me: the man is blind. Perhaps he understands nothing of what is happening to him, the world gone mad, this freezing hell. At the same moment, I feel strong hands grip my ankles and hear another's laboured breathing. I look over my shoulder. There is a pink-cheeked policeman with a thin yellow moustache stretched on the ice behind me. Behind him, two teenage boys are in the act of dropping to all fours, making a chain of bodies. A fifth person, a young woman, is running towards us. "He's blind," I shout. The policeman nods: he seems to comprehend everything in an instant. The man in the water has come to rest against a jutting point of ice a few yards away. The dog is much nearer, but I make for the man, crawling on my hands and knees, forgetting my coat. There seems nothing to fear now. Our little chain of life reaching toward the blind drowning man seems sufficient against the infinity of forces which have culminated in this moment. The crust is rolling and bucking beneath us as I take his wrists. His fingers, hard as talons, lock into mine. Immediately he ceases to utter that terrible, unearthly bawling sound. Inching backward, I somehow contrive to lever the dead weight of his body over the ice lip, then drag him on his belly like a sack away from the water. The cop turns him gently on his back; he is breathing in gasps, his eyes rolling frantically "T'ank you, t'ank you," he whispers, his strength gone. The others quickly remove their coats and tuck them around the man who now looks like some strange beached fish, puffing and muttering in the snow. Then in the eerie silence that follows, broken only by the shushing sound of traffic on the bridges, the distant whine of a siren coming nearer, the hissing river and my heart beating, I look into the smoky water once more and see that the dog is gone. I am dazed; I watch a drop of sweat freezing on the policeman's moustache. I stare into the grey flux where it slips quietly under the ice and disappears. One of the boys offers me a cigarette. The blind man moans; he says, "I go home now. Dog good. I all right. I walk home." The boys glance at each other. The woman is shivering. Everything seems empty and anticlimactic. We are shrouded in enigma. The policeman takes out a notebook, a tiny symbol of rationality, scribbled words against the void. As an ambulance crew skates a stretcher down the river bank, he begins to ask the usual questions, the usual, unanswerable questions.

This is not the story I wanted to tell. I repeat this *caveat* as a reminder that I am willful and wayward as a storyteller, not a good storyteller at all. The right story, the true story, had I been able to tell it, would have changed your life—but it is buried, gone, lost. The next day Lucy and I drive to the spot where I first saw the dog. The river is once more sanely empty and the water boils quietly where it has not yet frozen. Once more I tell her how it happened, but she prefers the public version, what she hears on the radio or reads in the newspaper, to my disjointed impressions. It is also true that she knows she is losing me and she is at the stage where it is necessary to deny strenuously all my values and perceptions. She wants to think that I am just like her father or that I always intended to humiliate her. The facts of the case are that the man and dog apparently set out to cross the Idylwyld Bridge but turned off along the approach and walked into the water, the man a little ahead of the dog. In the news account, the dog is accused of insanity, dereliction of duty and a strangely uncanine malevolence. "Dog Attempts to Drown Man," the headline reads. Libel law prevents speculation on the human victim's mental state, his intentions. The dog is dead, but the tone is jocular. *Dog Attempts to Drown Man.* All of which means that no one knows what happened from the time the man stumbled off the sidewalk on Idylwyld to the time he fell into the river and we are free to invent structures and symbols as we see fit. The man survives, it seems, his strange baptism, his trial by cold and water. I know in my own mind that he appeared exhausted, not merely from the experience of near-drowning, but from before, in spirit, while the dog seemed eager and alert. We know, or at least we can all agree to theorize, that a bridge is a symbol of change (one side to the other, hence death), of connection (the marriage of opposites), but also of separation from the river of life, a bridge is an object of culture. Perhaps man and dog chose together to walk through the pathless snows to the water's edge and throw themselves into uncertainty. The man was blind as are we all; perhaps he sought illumination in the frothing waste. Perhaps they went as old friends. Or perhaps the dog accompanied the man only reluctantly, the man forcing the dog to lead him across the ice. I saw the dog swim to him, saw the man fending the dog off. Perhaps the dog was trying to save its master, or perhaps it was only playing, not understanding in the least what was happening. Whatever is the case my allegiance is with the dog; the man is too human, too predictable. But man and dog together are emblematic—that is my impression at any rate—they are the mind and spirit, the one blind, the other dumb; one defeated, the other naive and hopeful, both forever going out. And I submit that, after all the simplified explanations and crude jokes about the blind man and his dog, the act is full of a terrible and mysterious beauty.

My wife and I decide to separate, and then suddenly we are almost happy together. But this was long ago, as was the visit to the Mendel Art Gallery and my time in Saskatoon. And though the moment when Lucy shakes down her hair and tucks it into her knitted cap goes on endlessly in my head as does the reverberation of that other moment when the dog disappears under the ice, there is much that I have already forgotten. I left Lucy because she was too real, too hungry for love, while I am a dreamer. There are two kinds of courage: the courage that holds things together and the courage that throws them away. The first is more common; it is the cement of civilization; it is Lucy's. The second is the courage of drunks and suicides and mystics. My sign is impurity. By leaving, you understand, I proved that I was unworthy. I have tried to write Lucy since that winter—her only response has been to return my letters unopened. This is appropriate. She means for me to read them myself, those tired, clotted apologies. I am the writer of the words; she knows well enough they are not meant for her. But my words are sad companions and sometimes I remember . . . well . . . the icy water is up to my neck and I hear the ghost dog barking, she tried to warn me; yes, yes, I say, but I was blind.

The Obituary Writer

We drifted along in this empire of death like accursed phantoms.
—DE SÉGUR

I

AIDEN IS IN ST. JOSEPH'S, dying of head injuries. Annie has a gone Catholic on me. She has quit school and taken a job at a home for retarded children in West Saint John. She works the graveyard shift so she can spend the day with Aiden. Mornings, she visits the hospital chapel for mass. I hardly ever see her.

Of all the brothers and sisters (there are a dozen O'Reillys, counting the parents), Aiden and Annie were closest in age and sympathy, though all they ever did in public was bicker and complain about one another. Aiden was the family clown, a bespectacled, jug-eared, loudmouthed ranter, given to taunting the younger children and starting fights—though he once sang in the cathedral choir and spent a year trying to teach himself the guitar. Annie is boyish and prim. She dawdles over her makeup, ties her red hair back and gets average grades in her university courses. But like many people who spend their lives reining themselves in, she has a soft spot in her heart for eccentrics and outsiders. One always knew that if anything happened to Aiden, it would be hardest on Annie. It is also natural that she should flail about, trying to locate beyond herself an agent responsible for this terrible tragedy. I say "beyond herself" on purpose, because, of course, Annie O'Reilly blames herself for everything first. Then me.

47

Mornings, in the chapel, she and God are sorting all this out. But I have little hope that He will see fit to represent my side of things.

We live in a brick apartment house owned by a police sergeant who is dying of cancer. He has told me about the operation he underwent, but not that he's still dying. Maybe he doesn't know. I know because the other day, returning from the scene of a fatal car crash on the MacKay Highway, I passed Sgt. Pye directing traffic. Father Daniel, Annie's priest-uncle, happened to be driving with me. He said, "That one's not long for this world. He's full of cancer, just full of it. I've seen enough to know." I was filled with envy then for Father Dan, for his knowledge of the mysteries of not-life, for his familiarity with the endless, dark ocean on which we float.

That's the sort of wisdom I sought when I first went hunting for a newspaper job. Mostly, though, I type obituaries and make lists of striking names to use in my short stories. Mornings, I rise early and type my dreams on a table beside our bed. Annie sometimes stops by on her way between the retarded home and the hospital. She'll lean on the doorjamb, smoking a cigarette and watching me type my dreams. My habits mystify her. The minutiae of my psyche seem frivolous next to her crippled children and dying brother. She lives in a world of mythic horror. I read my dreams like tea leaves, observing the signs, the motions of the universe as they ruffle the limpid pool of the unconscious. I want to know who I am before I sink back into the inanimate. I tell her this.

I go to the hospital. Aiden is in the head-injury ward, where old men mutter, fall out of bed or walk into the hall to be tackled and restrained by nurses. Once one of them grabbed Annie from behind and tried to choke her, a mad, fragile, leaf-dry, shit-stinking man.

I stand beside her chair and say, "He's in there. He's in there practising for death. It's been a shock. He never thought about it before. There's this little man inside the bombed-out control centre with the frizzed wires and smoking lights, all dripping with goop from the fire extinguishers. He's pressing buttons frantically, trying to get a line out, panicked, not knowing what to do.

"Later, the little man will give up, collect his coat and lunchbox, wrap a scarf around his throat, turn out the lights and lock the door. Then Aiden will be dead. Where will the little man go? I don't know. Home, probably. Back to the infinite split-ranch in the sky, with three pear trees in the back yard and a tire swing for the kids, and wait for his next job. What's the little man's name? He hasn't got one. But he's all there is."

Annie stares at me as if I were crazy; she prefers to pray. Aiden is taking it about as calmly as anyone, sleeping it off like a hangover. Life.

Old Mrs. Lawson who lives on the floor below persists in leaving her door ajar. She treats the landing as a parlour and has decorated it with antique tables and ornately framed prints of Saint John harbour in the days of the sailing ships, the port a forest of spars and sheets. When she hears me climbing the stairs, as likely as not she will think of an excuse to ambush me and talk. Sometimes her stove won't start—she'll tell me she hasn't had a hot cooked meal in a week. Sometimes she'll gossip about Sgt. Pye who bought the building from her after her husband's death.

Once she told me about the tenant who used to live in the apartment Annie and I share. (She insists on calling Annie "Mrs. Cary," though I have told her a dozen times we aren't married.

As in, "Is Mrs. Cary still keeping those late hours? Mercy me!")
It turns out that our bed was a deathbed, something I had long
suspected, though for no particular reason. Frank Beamish, a
retired foreman from the sugar refinery, died there in his sleep a
month before we moved in. Of course, Sgt. Pye cleaned and re-
decorated the place, but, said Mrs. Lawson, she can't help thinking she senses "something" above her head late at night when
the distant foghorns sound.

I think of Aiden in his bed and Frank Beamish and Annie in
bed with me (yes, there is a symbolism attached to beds, those
banal loci of love, death and dreams) and my strange dreams
since we moved in. This bedroom of broken dreams.

Mornings, when I type my dreams, my mouth is bitter and
clogged with dead cell detritus. It floats in the air. Those motes
you see in the sunlight in the window. Annie used to be a sack
angel—that was her revolt, everyone's really, the only thing we
do to reverse the current, twisting and snapping our backs like
salmon struggling upstream, against the flood of time, to spawn
and die. We would beat together like fighters in a ring, like tiger
moths against the killer light, and Annie would expire, whispering, "I love you. I love you."

She was a technical virgin when we met, though she had
had a lover in high school, an older girl she met playing bad-
minton. When this girl left for Montreal to study nursing, she
began writing Annie passionate love letters. Annie panicked,
burned the letters, flushing the ashes down the toilet, drawing
back from the aberrant entanglement, the suck and slop of
emotion, the dark flow. She became prim. At a party, drunk
and ironical and somewhat provoked by her coldness, I put
my hand down the back of her pants and felt her ass. "I don't
know what to do," she said. "Why are you hurting me?" Later,

I made her bleed. "I love you," she would say and die. "I love you."

After sex, she becomes formal, embarrassed, shy and neat, with every hair in place, her back straight. I sometimes laugh at her, laugh in her face. I say, "Abandonment is a commentary on primness, just as my dreams are a gloss on obituary-writing." She makes a sour face, reties her hair and takes an extra fifteen minutes with her makeup to drive me mad. We both understand that I am titillated by her dual nature and her lesbian past. I am a lover of paradox, of outré juxtapositions and jokes—this is the way we talk about death.

Across the landing, there is a single room Sgt. Pye rents to a middle-aged black man named Earl Delamare. Earl is the colour of dust, or he is one of those black people whose skin always looks like it needs a quick buff-up with Lemon Pledge. Earl lives on welfare and a disability pension for some back injury. He's unmarried. He has never spoken to Annie or me. The first week or two after we moved in, he would open his door a crack whenever we came or went—dusty skin, white eyeball. It gave Annie the shivers. She would shake her shoulders and skip out of sight, either down the stairs or into the apartment.

Now that we hardly ever come and go together, I rarely see Earl. Though mornings, when she stops by for a visit, Annie sometimes remarks that he is still there, watching. When she is cranky, she'll accuse me of being friends with Earl, or make believe we are twin brothers, or one and the same person. The truth is Earl and I don't get along well, this in spite of the fact that we have never even spoken to each other.

Nights, now that Annie's away, Earl will get drunk and stand outside my door shouting obscenities, taunting me about my lost sweetheart. I do not respond—at first, because I was afraid of him; now, because I am not afraid of him—which only infuriates Earl. He rants on the landing, getting drunker. (God knows what Mrs. Lawson thinks is going on. Perhaps this is the only "something" she senses.) He creates complex plots out of whole cloth, accusing me of devilish connections, quoting the *Book of Revelation,* speaking other names I do not recognize. He says he's going to call Sgt. Pye and have the police put an end to my racist cabal before my friends and I burn him out. Lately, he's been going on about some mysterious group called the *Numéro Cinq,* which he thinks is holding meetings in our apartment.

I do not tell Annie any of this. Perhaps none of it's true.

I tell her, "Without someone else we cannot exist." Of course, I mean this in the contemporary sense—the Other.

She hasn't forgiven me for taking a newspaper job. Or, more precisely, she hasn't forgiven me for being content, for burrowing into the warm mud of the daily press, like an ancient fish into its river bed, and waiting. She prefers my previous incarnation as a discontented junior lecturer at the university at Tucker Park, where we met—long hair and tattered jeans, waving my unfinished dissertation like a toreador's cape, the student's friend. Because she cannot bring herself to rebel, she adores rebellion in others—in this way all love is pathological. But I have grown tired of drawing attention to myself.

Moreover, it was her father who introduced me to the city editor. Of course, Annie worships her father, that gruff, taciturn patriarch. Yet their relationship is difficult, and she yearns for independence. Her father found Aiden jobs, too. The summer before Aiden worked on the Digby ferry as a deck hand to earn his university tuition. But Aiden made a show of accepting the job under duress, with an air of knowing his father had laid something on the line to get him hired, to which extent the father was now in his son's power.

Aiden boasted he could always go back to cutting pulp in the woods. But the last time he did this he nearly cut his foot off with a chain saw. Aiden's body is an archaeology of his experiences: the chain weal on his cheek from a fight with a biker, the knife scars on his arm from the time he and a friend intervened to stop a gang rape on the night beach at Mispec, the thick diamonds of white skin on his knuckles where he smashed his hand through the kitchen wall after an argument with his father.

Now Aiden is dying; he's only nineteen and; though we live together, I don't see Annie anymore.

The librarian is a fey, blond woman named Lyn Shaheen. She wears wire rim glasses and has long, thin breasts of exceptional whiteness. For weeks I went to the library hoping only to catch a glimpse of her out of the corner of my eye. One day I screwed up enough courage to speak. I said, "I'm writing a book, a novel, you might say. I need music to go with it. In the text, I mean. I need something mad, something eerie." She looked at me strangely, but led me to the record collection. Mussorgsky, she thought. *Night on Bald Mountain.* Cage, she suggested. But no, experimental music would be too rational. Lyn Shaheen. I played the records.

In truth, I am writing a novel. It's about a woman with epilepsy, a rare form of the disease in which the fits are triggered by the sound of music. The young woman is a concert cellist who develops seizures in her twenties following a car accident. Out of pity, her lover murders her. On subsequent visits to the library, I have told Lyn the plot of my book. We have had coffee together at the Ritz restaurant next to the bookstore on King Square. We have kissed in the street, though I was terrified one of the O'Reillys would see us and report me to Annie.

I don't want to make this depressing for you. This story does have its lighter moments. For example, Aiden lying dying in St. Joseph's has convulsions (not necessarily funny in themselves), which the doctors attempt to control with drugs. Occasionally a message fights its way from what's left of his brain to an arm or a leg and some macabre incident will ensue. Annie and I will be sitting next to the bed when, suddenly, Aiden's right leg shoots up to attention, exposing his catheter tube and waxy, shrunken genitals. Flustered, Annie will jump to her feet and try to press the leg back down on the bed. This always reminds me of those silent-movie slapstick routines. I half expect Aiden to lift his other leg as she pushes the first down, or his arms to fly up over his head, or his torso to rise.

Dying, Aiden has preserved his sense of humour. I am with him in this, considering irony to be the only suitable mode of comment on our universal disaster. I try to explain this to Annie. I try to tell her that if she would see Aiden as a different sort of symbol, she could remain in love with me, we could get back into bed together. Instead of praying to Christ, she could go back to being Christ every night.

I have always envisioned myself as the Roman soldier offering the sponge of vinegar, gambling for the robe, sliding his spear into His belly—irony, detachment and the ultimate kindness— that Roman soldier was the only interesting character in the whole drama, the only person who refused to react within the religious or political scheme of things, the only non-fanatic.

Well, I try to explain it, and she pushes me out of the head-injury ward, shushing me, whispering angrily for me to shut up, tears like jewels on the pillows of her cheeks—she has her point of view, too.

This is in Saint John on the Bay of Fundy, with its Loyalist grave-yard in the centre of the city, moss covering the bone white stones under the dark elms. City of exiles dreaming of lost Edens, it carries its past like a baited hook in its entrails. The O'Reillys, the Shaheens and the Pyes are descendants of Irish immigrants, sur-vivors of the potato famine and cholera ships; Earl Delamare is the grandchild of American slaves. Beneath the throughway bridges, on a swampy waste next to the port, lie the ruins of Fort LaTour, scene of an even earlier betrayal. It's no wonder these people see themselves endlessly as victims.

The place where we live, Sgt. Pye's ageing apartment house on Germain Street in the South End, lies between the dry dock and the sugar refinery. We can hear the boat sounds, bell buoys and foghorns in the night. When a fog blows in, as they often do, the streetlights look like paper lanterns hanging before the houses. Afternoons, when I finish work, I sometimes climb to the rocky summit of Fort Howe to watch the mist nose up through the port, threading the streets of the city like an animal trying to find its way in a maze.

Best of all is springtime, when the freshets swell the river, flooding Indian Town and Spar Cove above the falls. Television cameras mounted in chartered helicopters transmit aerial shots of a strange, watery landscape upriver. When the land dries, chil-dren set grass fires in railway cuts and vacant lots. Saint John is a wooden city, rebuilt hastily by ships' carpenters after an earlier fire. So this is always dangerous; the whole place could go up. These are the brilliant spring days after the freshets, when I take my position on high ground and watch smoke drifting over the sagging, pastel-coloured houses and hear sirens snaking through the streets and dream that everything man-made is being scorched clean, reabsorbed into rock and air.

Aiden is in St. Joseph's, dying of his head. This has been going on for three months. Annie, his sister, and I are breaking up. We are in the midst of the painful process of tearing down the lines of communication. Every time we talk it is like a fresh storm blowing a tree across a telephone wire, ice forming on the trans-formers, a flood washing away a cable. We are disentangling. Until all that will remain is the silence blowing like a cold wind against our faces. This is all right. You needn't worry about me. When I feel that wind, I know who I am.

Aiden is dying. He is asleep (in a coma) in St. Joseph's. He always seemed like a jerk to me, so it doesn't bother me much that he is dying. Except that his dying is contributing to our breakup. (Yes, I am jealous of a dying brother. God, how he used to irritate Annie. Once we had to rush to his girlfriend's apartment after she took an overdose of sleeping pills. We spent the night, brewing cups of coffee, walking her up and down. Annie swore she'd never speak to Aiden again—now, he has all the glory.)

He's suddenly moral. He's suddenly okay, with a ready-made excuse for missing mass. (Hell, they bring mass to Aiden. Those women have him right where they want him.) The story is that he got drunk (as usual) at a campus party in Halifax, tried tight-rope-walking on a balcony railing and fell three storeys onto con-crete slabs. The impact crushed the left side of his skull, but a surgeon kept him alive by cutting away the bone and draining the fluid build-up. That first week he nearly died a dozen times. (I was there. I was a tower of strength, escorting his mother back and forth from their hotel, playing cards and word games with his brothers and sisters in the waiting-room. Briefly, I was for-given for corrupting Annie.)

I recall the surgeon coming to tell us pneumonia had set in, that the case was hopeless unless he suctioned Aiden's lungs hourly through the night. It was clear, from the doctor's tone, his kindness and the set of his eyes, that he was telling Annie's father: "I can let him die tonight, which would be better for everyone, or I can prolong this." But you only had to glance once at the father's face to know what his answer was. These people are Catholic; they have met the Pope. On top of their upright piano, which stands next to the TV and the police-band radio in the living room, there are back-to-back photos of John Paul II and John F. Kennedy. They toe the party line. Whatever happens, they come down blindly on the side of life.

Sgt. Pye evicts Earl Delamare. It's my fault, too, because I was taunting Earl, playing on his fantasies. It's possible I have driven him mad. One night he came to my door, first listening, then mumbling, then beginning his litany of wild accusations. Instead of responding with my usual silence, I put *Night on Bald Mountain* on the stereo. As the music rose, I began to intone the French advertisements on the backs of cereal boxes in my kitchen cupboard.

The music gave Earl fits; he practically howled with rage. "*Numéro Cinq! Numéro Cinq!*" he cried. I played John Cage on the stereo and began to read the cereal boxes backwards, imitating several voices at once. Earl began to beat the door with his fists, perhaps even his head. I could see the panels giving with the force of his blows. In the midst of this I heard Sgt. Pye climbing the stairs. When he came into my apartment, he found me sitting in an old Morris chair, eating a bowl of Rice Krispies, with the stereo low. He had a face like a yellow skull. Earl had retreated to his room, like a mole going underground. But I could still hear him shouting, "*Numéro Cinq! Numéro Cinq!*" When

Sgt. Pye let himself into Earl's room, the black man went through the window and down the fire escape.

After Earl's things were moved out, I sneaked into his room to look around. There were five bags of empty Molson's bottles in the kitchenette. His closet was papered with cut-out magazine ads for automobiles. On the bare hardwood floor of the bed-sitting room, under the single, naked light bulb, I found the photograph of a young black woman.

One afternoon, I stop by the library. I am on my way to Connor Street to have dinner with Annie and her family. Oddly enough, I think her father is trying to patch things up between us. Lyn Shaheen is pleased to see me. We chat by the record collection, then we meet again in the stacks, near philosophy where no one ever goes, and kiss. When I look up, I notice we are next to the Ms for Mortality, Metaphysics and Man. She has strange lips and a tongue that she runs over my teeth. I stroke her long breasts beneath her sweater. Her hair smells like old books.

I wait for her to get off work, then, for a while, we snuggle together in the front seat of her Volkswagen. I undo her pants and masturbate her with my fingers. Outside, a blizzard whirls around us, obscuring the Viaduct and the bridges across the river. Her Volkswagen is white; in all that snow, we are invisible. Without saying a word, she takes my cock in her mouth. She is the keeper of the words. She is the beast in the labyrinth. When I come, I am, briefly, nowhere, lost, swirling in a semantic ocean. Then she drops me a block from Annie's house.

There is no fiction in this story. I have, on the other hand, like any author, permitted myself occasional legitimate assumptions.

I am the obituary writer. I do other things as well. But mornings I begin the workday by typing up the form obituary notices dropped in the night mailbox by representatives of the local funeral homes. The format is pretty much set in stone, and I have little leeway in the manner in which I choose to present my material. Nevertheless, I try insofar as I can to add some colour and meaning to the bare facts I have to work with.

Let me tell you, it makes all the difference in the world if you can say so-and-so died "suddenly" and "at home." Age can be a factor. From a human interest point of view, the younger the deceased the better. Death at an advanced age, say, past a hundred, elicits only a mild exclamation from the bored reader. But give me a little girl who dies at three, and I can bring tears to the eye. Personally, I enjoy the stories of early retirement deaths. A welder, say, works all his life for a single firm (I bring in such telling details as his union affiliation, his membership in the Knights of Pythias, his forty-five year watch), then retires at sixty-five, only to die a few months later "after a brief illness." What I feel is that the obituary writer is a moralist, a prophet. Everything I type tells the reader, "All is dust; all is vanity." A salutary message in this age of rampant materialism.

Soon I will be typing Aiden's obituary. The thought, I am sure, has crossed Annie's mind and makes her uncomfortable. But these days everything I do seems to make her uncomfortable.

Aiden is in St. Joseph's, dying of head injuries. Annie shaves him, washes him, rubs salve on his bed sores, feeds him (I find this amazing—a man in a coma can be made to swallow a little Jell-O from time to time), changes his catheter bag, plays him music on the radio and reads him his favourite science fiction novels—Bradbury, Heinlein, Asimov and Wells. Sometimes, when Annie cannot be there, I go and sit with him myself.

It is curious how involved you can become in gauging his level of wakefulness. I tell jokes, insult him, instruct him to blink an eyelid, yes or no. I tell him secrets, shameful facts about my relationship with his sister, just to get a rise out of him. But Aiden is unflappable, and I quickly grow tired of the game. I recall a religious (though not Catholic) friend of mine, describing her mother's death: "The last week was difficult, you know, the terribly difficult time when the soul is separating from the body." Something like this is happening with Aiden. His existence is entirely passive, and he has lost even the sense of the sense of loss.

(It is during one of these clandestine visits that Annie suddenly appears and, in a fit of pique at finding me there—somehow this confuses the pristine relationship she enjoys with her brother, implying that, even as a vegetable, he might have a life of his own—she reveals that she has learned "everything there is to know" about my affair with the librarian.)

Two things drew me to her at the beginning: the way she blushed when she failed to pronounce Dostoyevsky correctly in my literature class, and the way, once, in an unguarded moment, I saw the pink band of her underwear show above the waist of her jeans. These images of self-betrayal, Annie's tiny pratfalls, are the imperfections in the other we attach ourselves to and which they strenuously deny and hide. These are the buds of conflict, the rifts. I have not loved Annie for that for which she desires to be loved.

I find out from Sgt. Pye that Earl is staying at the Sally Ann. In a few weeks, a judge will hold a hearing for his committal to the provincial hospital on the other side of the river. I buy a six-pack of Molson's and go down to see my former neighbour. He doesn't recognize me, but the beer is a fine introduction. We walk through King Square to the Loyalist Burial Ground to sit amongst the stones and drink and talk. Earl used to be a checker at the port before the new container terminal and his chronic back injury forced him out of work. He once owned a house in West Saint John, near the Martello Tower. Now his family has all moved to Halifax; his wife is dead. He's actually a good-looking man, with that dusty skin and his woolly, white sideburns.

When we finish the beer, I take a deep breath and hand him the photograph. It turns out, as I had begun to suspect it would, to be a photograph of his dead wife, a woman he loved deeply but who betrayed him with another man. I tell him I am researching a newspaper story about a secret terror organization called the *Numéro Cinq,* that I'd appreciate him telling me anything he knows about it. Earl is silent, but tears come to his eyes. I say, "I don't know much. I've been tracking them for years." Earl nods vigorously. "But they're everywhere," I say. Earl hides his face in his hands. "Everywhere," I say, "and we're doomed."

2

I WILL TELL YOU now that Aiden dies. Perhaps you have already guessed it. Annie and I finally will have separated for good. I will have gone away to another city and another newspaper job. I will fly back for the funeral. I do this only partly because I hope to patch things up between us. Mostly it is because I like her family, her mother and father, who have often been kind to me, especially when Annie no longer loved me, and all the countless little O'Reillys. (There will, it appears, be additions—Annie's sister, Amelia, a soft, kind, simple person, has fallen in love with a dreamer who will never support her but has made her pregnant.)

I fly back for the funeral and book myself a room at the old Admiral Beatty Hotel. I recognize one of the bellhops, a homosexual classmate of Aiden's. I invite him for a drink in the bar when he goes off work and he tells me how the other boys used to tease him for being a sissy. In those days, Aiden was the only one who stuck up for him. Sometimes, he tells me, he thinks Aiden was the only person who was ever decent to him. I am shocked and chastened. I do not like to think of Aiden as a hero, but life always has a way of complicating itself.

I will fly back for the funeral and my faint heart will ache for the beauty of the New Brunswick forest as we descend through its autumnal aura. I will see the pulsing veins of its rivers and the gashes of civilization and the encroaching, all-blessing forest, and know that I too am only temporary, that this fever will pass, that the universe is only a bubble of my dreams.

I will take a taxi to the funeral home. I will see Aiden cradled in his coffin, so very thin and frail, not at all the laughing boy I remember, not mischievous at all, but thin and gaunt, with his skin sunk into his cheeks, and so small it seems even his bones have shrunk. Eleven months he will have been dying, eating Annie's Jell-O, listening to her lover's words.

Aiden's mother will sit by his head in mournful majesty. For a woman who has borne ten children, she is remarkably beautiful, possessed of a serenity I have always envied. I will kiss her cheek and say my say. And shake his father's hand. They will call me Flip in the old way. Annie will not be there—away somewhere, they tell me, sacrificing herself, cooking for the wake. (It is clear to me suddenly, as it must be to everyone I speak with, that I have been desperately in love with her all along.) Nights, her eldest brother says, after the public hours, she comes and sits with him, talking and talking, as if he understands. Aiden, the world. It will seem so strange, the terrible present, the irretrievable past. The world is not supposed to be this way, I will think to myself. The world is not supposed to be like this at all.

I will fly back to Saint John for the funeral. I will have written other stories about the place. I will have made fun of it—the Loyalists, the Reversing Falls, the petty pride. I will have had some vengeance. But when the time comes, I will want to go back. I will always want to go back.

    After the viewing, I will take another taxi to visit Lyn Shaheen in an out-lying village called Ketepec, where once (I recall) when I was a reporter, a black bear stumbled out of the woods and was shot to death. She will have married a man in a wheelchair, a man she knew before she met me, a man she returned to because I hurt her. Because I will feel badly about myself, because things have all gone downhill for me, I will try to kiss her when she goes to make coffee in the kitchen, out of sight of the man in the wheelchair. And to my surprise, she will kiss me back, running her tongue over my teeth, licking my face, searching with her fingers between my legs, finding that which she only half-wishes to find, the instrument that offers yet separates us forever from ecstasy.

The next afternoon I will walk the gritty streets from the hotel to the funeral home in silent despair. Annie meets me at the door; she shakes my hand. It is clear that I am nothing to her. And her grief is practical, not mythic as I had expected; she has done with wailing. But I am happy enough just to be near her. Going to Aiden, she proved I could not satisfy her, or that she did not wish to be satisfied, that she had accepted some sad truth about hunger and miracles.

Leaving the family for the closing of the coffin, I head up the hill toward the Cathedral of the Immaculate Conception, where the funeral mass is to be held, Father Dan officiating. But at the last moment, as I climb the cold, granite steps to the door, I turn aside like one accursed. Instead of waiting for the O'Reillys, I climb further up the low, clapboard canyons of the city to Carleton Street, past the stone Anglican Church, and turn down Wellington toward Germain Street and the South End.

Mrs. Lawson is alive and pleased to see me again. ("And how is Mrs. Cary?" she asks, oblivious to my personal misfortune. Because I am wearing a suit, she thinks I have come up in the world.) Sgt. Pye is dead. Some anonymous corporation has bought the building from his widow, and Mrs. Lawson is in danger of running through her tiny savings to pay the rising rent. Also, the new landlord has made her take in her tables and shipping prints. She tells me that Earl Delamare has been released to a halfway house in West Saint John.

It takes me half an hour to get there by cab, what with a stop along the way to buy beer. (We drive over the Reversing Falls Bridge with its fine view of the mental hospital and the Irving pulp-and-paper mill.) Earl is watching television with a number of other depressed-looking people. At first he doesn't recognize me (he has a difficult time just tearing his eyes away from the TV screen), but I finally convince him to take a walk through his old neighbourhood. (A social worker confiscates my beer at the door, so the first thing we do is head for the nearest liquor store and buy a fifth of Johnny Walker.)

We walk in silence until we reach Earl's former home, the seat of his many sad memories. There is no one around, so we walk through the yard, peering into windows, eyeing the shrubbery that Earl planted many years ago. For a while, I sit on the grass, drinking from a brown paper bag, while Earl does a little weeding and tells me what it was like to be newly married in this snug little house. The cheerful domestic tales he tells have the quality of dreams frozen in time.

When a neighbour comes out to ask us what we are doing, we move on. We stop at the Martello Tower (built in 1813 against possible attack from the United States; during World War II, there were anti-aircraft guns mounted on the roof) to admire the sweep of the river, the harbour and the roofs of the city beyond. Earl points out the old shipping-sheds, where he used to work, and the new container port with its vast spidery cranes. A chilly wind is blowing off the bay, bringing with it little runners of mist.

As we swing down St. John Street toward Dufferin Row and the Digby ferry landing, we turn up our collars for warmth and drink deeply from the bottle. We joke about taking a return trip on the ferry, drinking our way to Digby and back in the ship's bar. Earl is in an upbeat mood, and, to my surprise, I find my own spirits beginning to rise. But the ferry slip is empty, and we change plans in mid-stride, heading past the gate and plunging down to the empty shoreline.

The tide is out. The beach is strewn with bits of driftwood twisted into anguished forms, rusty pieces of machinery, shards of coloured glass and cobbles worn smooth and round by the action of the waves. We pick our way carefully toward the headland and the breakwater that stretches away from it into the fog. We shiver in the heavy, moist air. Just past the foot of the breakwater, we come upon an abandoned concrete bunker, built to protect the harbour from the threat of German U- Boats.

Dusk is falling, but we can no longer see the lights of the city for the fog. We are conscious of the city, rushing with cars and people (in spite of everything, I have not forgotten Aiden's funeral), just across the cold, gray water, but we are temporarily isolated from it. As we sit huddled together against the bunker wall, peering at the point where the breakwater disappears, it is as if we have entered some other alien, yet beautiful universe.

A Man in a Box

I

A WOMAN FOLLOWED ME HOME to my box today, claiming to be my wife.

I did not recognize her.

According to notes gummed to the wall of my box (n wall, ur quadrant, very early notes scribbled in a vehement hand on curled and faded yellow Stick 'ems—vestiges of an earlier denizen, no doubt, unknown to me personally), there once was a wife who abandoned her husband (referred to as "I," "me" and "the innocent in all this") for the manager of a Toys "R" Us store in Paramus.

This is the only reference to a wife I can find in any of the texts affixed to the cardboard walls of my home. It doesn't seem possible that this is the same woman. I don't even know what a Toys "R" Us store is, nor have I ever been to Paramus.

The woman seemed distraught. She tried to speak with me. But I have a policy against addressing people I don't know personally.

Personally, I don't know anyone.

My closest acquaintances are the dirty man with the beard in the next box (we share a common wall) and an elderly black woman who camps under green plastic garbage bags, from time to time, at the end of the alley. I have never spoken to either of them.

Stick 'em #131108 (on the s wall, there are several dozen numbered notes, printed in careful, resolute ballpoint ink) mentions a theory about the verbal origin of certain diseases (shingles, bad smelly farts, fibrodisplasia ossificans and plantar warts) and advises against exchanging words without a physician's certificate.

I am not the sort of man to be stampeded by medical gossip. I don't recall having read of this particular pathogenesis anywhere else. But in my study of the numbered Stick 'ems, I have found them, on the whole, to be measured, rational and strongly argued.

Therefore, a word to the wise.

My name is It. The woman called me Tom, a clear case of mistaken identity. I find no reference to anyone named Tom on the walls of my box.

Some of the Stick 'ems are so old they have fallen down (especially those which hang upon the wall I share with the dirty, bearded man; he brushes against his side of the wall in a most annoying fashion, deliberately, I think sometimes, causing it to bulge inward and shed its burden of yellow papers). I have gathered these up carefully and keep them safe in another box, formerly used to store a pair of size 9 ½ shoes. (I can still smell the fresh, clean leather smell—it makes me feel very rich.) I never know when the writer of the words might return to claim his property.

Some of these oldest notes bear the scrawled initials T. W. It could be that Tom, the woman's husband, used to live in my box. Perhaps he even built this fine cardboard home.

This might explain her tearful insistence.

I could not, however, find the words to reveal my thoughts to her. I racked my brains while she stood outside weeping and I crouched inside thinking. But I had forgotten the first thing about communicating with another person.

Did I address her as "my dear madame" or "Hester" or "you fucking pig"?

I wanted to be polite; I wanted to make a good impression. I wanted to open myself right up to her so that she could see she was mistaken and yet not be embarrassed about it. (Often in the streets, I see myself coming along and only realize when we have passed that it was some other person entirely. If a man can have this much trouble simply distinguishing himself from casual passersby, how much more difficult must it be to keep track of someone named Tom?)

In vain, I switched on the penlight attached to my cap to facilitate indoor reading (in the interests of conserving heat, there are no windows in my box; this also has the effect of increasing the amount of useable space for Stick 'ems) and perused notes at random, searching for a hint as to the proper mode of address.

Stick 'em #119735, s wall, ll quadrant: *She hath the loyalty of a windsock, the passions of a he-goat and the judgment of a golf tee. I have fixed her wagon though. I have put the darning needle through her diaphragm.*

Stick 'em, unnumbered, ceiling collection, sw quadrant: *The male organ is a thing of wondrous beauty but requires strict attention in matters of hygiene or it will drop off. Other names for male member are my little man and one-eyed trouser snake.*

Ed. Note: It is clear from internal evidence that the wall Stick 'ems, taken as a whole, are a composite work. I have identified no less than eighteen distinct authorial styles to which, in interests of future scholarship, I have given the following provisional designations: A, B, C, D, rabbit dick, Leffingwell, Quisenberry, T. W., Ronald, hammer toe, heartsick, Hester, my little man, Arturo Negril Q and W, Edward Note and Z.

It is not obvious from the texts when any of these notes were written or the events described therein occurred. But the numbered Stick 'ems clearly relate to a partial concordance on the s wall (ll quadrant) where water seepage has destroyed alphabetized listings from the letter F on. I myself have begun a reconstruction of the missing indices in conjunction with an overall cross-referencing to include unnumbered Stick 'ems, boxed Stick 'ems and a stack of old issues of the *New York Times* which I use as a mattress (also a tattered paperback biography of Julio Iglesias, with the last fifty pages missing, which I found in the corner).

Mysteriously, several articles have been clipped from the newspapers and have disappeared. At some point, I intend to visit a library and track down the lost news items so as to include them in my global concordance under a separate heading for non-existent words, words thought and not said, words better left unsaid, forgotten words, words said in haste and regretted, words said too late to do any good, and words said when there is no one to hear them.

My name is It. I know no other.

A woman followed me to my box, claiming to be my wife. She addressed me as Tom, a clear case of mistaken identity. She had red hair.

My closest companions are the dirty, bearded man in the next box and an elderly black woman who camps occasionally under a tent of plastic garbage bags at the end of the alley. I speak to neither of them; we guard our privacy.

The red-haired woman tried to crawl into my box after me, and I was forced to use violence to protect my property.

I blacked her eye for her.

She crawled in after me on all fours, resting her gloved hands on the foot of my newspaper pallet, and said, "Tommy, we have to talk. I know you're coming around to the apartment at night and ringing the doorbell and running off. Lance followed you in his car. We have to talk."

So I blacked her eye for her.

Boo-hoo.

I was nearly undone by the gross intimacy of it all, the closeness of the red-haired woman, with her bosoms hanging down, her rump in the air (I could, of course, only imagine this), the smell of her pomatum mixing with the foetid, cardboardy smell of my box, and the casual and familiar way she referred to Lance.

She backed out with a kid glove over her eye, whimpering.

Hester, I thought, in a fugitive sort of way, not knowing of whom I cogitated.

She sat splay-legged against the front of my box, with her feet standing up at right angles to the damp pavement, nursing her eye and sobbing. Her back made the inside ul and ll quadrants (e wall) buckle alarmingly (the ur and lr quadrants had been cut away to facilitate ingress and egress, i.e. the door). A half-dozen Stick 'ems dropped off, making a papery clisp-clisp sound as they fell.

I was overwrought and upset at the intrusion (Stick 'em LOAT #81: *A man's box is his castle*) and the outrageousness of her insane accusations, not to mention the implication that unseen spies were shadowing me to my very doorstep and the horrifying thought that total strangers might have free access to the premises in my absence.

The dirty, bearded man coughed in the next box, a kind of sniggering cough, a cough that screamed collusion with my enemies.

Hester, I thought again, uncontrollably.

Her breasts, I'll have to move, I thought.

I have begun renumbering the numbered Stick 'ems using a system of my own devising, prefixed by the letters LOAT, an acronym for the phrase List Of All Things. Hence, for example, Stick 'em #131108, under the new system, becomes Stick 'em LOAT #92.

The LOAT system itself raises a host of philosophical and grammatical—not to mention medical, lexicographical, numerological and gnostic—questions, questions which I intend to deal with in a separate preface to the LOAT Concordance.

To name only one:

1) What is the relationship of the LOAT numbers to the original numbers? Take, for example, the Stick 'em in reference, LOAT #92 (a brief, yet scholarly disquisition on the theory of word-borne disease vectors), formerly designated as Stick 'em #131108.

Divide 92 by 131108 and you get .000701. Multiply them and you get 12,061,936. Are these results simply random arithmetical products or do they refer in some obscure way to other, lost or as yet unnumbered, Stick 'ems?

Do the walls of my box conceal a hidden pattern discoverable only on mathematical grounds?

2) Why have I been able to trace and renumber only three hundred and eighty-seven numbered Stick 'ems, when my predecessor or predecessors were able to number them in the hundreds of thousands? Does this mean a vast trove of painstakingly inscribed notations has simply disappeared?

It has occurred to me that the dirty, bearded man and the elderly black woman, with her sinister green garbage bags, are not above suspicion in this regard. It could be that they have entered my box on occasions when I have been out foraging for food and deliberately stolen or rearranged my Stick 'ems in order to torment me.

Thinking about this possibility often drives me to despair. Someone meddling with my Stick 'ems, even the slightest pencilled alteration to a text, would render all my efforts otiose. The text must be pristine and untouched for me to be able to read the correct meanings into it.

The uncertainty caused by thoughts of lost or stolen Stick 'ems or false entries (of comic or sadistic origin) causes me to alternate between profound fatalism and extreme paranoia (see relevant psychological notes—s wall, both u quadrants).

The red-haired woman went away, but I was a shaking wreck.

Her sobs and the texture of her sturdy brow and cheek bones against the knuckles of my hand had left me completely undone and exhausted.

A fragmentary thought crossed my mind—*Depleted by passion . . .*

Then I realized the words were a phrase on Stick 'em LOAT #153, sw quadrant, ceiling collection (I noted with satisfaction how easy it was to use the new system) which read: *Depleted by passion, the successful lover withdraws into himself after coitus in order to recuperate the energies discharged into the amorous and unassuageable female. The cycle repeats itself, though each time he becomes weaker. His very success creates in her the desire, the lack, the absence, into which he, driven by instinct, throws himself again and again until released from this onerous duty by Death. The female is apparently able to have multiple organisms without any ill effect whatsoever.*

There were several LOAT cross-references, this being a key text, alarming in its implications, including a reference to LOAT #1107, a little etymological essay which I had written myself on that troubling word "organisms."

I felt better after reading this and spent the remainder of the day supine on my *New York Times* mattress, staring at the Stick 'ems above my face. After a time, the penlight on my hat went out and I was in the dark. It was better thus. In the dark, I could brush my fingers ever so lightly across the Stick 'ems as if they were a woman's nape hairs I happened to be caressing.

In the morning, when I awoke, I discovered that several ceiling Stick 'ems had fallen on me in the night, dry and quiet as autumn leaves. I urinated in an old milk carton and spent a happy hour with my glue pot re-sticking the Stick 'ems in their proper places.

Ed. Note: Here follow several unnumbered Stick 'ems to be cross-referenced using the key word "morning."

Mornings, now that it is cold, the dirty, bearded man and I rise late and sit at the doors of our respective dwellings, stuffing old newspapers under our clothes for added insulation. Wordlessly, we pass individual sections back and forth. He is a shallow fellow, dressing himself in the *Post* or the sports and business sections of better papers, to the exclusion of all else. I myself love the feel of the *Times Book Review* and the Tuesday *Science Times* next to my skin.

The ink rubs off, leaving snippets of articles and headlines on my chest, back and thighs. When I go to the mission for my monthly shower, I often enjoy reviewing past events in the mirror, before getting under the water. The chance juxtapositions and inter-cuttings make a kind of found poetry that is often delightfully witty.

Of course, there were other men at the mission who use newspapers for underwear. The dressing room is the next best thing to a library reading room. Certain lower class types sport huge headline smears from the tabloids. Others bear smudged, yet incisive, economic analyses from the *Wall Street Journal*.

I am the only real reader in the group. Sometimes this has led to misunderstandings and embarrassments.

The woman who claimed to be my wife has red hair. She returned this morning and spoke briefly with my neighbour, an act which filled me with foreboding.

I was unable to continue my work and had to go out.

In the street, I encountered several well-meaning individuals who pressed money on me (though I make a good living carrying a sandwich board around Times Square three evenings a week; I am a human sign which reads: GIRLS, GIRLS, GIRLS! LIVE SEX ACTS! HE-SHES! GREEK AND FRENCH TRANSLATIONS! NO COVER! FREE HOTDOGS AT MIDNIGHT!).

I went to the mission for my monthly shower though it had only been four days since my last. The concierge remarked upon this, a liberty and invasion of privacy to which I could not respond because of the angry feelings which welled up inside me. He told me to stop reading to other people in the shower as this annoyed them.

In spite of the concierge's injunction, I read parts of several informative *Times* pieces while I soaked under a thin stream of lukewarm water. One article dealt with the mysterious disappearance of Pancho Villa's head, another discoursed on the End of History, an event that apparently occurred only a few short weeks ago.

When I returned to my box, the dirty, bearded man was pacing up and down before my door in an agitated manner. As soon as he sighted me, he came running over, shouting, "There was a woman here to see you. She talked to me. I think she wanted sex. I've always had that effect on women. That's how I ended up here. My health cracked."

I didn't know what to say. He seemed so excited, so very pleased with himself *her breasts and red hair,* giving me his whole history and health record like that. I couldn't just turn away from him.

So we sat a while with our backs to the alley wall, watching the elderly black woman rummage in a dumpster. This was a profound moment of communion, let me tell you, though it ended abruptly when I tried to share my thoughts on the LOAT Concordance with him. The dirty, bearded man said something rude, and we ended up wrestling and spitting in one another's faces.

The elderly black woman screamed at us, "Aaaooorrw! Aaaooorrw!" She seemed to derive some evil pleasure from our conflict.

(Aged Stick 'em, shoebox collection: *The most common human experience is betrayal. All our relations are contaminated with sadness and terror* [Ed. Note: A depressing thought.])

3) Then there is the infinity problem.

I am composing the LOAT Concordance and its explanatory preface on fresh unnumbered Stick 'ems (there is a large supply in another corner of my box, origin unknown), which I glue to the ceiling in orderly rows easily readable from a recumbent position (sometimes jokingly referred to as "the missionary position") with the aid of my penlight.

I intend to begin numbering the ceiling Stick 'ems sequentially as soon as I finish numbering all the previously numbered and unnumbered Stick 'ems and the *New York Times,* also the trademarks, logos, company slogans and shipping instructions on the cardboard walls of my box (some of the box panels face inward, some outward, thus creating horrendous cataloguing problems).

Each numbered Stick 'em generates at least two concordance Stick 'ems and an abstract to which I append some brief, preliminary conclusions, a tally of possible connections (semantic, spatial or mathematical) with other texts, and assorted stray thoughts. To achieve my goal of total list integration (LOAT), I shall have to include the new concordance Stick 'ems as a special subset of all Stick 'ems. This means that the set of all Stick 'ems grows at a faster rate than my system list, making the job of including all Stick 'ems within the list impossible to complete.

A task which I once undertook with a light heart, thinking perhaps to while away a few idle hours putting in order the thoughts, observations, quotations, theories, apophthegms, limericks, hypotheses, phone numbers and laundry lists earlier tenants had affixed to my cardboard walls, has turned into a pointless burden.

I worked on reconstructing the water-damaged notes on the s wall. When the red-haired woman knocked at my door, I had finished eighteen LOAT references, a good morning's work.

"Tom?" she inquired, softly and wearily.

She had a black eye, a stunning instance of the convergence of text and reality.

"Tom?"

She was clearly deranged. I was not Tom, though I felt myself beginning to acquire a veneer of Tom-ness through repetition and association. (Ed. Note: See LOAT #437, Arturo Negril Q, s wall, ur quadrant: *The lover attempts to reflect the image of himself which he sees in her eyes. He steps outside of himself and becomes an other, a stranger. This stranger then has an affair with the poor fellow's girlfriend. Ha!* See under Lovers, Paranoid Schizophrenia, Betrayal, L-words, Doubles, Out-of-Body Experiences and Impossible Things.)

Who was Tom? Who was the red-haired woman, for that matter? And the ineffable Lance? (Ed. Note: See under Love Triangles, Real and Imaginary.) I found myself adrift in a phantasmagoria of things which did not exist: missing *New York Times* articles, Pancho Villa's head (stolen from his grave in 1926), Tom, words left unsaid, not to mention the numbered Stick 'ems which I had failed to locate.

I started to weep, abruptly aware of the futility and hubris compassed by my life in a box.

The red-haired woman seemed to understand. She placed a gloved hand on my ankle and pressed it. Her hair was heavily lacquered. She was wearing trousers and a short jacket made from animal skins. The odour of her perfume—Mankiller— was everywhere.

She was clearly ablaze inside whether I was Tom or not. I tried to resist, but she was too strong for me, and soon we were involved in an embrace.

To the casual observer, there was little difference between our embrace and the wrestling match I had recently had with the dirty, bearded man.

We knocked over the urine carton.

I caught sight of Stick 'em LOAT #57: *His life was haunted by a sexual sadness.* This made no sense to me whatever.

"Stop it! Stop it, Tommy," she said. "I'm with Lance now. You have to stop living in the past. It's not right what you're doing, making a public spectacle of yourself, hurting your Mom and Pop, harassing Lance and me. Dr. Reinhardt wants you to come back."

Ha, I thought. I knew I was living in a box and that the *Times* had reported the End of History several weeks before. But her beauty gave me pause. I felt sorry for Tom, clearly a man like any other, like myself perhaps, a scholar equally obsessed by his work and this red-haired Siren, a tragic figure.

Her black eye, partially concealed with cream and powder (the smell of which reminded me of my mother), was exceedingly attractive.

I wanted to speak, though when I opened my mouth, I had nothing to say. I felt the need to come to an understanding, for some sort of communication to take place, but the words to express this failed me.

From the first onslaught of passion, I had felt my desire begin to wane. I had begun to think of the Stick 'ems, ponder the meaning of the relationships, so far undiscovered, between the various authors. The truth was I felt my body dissolve as soon as she touched me. It became evanescent and airy, a thing of dentals and labials; I became nothing but words, ambiguous, ironic, fleeting and slippery.

The moment she touched me I was gone.

She knew this. I could see it by the tears in her eyes.

A new Stick 'em has appeared. Blue. A different colour from all the rest. Provenance unknown. I should resolve to stay in my box continuously, but nature drives me out, not to mention the constant hacking and snuffling of the dirty, bearded man next door, his amorous sighs—my mind boggles at what is going on in the next box.

Blue Stick 'em LOAT #492 (it was such an event, finding a new Stick 'em, that I registered it immediately in the List Of All Things): *Dr. Elkho Reinhardt, 3:30 P.M., Thursday. H.*

I think the dirty, bearded man and the elderly black woman have formed a liaison, a cabal, a plot, against me. Alternatively, it has occurred to me that the dirty, bearded man and I are identical (he bears the marks and scars of It-ness), or that he is the author of at least some of the Stick 'em entries, the ones exhibiting a peculiar sexual obsessiveness, for example LOAT #12: *She hath an organ that smells like a wet horse blanket; by the size of it, I warrant she hath been entertaining large herbivores; she pisseth continuously, noisily and in huge volume. The house is awash!* (Ed. Note: See under LOAT #92.)

I took off my clothes to examine myself. On my shrunken member, I found the words: *Several women in the chamber broke into sobs. Some men buried their faces in their hands.* Under my left nipple, I read: *Wandlitz, the name of the elite compound outside East Berlin, soon became a synonym for corruption.* And using a hand mirror, I discovered, imprinted on my buttocks, the words: *The most serious allegations for now are those against Mr. Schalck-Golodkowsky, but his dealings could not compete for public indignation with the revelations of the lifestyle of the elite.*

I made appropriate notes and stuck them to the common wall.

I was extremely pleased. Clues were beginning to point to this man Schalck-Golodkowsky as the agent of all my distress. I barely thought of the red-haired woman *her breasts* until I perceived that she was walking up and down outside my box, slapping her hands against her sides to keep warm, her breath going up like smoke.

How long had she been there?

I felt a sudden thrill of fear. Having decided at the outset to eliminate the time element from the LOAT Concordance and Preface on sound philosophical grounds (the number and contents of the original Stick 'ems being fixed, time references were assumed superfluous), I now found myself with no objective scale for determining the sequence of events referred to on the walls of my box.

How many times had she visited? The words "morning" and "Thursday" suddenly appeared less fixed and precise than hitherto assumed. The morning of what day? I thought, *Hester I am all alone and you with your toy man.* Or were they all the same morning? The urine carton was full again, so one could deduce that time had passed since it was overturned. But how much time? How long had I been there? Where did I come from?

The red-haired woman had cast me out of the Eden of my certainties and flung me into the Hell of relativity. (LOAT #87: *Her nether hair hangeth even to her knees.*)

When I poked my head out of my box, she said, "It's Thursday. You're late. You were out at the store yesterday, bothering Lance's customers. I've come to take you."

I threw the milk carton full of urine over her and walked to the door of the box occupied by the dirty, bearded man. In the murky darkness of his dwelling, I could see him and the elderly black woman with their ears pressed against the common wall.

I have you now, Mr. Schalck-Golodkowsky, I thought in triumph.

Clicking my heels with aristocratic disdain, I gave them a curt nod and said, "*Guten abend.*"

I went to the mission for my monthly shower. The concierge mentioned quite rudely that I had only been there the day before. I went into the common shower and immediately noticed, on a fellow bather's shoulder blade, the words I had so recently (?) recorded: *Several women in the chamber broke into sobs. Some men buried their faces in their hands.*

The concierge ushered me into the street once more, begging me never to return. Apparently, I had been following the words with my fingertip, my devil's finger.

I felt the same painful embarrassment a boy feels when caught touching his member by his Mom. I want my Hester, I thought, in a bleak and fleeting sort of way. What was a Hester?

I thought of going to the library to check on this, but went by the alley which I now believed was called Wandlitz, a place of vice and corruption. Old Schalck-Golodkowsky invited me to share a bottle of Thunderbird with him and the elderly black woman. They had the sign of venery over their door, but I could not refuse their kind offer. I wiped the mouth of the bottle with a dirty sock before taking a sip.

"Yer missus were har win you wuz out," said Frau Schalck-Golodkowsky. For the first time, I noticed she had only one eye. She was very old, upwards of one hundred and fifty, I should have guessed, looking into that morbid orb. Her words struck me as having a persecutory ring.

She broke wind alarmingly. Old Schalck-Golodkowsky giggled.

What did it all mean? I asked myself—the red-haired woman and the sudden unreliability of words; Tom and his evil twin, Lance; their collusion with the dirty, bearded man and the elderly black woman, now unmasked as the nefarious Schalck-Golodkowskys; the fresh note of asperity in the voice of the mission concierge; and the messages on the walls of my box, which had once seemed so open and eloquent, so ready to give up their meaning, to body forth for me their laws, structures and universal explanations in simple lists, diagrams and equations?

I had wanted to thank the old couple for the wine, but words failed me.

In fact, I began to suspect I was suffering from some sort of speech impediment—fibrodisplasia ossificans progressiva of the vocal line-out. I had become the words on my walls, but had lost my voice. It was a strange condition, let me tell you (though I won't, or I wouldn't, except for the large number of fresh Stick 'ems which allow me to make notes on the progress of my disease *her heart beneath her breasts, Hester* and leave them here upon the wall—LOAT #401 et passim—for later scholars of boxology, psychoarchaeologists and linguists of all persuasions; make no mistake, I am on the cutting edge of *a nervous breakdown* research into the limits of dis*(inter)*course, the pathology of s*(ex)*peech acts, the drag net of language, which floats through the sea of life killing everything that comes to it).

The wine had made me paranoid.

After an immense effort, I found a library.

I was able to trace one of the missing *New York Times* articles, a report on new developments in cosmology. Indications are that the universe would not have turned out the way it has unless there existed huge amounts of matter as yet unnoticed and unaccounted for. This missing stuff, the source of mysterious and powerful gravitational forces which shape our destinies, is called dark matter.

I knew at once that the red-haired woman and her minions, the synecdochic Lance and the S-Gs, were at the bottom of this. It wouldn't have surprised me to discover that the S-Gs had been secreting vast amounts of dark matter in that box next door to mine (suspicious coughs, amorous noises, cries of joy).

I left the library vindicated and went over to the mission for a shower but was not allowed inside.

Stick 'em, unnumbered, shoe box collection: *The messages from the past rustle on the walls of my little home when the wind blows or when the dirty, bearded man brushes against the wall. I feel a kinship with the mysterious, lost writers, the ancient ones who penned their thoughts and stuck them inside the box—strange cardboard bottle floating on the concrete sea-pavements of the city.* (Ed. Note: The concluding sentences are in red ink and written by a different hand.) *The ancient anatomists were wiser than they knew when they chose to call the exterior female organ "labia"— lips as in mouth and as in the phonetic designation labial—thus etymologically linking the power of speech with a woman's nether parts (which, I have heard it said, are capable of generating sound and rudimentary speech acts by the sucking in and sudden expulsion of air). The noble male member, by contrast, is mute, stoic and incapable of falseness. It is the source of univocal meaning. When a woman speaketh, so says the Sumerian prophet Raz-el-dorab, it is prudent to stand up-wind.*

The trick is to read all individual texts as part of one vast narrative the meaning of which will become clear as we approach textual totality (TT), that is when we have arranged enough or all of the individual texts (textuals or textettes)—the jigsaw puzzle analogy is helpful here—in their proper order.

At TT, for example, it will be possible, at last, to decide if life (L) is meant to be read as a comedy or a tragedy, as romance or thriller, or some combination of genres, styles and points of view.

It will also be possible to arrive at some *endlich* theoretical conclusions as to the nature of AOAT (the Author Of All Things, God, Amenhotep, Tom Wyatt, Herr S-G, or whatever name it will be proved He goes by—all clues pointing to the writer being blessed with possession of a one-eyed trouser snake [Ed. Note: Except for the blue Stick 'ems!]).

Of course, it must be admitted at the outset that TT, L and AOAT are all hypothetical constructs, moot, unproven and highly speculative. The LOAT Concordance and Preface are meant to be a sort of prolegomena, a kind of ground-clearing exercise and first attempt at TT, a preliminary structuring, if you will, of the hard data.

I returned to Wandlitz in haste, eager to put to paper my most recent impressions. It seemed to me, all things being equal, that $TT = (t)n$, where t stands for any individual textette and n is *Hester's bra size* the number of all existing, possible, putative, potential, virtual, spurious, forged, false and inspired textettes (or textuals. [Ed. Note: It seems that the use of the technical terms "textette" and "textual" formed the basis of a heated scholarly debate among the authors represented inside the box. Half seem to follow Arturo Negril W in preferring the feminized "textette," while the other half swear by rabbit dick who coined the designation "textual." There is even some internal evidence to the effect that C and Ronald were living in the box at the same time as rabbit dick and that the latter was forced to leave after promulgating his heretical jargon.])

The following equation then describes, in a form at once succinct, perspicuous and elegant—after all, scientific criteria are ultimately aesthetic—the meaning of existence: $(t)n/AOAT = L$.

I was tremendously excited by this discovery and only slightly worried about thoughts of dark matter, words left unsaid, Pancho Villa's head and the mysterious blue Stick 'ems. I resolved not to spare myself in my efforts to complete the LOAT Concordance, but as I turned the corner into the alley (Wandlitz, East German Sodom, Box City) I was nearly run down by a bright-yellow city sanitation truck.

The elderly black woman (a.k.a. Frau Schalck-Golodkowsky, the Whore of Babylon, paramour of my neighbour, dark twin star of the red-haired woman *Hester*—in a flash, terrible doubts assailed me; what if L = Labia, Lance, or Lovelorn? Alliteration was only a circumstantial clue, yet no scientific or scholarly mind could ignore it; only a painstaking series of experiments could settle the issue) sat weeping in the doorway of Herr S-G's box, wiping her tears and blowing her nose in a green plastic garbage bag.

She said, " 'e was takin' a shit in da dumpter an' det took oom away!"

I was struck speechless. (Ed. Note: Progressive fibrodisplasia ossificans was first diagnosed by the French physician Guy Patin in 1692. In the course of the disease, muscle turns to cartilage and then calcifies. As the tongue is a muscle, speechlessness is often the first symptom of onset. The patient generally dies after a few years by shattering, either from being dropped on the floor by clumsy attendants or by being knocked accidentally against door jambs. This is, of course, the origin of the term "broken hearted.")

As you know, I had never trusted these people. I could tell they held some mean-spirited grudge against me, perhaps through nothing more than sheer envy at my superior ambition and intellect ("Snob!" he would hiss every time I stuffed a fresh *Book Review* down the back of my pants). Sometimes, however, I suspected them of more facinorous motivations, suspected, yes, that they were in league with (dupes, paid informants, hit men) unseen forces (dark matter, Hester, the Toys "R" Us corporation) out to compass my ruin—on the whole things had been going badly for me, oh, for the last thirty or forty years.

Still, it was a shock. We all used the dumpster as a comfort station, careless of the dangers involved. I thought of old S-G, neighbour, drinking companion, fellow cardboard troglodyte, honourable opponent, cut off and swept away in the act of defecation.

Sic transit gloria mundi, I said to myself.

My heart went out to the sad, old woman in her hour of sorrow. I wanted to say something comforting, but words failed me. (Ed. Note: As usual. See *supra.*)

I reached out a hand and touched her trembling shoulder.

This is what life is like, I thought, loved ones disappearing for no reason, when your back was turned, going off in city sanitation trucks or with fast-talking toy entrepreneurs from New Jersey, leaving you bereft, empty and wordless. What could it all mean?

At this moment, the red-haired woman drove up in a car with New York licence plates (I had thought, from internal evidence, that we were living in East Berlin), a dozen or so new blue Stick 'ems in full view on the dash. She was wearing a plastic raincoat with the hood up.

I started off to the mission for my monthly shower, when she screamed, "Stop!"

She went over to the elderly black woman and asked her what was wrong.

Frau S-G repeated her obscure but heart-rending story. I really wanted a shower, having, in the red-haired woman's presence, a strong desire to scrub my little man. But I could find no words to express my desires.

What I had begun to notice was that I had times when my energy was up, when all things seemed possible, when I would throw myself into my work with a positive and optimistic attitude; while at other times I was confused, fearful, melancholic, assailed by doubts, uninterested in even the simplest words. (What if, I suddenly thought, L = Laminate, Lobworm or Laxative? Once the argument for alliteration was admitted, all sorts of horrific and Lunatic possibilities became thinkable.)

I felt the latter most strongly, as I say, in the presence of the red-haired woman, who at that moment was busy trying to squeeze Mme S-G into the back seat of her car.

I craned my neck and tried to read one of the new blue Stick 'ems—LOAT #92. With a growing sense of alarm, I realized she had fathomed my system, had tumbled to the LOAT Concordance and had begun fabricating false (though blue) entries to the List Of All Things *en masse*. This filled me with dread.

The red-haired woman had subdued Mrs. S-G who was blubbering in the back; I found myself in the front passenger seat of a BMW sedan (proof, I thought, of the German connection) with a Blaupunkt tapedeck blaring my favourite Julio Iglesias tape. We sped off at once, leaving the Sink of Sin, Wandlitz, in pursuit of the yellow city sanitation truck.

Though I still had nothing to say, I admired the red-haired woman for her decisiveness, her quick-witted willingness to intercede on behalf of old Schalck-Golodkowsky and his stricken lover. My own obsession with words, with the LOAT Concordance, with *her breasts* subterranean plots, infidelities, ambiguities, showers, Stick 'ems, concierges, etc., rendered me useless in a situation that called for action. At the same time, I really despised her for foisting her vision of reality on me, for her constant references to Tom, her persistence (the black eye had all but healed), and the truly insidious scheme to introduce spurious Stick 'ems (blue) into the box at Wandlitz.

I caught a glimpse of my face in the side mirror. On my cheek I could clearly make out the words: *Several women in the chamber broke into sobs. Some men buried their faces in their hands.* I carefully laid a hand over my cheek so as to preserve the message till I had a chance to transfer it to a Stick 'em.

The sanitation truck came into view just ahead of us. Old Schalck-G was in the process of climbing out the back, though his progress was impeded by the circumstance of his pants being down around his ankles and also somehow caught in the machinery.

With my free hand, I rifled through the stack of blue Stick 'ems on the dash. Out of the corner of my eye, I noticed the red-haired woman glance at me as she threaded the grid-locked traffic. (It was a strange city; sometimes it seemed to me that cars stood motionless at blocked intersections for years on end, their bodies dissolving into piles of rust, mice making homes in their engines, their drivers growing old at the wheel.)

Horns were blaring.

Frau S-G was screaming, "Aaaoorw! Aaaoorw!"

Blue LOAT #1287: *We all love you and pray for you but Lance is about to call the police. He says somebody tried to jimmy the back door of the store.*

Blue LOAT #37: *You wrote all those Stick 'ems yourself. H.*

My mind was in a state of ultra-confusion.

The dirty, bearded man fell off the sanitation truck into the path of a Yellow Cab. A Haitian cabbie jumped out and began to shout French epithets.

I recalled LOAT #37 in the box (yes, in her haste, she had duplicated an already extant Stick 'em number): *Man hath an eye for eternity; his works are multifarious, austere and transcendent; his Organ is the Rod of Justice. Woman hath a wayward eye; her purpose on Earth is obscure; she is a Temptress, and her Organ is the Swamp of Iniquity.* (Ed. Note: Once again the handwriting changes in mid-text.) *She says she loves me, but she just woke up one morning and knew she would die if she didn't change her life. She says I don't listen to her, that I make funny whistling sounds with my nose when I sleep, that I gobble my food in barbaric and gluttonous haste (watching me eat makes her want to be sick), that I bore her with my constant complaints against Fate and mediocre people ("Look who's talking," she says). She hates Julio Iglesias and the* New York Times *and thinks my nervous laugh is maniacal.* (Ed. Note: Not exactly what one would call a ringing indictment.) *Evidently, changing her life means going out with L., who once gave her a t-shirt with the motto "Life's A Beach" printed on it. How can she take seriously a man who has made a career in Barbie dolls?*

We passed the mission, which was only three doors along from where Mr. S-G lay in the street. I tried to get out, but a Yellow Cab prevented me from opening my door.

"Why don't you say something?" asked the red-haired woman (pretty, eyes the colour of blue Stick 'ems; only my dedication to the LOAT Concordance and a certain ratine—of or relating to the genus rat—toy drummer stood between us).

Hester's name *her breasts, her heart, her dear heart* were on the tip of my tongue, but the curse of silence was upon me. (Ed. Note: *Supra.*) Speech—evanescent, hasty, unconsidered, polysemous—evaded me; far more did I trust the written word which had a tendency to stay put (unlike women, viz. Stick 'em #128777: *A woman's words are as substantial as a ferret's fart. Trust them not.*)—grapheme over phoneme, those were my watchwords.

I wanted to get back to my box, to lose myself in my work, to drug myself with the infinite and loving analysis of the notes, signs and commercial heiroglyphs which festooned the walls of my corrugated home.

(We had, by this time, crawled through the car windows and retrieved the dirty, bearded man—a.k.a. you-know-who—much soiled by his recent proximity to the interior of the city sanitation truck. We helped him pull up what was left of his pants—all sorts of surprising and interesting reading material falling out of his clothes as we did so: several issues of the *Guardian,* a December 12, 1989, *Pravda,* sports pages from *Rude Pravo* and the *Frankfurter Zeitung,* and five identical copies of the *Partisan Review* dating from the spring of 1984. This sanitation truck incident had revealed new qualities to me; already I liked him better. Several of the Stick 'ems, I was certain, had been written in a little known Croatian dialect. Now I felt sure the dirty, bearded man was just the person to help me decipher them.)

Ed. Note: I had a dream last night. I dreamt that the elderly black woman wasn't: a) elderly, or b) black. We were making love in the box next door, this Cyclopean woman and I. She was about twenty, with one eye like a green grape and the other normal. Her lustrous red hair seemed to wreath her head in flames. As time passed, I became aware that the blackness of her skin had nothing to do with her pigmentation. She was covered from head to foot with a tattoo. Upon closer inspection, the tattoo resolved itself into incredibly tiny letters, words, sentences, paragraphs and chapters. I took out my magnifying glass—having lost interest entirely in our love-making—and began to read her body. I read and read. It seemed as though it would take a million years to read the whole book. I was only down to her left nipple (an amazing spiral nebula of a tone poem made up of concentrated miniaturized letters totalling upwards of one hundred thousand words) when I woke up. I could remember nothing of what I'd read, except that it was wonderful, better than the best sex. When I woke up, I felt as if everything was going to be all right, as if, finally, I would be happy again. I thought, She is the Mother of the World.

2

IT DID NOT FULFIL HIS GOAL of translating the Croatian Stick 'ems with Prof. Schalck-Golodkowsky's help. Old S-G returned to Wandlitz, but he had clearly lost heart after his accidental run-in with the city sanitation truck.

Constipation was perhaps his main problem.

His wife, growing less and less articulate, began to beat him mercilessly with old shoe boxes.

Eventually, he abandoned his surface home altogether, went to live in the subway and was heard from no more. He had tears in his eyes and stopped to give It a fond little wave of farewell as he staggered out of the alley the last time.

The elderly black woman pined for him (this is one of the mysteries of human existence: how a woman can hate a man, beat him mercilessly with shoe boxes and then dwindle as though she had a tape worm when he is gone). She and It had a brief, frenzied and melancholy affair, a relationship they both regretted later.

It probably summed it up best when he wrote in LOAT #2073: *We were both lonely, sad creatures. We had both suffered grievously in life, had both felt love and been abandoned. It was natural that, without thinking much, we should lurch toward one another in the hour of our need. But she was not a reader, and we both soon realized there could be no lasting attachment.*

Eventually, the elderly black woman left Wandlitz, too, heading, she said, for El Cajon, a San Diego suburb where she believed she might have family.

The neighbouring box fell into decay, and It had to take special measures to ensure the structural integrity of the common wall.

But Wandlitz had lost its Weimar Republic charm for him. The fruitful period, when moral decadence strode hand-in-hand with intense intellectual activity (like Nero fiddling while Paramus burned), had given way to an era of stagnation, cultural anomie and mounting anti-Semitism.

In this atmosphere of malaise, It quit his job as a human sign and began to take money from the red-haired woman and her toy mogul boyfriend on the condition that he make twice-weekly visits to Dr. Elkho Reinhardt, a prominent Upper West Side analyst. For a month that spring, It sank so low as to impersonate Tom Wyatt, the red-haired woman's former husband, in order to encourage the doctor and extort additional funds from the guilty (if deranged) couple.

This time of drift came abruptly to an end one afternoon when It (who never lost his native fastidiousness) adjourned to the mission for his monthly shower. There, for all to see, wrapped around the broad buttocks of a fellow mission client in sixty-point type, was a *New York Post* headline: PARAMUS TOY STORE FIRE BOMBED / MANAGER DESCRIBES BARBIE DOLL "HOLOCAUST."

He knew at once this was the proverbial writing on the wall, though how he knew he could not tell. Only, the sudden and mysterious linkage of the words "Paramus," "toy store," "fire" and "manager"—words which had hitherto appeared exclusively within the confines of his box—struck him as evidence of a disturbing synchronicity, a gathering of *her breasts* forces (Lance, dark matter) bent on his destruction.

Alarmed, yet lucid, realizing he must somehow save himself, he went underground within hours—first sealing his box with duct tape and mailing it to himself under an assumed name (Leffingwell), c/o General Delivery, El Paso, Texas.

Such practical action on It's part may surprise the casual reader. But he had always possessed a special affinity for the phrase "parcel post," and the sight of a Federal Express truck parked in the street beyond the alley never failed to inspire in him the frisson of adventurous anticipation other people feel at airports and train stations.

(Also, he had eaten a Mexican orange that morning, which he regarded as a sign. From his investigation into the disappearance of Pancho Villa's head, he knew El Paso was on the way to Mexico.)

It took two weeks to make his way across the country, travelling at night on Greyhound buses, using money he had saved from his therapy job for food and tickets.

In El Paso, he collected his box, then slipped across the border in the back of a crowded cattle truck.

Changing his name yet again (A. Negril), he journeyed south to the village of Ococingo near the Guatemalan border, where he now resides in a small, rented room above a brothel that goes by the name of a large American battery manufacturer. He earns his living as a letter-writer among the credulous and illiterate Chiapan peasants, while continuing his boxological research.

It is neither happy nor sad.

The passions of his youth are spent. He has to wear eyeglasses to read and make notes.

The brothel denizens regard him as a harmless and amusing eccentric and delight in spending a restful hour or two sitting in his box (it just fits inside the rented room, with space to spare for a hotplate and icebox), listening to Julio Iglesias tapes and sipping iced tea while the old man scribbles on his little yellow pads.

Sleeping, he dreams tropical dreams, full of talkative parrots and red-haired women.

And if, by chance, some distant night sound disturbs him and he wakes, It will step out on his tiny balcony, wipe his glasses and peer upward, marvelling at the innumerable pinpricks of light which spangle the firmament. At such moments, he feels the deepest peace. For in his heart, he knows that what he sees is nothing but the ceiling of yet another vast and mysterious box.

Edward Note

Calle Borracho
Ococingo, Chiapas

A Guide to Animal Behaviour

I AM IN BED with a woman who looks like a movie star, and I have lost my memory.

The movie star woman is asleep, which is lucky and gives me a chance to try to remember who I am and how I got here. She is evidently a person of low virtue. I can see she is shamelessly naked, as I am myself, I might add. And she is snoring. I find the combination of her beauty, her shamelessness and her snores moving in strange and delightful ways.

When she wakes up, she is almost as suspicious of me as I of her, though she has the advantage of knowing who she is.

"How did this happen?" I say.

"You were cute," she says. "When I asked you your name, you looked at your watch and said, 'Seiko Quartz.'"

Her name is Tracy Mondesire—used to be Tracy Gittles from Boogie Ridge, Levy County (the only county in the U.S.A. named for a Jewish person), Florida. Her family were Flat-Out Baptists, but died young, and she was brought up by Grammy and Grampy Gittles in a car-part heaven outside Ocala.

Grammy and Grampy Gittles were fat and blind and stood four square for the Bible and segregation. Grampy Gittles swore he'd die before they had a "coloured" TV in the house. He wrote verses for the local paper and communed with the dead with the aid of a hollow cow horn.

Several strange men interfered with her while she was growing up, but it was nothing she minded.

Glitter is the only life she ever wanted.

They tell me we are living in Bel Air. Does Washington know about this place?

Our swimming pool has an undertow.

I have set off the burglar alarm eighty-two times since moving in.

She sells real estate to Arabs, nothing under a mil and a half.

She can suck air into her hole and blow pussy farts. It is the damnedest thing to see.

She reads pornographic books to raise her spirits and sometimes will sit home of an evening with a stack of filthy cassettes as high as your elbow. I am not much for seeing it on the screen myself.

Wherever you go in this house, there is odour of muff.

One morning, I tackle Juanita, the maid, out of pure aggression. Evidently, Juanita has had her eye on me as well. We do it in a chair until there is nothing left of me but a little pool of sweat. I wake up on the living room floor, with Tracy trying to get my thing between the blades of the garden shears.

She fires Juanita without notice, then hires her back a week later because she cannot bear to be cruel to anyone who makes less than two hundred thousand a year.

After a year or so, we get married. It is a clamouring and tasteless affair with eight hundred guests and house ads in the toilets.

"Eat me," she says, lying on the bed with her legs in the air. This is an inviting subject for the Old Masters, let me tell you. I am not certain it is the manly thing to do, but I love to mumble her pussy, and it drives her wild.

I read in the *Enquirer* that I once flew DC-3s up from Colombia but turned for the state after crash-landing three tons of high-grade in a peanut field surrounded by federal agents. I fingered Richard Estramadura, arch-international crime king-pin, before he went into hiding. He has taken out a million-dollar contract on my life.

I ask Tracy if this is true. "He made it up," she says, pointing to Don, her publicist. I do not know if I should be upset that this over-sedated weeny is inventing my life.

To keep in shape, I do daily workouts with an S & W .357. Nights, I do speed and sneak up on coyotes in the backyard.

I drive a pink Fleetwood with zebra-skin seatcovers and an oog-gah horn. She gave it to me for my birthday. How do I know when my birthday is? I don't. But she says I must have had one some time.

Ten years have passed. I have learned to walk sideways in the street to cut down wind resistance. I have only strayed five or six times, that Tracy knows about.

I don't know how this happened, but we are having one hell of a time together.

A woman stopped me in the street the other day. I was wearing aviator shades, eight gold chains, a button that said "Drugs Saved My Life" and expensive white shoes made by poor people in Brazil. She said she was my wife. She said she had married my brother Daken after I left like that. She and Daken had just flown in from Kentucky to be on "Wheel of Fortune." We have three children, all brought up Christian.

The Indonesian Client

THE INDONESIAN CLIENT was due at 2:15 P.M., in exactly ten minutes according to my watch. But Bove, the CEO, had taken suddenly and mysteriously ill over lunch and had failed to return to the office. This left myself and Janet Louth, my assistant, to handle the Indonesian client even though, till now, Bove had zealously and, as it seemed, short-sightedly arrogated all client relations to himself. Neither Janet nor I had ever seen a client, let alone conducted any of the intricate negotiations necessary for a sale. Nor were we at all experienced in the fine arts of wining and dining clients. Yes, of course, it was the wining and dining Bove loved. The wining and dining were no doubt responsible for his corpulence and for his sybaritic leer whenever I hinted at the advantages of my presence during a sale.

Bove was a man of the world and a philosopher; neither Janet nor I could make such a claim. Though Janet had long ago confided to me that she was the victim of a sexual addiction, neither of us counted this as worldliness so much as an aberration of her wounded innocence. And Janet was obese much the way Bove was, except that Bove carried himself with grace and delicacy while Janet kept a large plastic pig hanging from her key chain. "He's an animal," she once said, speaking of Bove, not the pig. "It's all a hunt for him." When she said things like this, she would blush and excuse herself to go to the ladies' room.

I myself was thin and hairless, the result of a childhood disease the nature of which my mother failed to explain before she died. I was, according to Bove, his idea man, a copywriter, a wordsmith (or, as I sometimes thought, simply a high-priced interlocutor with whom he could indulge his love of philosophical badinage). Our product did not speak for itself; on the other hand, I had never seen the product—I worked from technical specifications written by our engineers and looked to Bove for inspiration of a more practical and utilitarian nature. Bove, who was Dutch, had travelled briefly in the East and had a Zen approach to business which alternately fascinated and mystified me. He would wave his hand airily and say that any vagueness inherent in my copy could only help in selling the product to clients who, when they came to him, often did not know what they wanted, that the product, defined open-endedly, as it were, could mould itself to the desires of a client more absolutely than any single-use gadget of the more mundane variety.

Bove decried the sales philosophy of market niches; when he came to the plant after the takeover, he specifically charged our product development staff with the job of finding something we could build that would be niche-less and yet fill every niche. That this revolutionary concept was not easily embraced by, among others, the product development staff is attested to by the statistics: one suicide, one voluntary committal, four resignations, half a dozen forced retirements. Bove, in restructuring the department, committed funds for eighteen new hires of which only three—Montag, Straith and Naylor—survived their three-month probations.

The new product owed much to these three men, and yet I had never grown comfortable with them. They were evasive, edgy and paranoid. Montag, especially, had washed-out eyes of aquamarine which seemed to conceal some murderous intent. Janet, who blushingly confessed to having had sex with Naylor in a men's room toilet stall on two or three dozen occasions, said he was not even an engineer, that his previous experience consisted of selling ad slots for a CBS-TV affiliate in Norfolk, Virginia. According to Janet, Montag, Straith and Naylor reported independently to Bove, who encouraged them to compete with and even betray one another. She also said the engineering specifications I used to produce copy may have been falsified by one or all three in order to conceal from the others the true nature of their research. Add to this the fact that the product was built simultaneously in parts on eight production lines, each effectively sealed from the others by concrete walls, safety doors, air-locks and employee fraternization bans (there were separate dining and parking areas), and you can see that there was considerable backing for my theory that only Bove really knew what was going on in the plant.

But what did Bove know? I asked myself. And how was I to deal with Mr. Wahid, the Indonesian client soon to appear at the electronic surveillance gate which functioned as a reception area in front of the burnished steel doors of Bove's office? I switched on a bank of security video monitors which Bove had installed over Janet's desk and with some relief noted that the elevator remained empty and stationary at the bottom of its shaft. Above my head, an illuminated stock ticker flowed hypnotically like a ribbon of light around the walls of the room just beneath the ceiling. I noted with surprise a five-dollar uptick in our stock price and an equally sudden rise in volume over the morning lull.

Like myself, Janet is a Canadian. The plant, which housed our company headquarters, sprawled over fifty acres of a North Carolina industrial park just outside Winston-Salem. How we came here was nearly as much a mystery as the nature of our product itself—Janet Louth from North Battleford, Saskatchewan, I from Toronto, where I had edited trade magazines before a series of buyouts and job tenders sent me on an international tour: Brussels, Capetown, Vienna, San Remo, Kuala Lumpur and Winston-Salem. I had stock options in a company once called Trans-Ocean but since renamed eight times and now calling

itself eTrans.com. When Bove arrived, he said I could stay, that
he had had his eye on me since Vienna, that he preferred Canadians because, like the Dutch, they are culturally blank, an asset
in modern business. Canadians are like suburban architecture,
shopping malls and McDonald's franchises, he said. They are
forerunners of the universal world culture.

Bove himself was large, bland and featureless. His white-blond
hair and eyebrows, his Buddha-like corpulence, his strange, whis-
pery voice (in which he affected an accurate but slight Midwest-
ern accent) seemed, all in all, to project what might be called a
negative affect. That he preferred e-mail for in-plant communication went without saying. He liked to say that a document trail
was worth a hundred decisions, and it was rumoured (Janet told
me this) that he routinely had inter-office mail screened for key
words or suspicious flow patterns he called vectors. What key
words? I asked, trying to recall any incriminating diction I might
have let slip in the past. Janet shrugged.

She was wearing a pair of silver earrings shaped like piglets
which I had given her when we were still lovers, before Bove arrived. I do not say that we were in love then, only that some residual yearning for home drew us to one another. It is strange to
think that being Canadian might influence what otherwise is a
matter of hormones and genital reflex. But we were both a little
lost in this weatherless new world of antiseptic pine barrens, featureless blue skies, gated communities for the new techno-elite (as
we saw ourselves) and dust-free cutting-edge industrial synergies.
Janet had grown up on a hog farm on the bank of the North
Saskatchewan River, highway of the ancient Indians, fur traders
and imperial raiders; she remembered the harsh shrieks of dying
pigs, her father's arms drenched in blood and the sight of a sow and
her young frozen hard as rocks one cruel winter. Janet's sexual allure was all in the sudden, almost pathetic eagerness of her desire,
while her desire itself was a combination of nostalgia for the gluti-
nous blood-and-excrement-drenched mud of that distant river farm
and her equally violent revulsion for a past she could not disown.

All sex, it seems to me, is the manipulation of guilt for pleasure. That Janet was aware of the compulsive sadness inherent in love goes without saying. She is an intelligent and perceptive young woman who yet could not help herself when the handsome and articulate foreigner, Bove, appeared so energetically upon the scene. (She claimed to have experienced a spontaneous orgasm as she watched him emerge from the gleaming, sweptback, erectile fuselage of the company Lear jet.) And it is a comment on Bove's insidious management practices that when he was finished with her, he reassigned Janet to me, so that all our relations would thenceforth be contaminated with triangularity, suspicion, jealousy and hatred. In a sense, this was simply an instance of the naked exercise of power symbolized by the exchange of women. But in my bitterness I perceived a subtle and perhaps more horrifying pattern. It was as if, as our product purified itself of mere functionality, we ourselves turned increasingly corrupt, petty and, yes, sinful, as though we were destined to sacrifice something of our humanity for the product to succeed.

Following another of Bove's injunctions, to hide nothing from me, Janet described sexual congress with our chief as "weird" and based on an anorgasmic latex fetish which involved Janet and Bove zipping themselves into identical rubber suits and breathing masks. Bove would then "doctor" Janet, that is, he would listen to her internal organs with a stethoscope until, encountering a heartbeat, he would throw off his mask and begin to weep. When she told me this, her cheeks blushed red with desire and humiliation, and she excused herself to go to the ladies' room. At that moment, I realized that she was lost to me, also that I was in love with her, and that the two propositions were identical.

Once I wanted to write the Great Canadian Novel. I had even composed the opening sentence: As they ate breakfast, it began to snow. Once I watched Saturday night hockey games on television with my father, dreamed of going to live on Baffin Island with the Eskimos and masturbated to fantasies of Jesuit martyrs writhing upon the stake. Once I slept with a sixteen-year-old figure skater named Paula Singleton, who simply and passionately opened her shirt for me one afternoon on her family room carpet. The world was a place of ambition, mystery and glory, which somehow, in the years that followed, translated itself into senior editorships on *The Wool Newsletter, Canadian Sugar Beets Notes* and *The Northern Hog Growers Association Monthly*. (Admittedly, the latter did help me attract Janet's attention at the outset. Not everyone can casually interject: "Did you know that out of the 293 hog growers in Saskatchewan only 23% had the capitalization to introduce bulk feeding systems prior to 1995?")

At 2:15 precisely the elevator bell chimed and the UP light blinked on, though a glance at the video array showed me the elevator was still empty and stationary on the first floor. Janet noticed my furrow of concentration and sighed. Her chubby fingers swept over the keyboard and, abruptly, the video images shimmered and changed. Eight people boarded the elevator and began to ascend, even as the elevator doors slid open and a solitary black man in an orange eTrans.com maintenance uniform emerged into the arbour of security sensors. I recognized him immediately as one of a crew of state-sponsored employees hired from a local home to enhance the company's image of social responsibility. Another screen showed Bove seated at his monolithic desk speaking into a wireless phone; another showed Janet working industriously at her computer; another showed me urinating in the men's room; and yet another showed Bove inspecting the shop floor in the company of Montag, Straith and Naylor, all clad, somewhat comically given their self-important attitudes, in anti-dust, anti-static suits.

Evidently, and no doubt at Bove's insistence, even our security apparatus had been turned into a beacon of internal disinformation. Again, as had happened increasingly in the past months, I asked myself, What is real? Why am I here? What is the purpose of all my work? Was Bove really ill? How much did Janet know? What is love? Perhaps nothing, aside from the image of Janet pursued by Bove in a rubber outfit and stethoscope, had shaken my faith in the routine trustworthiness of things more than this display of out-and-out fabrication. Although my faith in Bove as a brilliant, if eccentric, business manager remained unshaken, I now realized I would never be privy to his system, that I would always be manipulated and never manipulate, that my sense of self would always be secondary to someone else's sense of me, that reality was someone else's perspective. The screens shimmered once more on Janet's signal, and a new set of equally false images appeared. I looked at her aghast, and she shrugged, causing the little piglets dangling from her ears to bobble seductively.

But I had no time to consider this development because the maintenance man, trapped in a web of automatic safety gates, was waving energetically in our direction. When Bove was on watch, the office systems worked perfectly—yes, it occurred to me now that possibly, in his Zen-like detachment, he simply turned everything off. It took a few minutes, but we finally extricated the maintenance man with no more damage than a superficial radiation burn on his left hand because he would, against all advice, attempt to view parts of himself in the bomb detection unit. His name was Harley, I remembered now. I had seen him in several of our commercials, posing as a typical eTrans.com employee and spokesperson, symbol of the democratic benevolence emanating from the new product.

We sat him at Janet's desk before the video array, which captured his attention immediately. It was now 2:30 and evident that Mr. Wahid was either delayed or had skipped his appointment or did not exist. Both Janet Louth and I began to experience an existential vertigo, the effect of trying to divine Bove's intentions when his prime intention was always to conceal his intentions. His absence, coupled with Mr. Wahid's failure to appear on schedule, now seemed dense with implication. With

Harley, we remained glued to the video array, watching events we knew were not taking place, even catching ourselves from time to time performing actions we could not remember having performed. Harley, who had clearly achieved some Zen state himself, was not bothered by this at all; somehow he had already accepted the completely fictional nature of reality.

I considered whiling away the time with my usual work, though the thought of translating falsified technical summaries into fact sheets, instruction manuals and promotional brochures now seemed, frankly, a waste of time. On the ticker, eTrans.com was up eight points, volume was surging. Suddenly, it occurred to me that Indonesia had once been a Dutch colony, that there was at least an associative as well as a historical link between Bove and Mr. Wahid. What this meant, I did not know.

In Canada, snow was falling. Snow was falling generally on the great northern lakes, on the western mountains, on the glaciers crouched over Baffin Island, on the cedars bordering the slough where Janet lost her virginity to a boy named Michael F. who sang in the church choir and caught the flu from her, on the empty streets of Toronto, on the statues of Victoria and Sir John A. Macdonald in Queen's Park. I had once had a bitter fantasy that one day snow would begin to fall and never stop and that the whole continent, down to about Cincinnati, would disappear under the awful weight of a new Ice Age.

Yes, I will not gainsay the fact that Canada had become a symbol of everything about myself I wished to leave behind, that my constant dream of snow, glaciers and, occasionally, amnesia was a childish dream of grace and redemption, that all Canadians know the true meaning of Original Sin, of not being among the Elect. (My parents were Presbyterians, my degree was in English and Theology—I was bound to speak this way on occasion.)

An hour passed at eTrans.com (now eighteen dollars above its record high). Janet passed much of this time nervously rushing to the bathroom, a sign that she was succumbing to her addiction. In her eyes, her rubicund cheeks, her shaking hands, one could see the humiliation, the almost voluptuous submission to her weakness. Harley and I played two-handed bridge for stock options while watching the video array, which, when you watched it carefully, presented nothing more than a randomly repetitive sequence of ten-minute video loops.

There was something disturbingly inept and shoddy about the thinness of the illusion. Bove had counted on carelessness, boredom and inattention to collaborate with him in fostering this fake reality. And, of course, he had succeeded. The fact of my own unwitting collusion struck me with the force of a religious revelation just as Harley (who had turned out to be something of an idiot savant at cards) took the last trick and relieved me of $500,000 from my retirement fund. He kept chortling to himself, saying over and over, "Who's the dummy now?" Though it was all in good humour, and I had grown to like and admire him as a sort of natural man whose impulses, judgements and perceptions were all unmediated by ulterior motive or outside influence.

I still believed in the product, mind you. And Bove. But nothing else was what it seemed. And possibly it was only belief I believed in. In other words, I still believed things must make sense, and the only way anything made sense was if I believed Bove had some reason for all the manipulation and fakery at eTrans.com. There was a product, we sold untold millions of units, capital expansion continued at an incredible rate, shareholder value increased as the stock went up, split and rose again.

Admittedly, the company was still unprofitable. In fact, the steady seepage at the bottom line had lately become a hemorrhage of red ink. But this did not discourage investors, who flocked in ever-growing numbers to buy our stock. I myself had played some small part in this—following Bove's suggestion, I had written a series of press releases outlining a company policy that put expansion before profit, implying that it was Bove's sagacious plan to lose massive amounts of money now to ensure future profits that would be proportionally greater, that the huge losses at eTrans.com somehow actually guaranteed future profitability. At the time, I believed this. After all, we had created a product that everyone wanted. But what was the product?

At that moment, as if in answer to my unspoken question, Janet Louth re-emerged from the ladies' room, this time completely naked. She was huge, a Canadian Venus of Willendorf. In the crook of one arm, she carried a fuzzy stuffed pig; from the other hand, she dragged a dolphin-blue rubber suit made of latex as thin as those ultra-thin condoms. She was weeping, her great breasts heaved like tectonic plates. She was clearly in a paroxysm of desire or a crisis of faith or the afterglow of some primal orgasm or all three. Her eyes were glassy, she seemed unaware of our presence.

Harley muttered, "Wow." Then, "Fuck me, Mama." Which I took to be his ur-reading of the situation. I myself, naturally, wanted to go deeper. Janet and I had been lovers once. I had seen her naked before, but never so naked as now, if you see what I mean. Her nakedness now—under the full-spectrum gas tubes Bove insisted upon—seemed shocking, ancient, unutterably painful and yet achingly innocent. Women, as was ever evident in Janet's case, are pure signs, objects of desire whose desire is all that is desired of them. It has always been difficult in our culture to see women as anything but two-dimensional, as having souls or even brains. Even now, when women have been accorded a certain grudging place in society, evidence of female thinking is often greeted with nothing more than irritable forbearance. "Yes, yes, my dear, always interesting to hear from the women in the audience, but as I was saying..."

All at once, I began to wonder what Janet actually thought, trailing that disgraceful carapace of passion. What secret knowledge had been vouchsafed her in the sanctum of the eTrans.com executive ladies' room? What did she think of me? Of my hair-lessness? Of love? How had she been convinced to conspire with Bove to doctor the security video array? Like Bove, she seemed to be hiding something; in her nakedness, more now than ever.

It occurred to me suddenly that some of my earlier inferences might be faulty. With a sickening sense of déjà vu, I realized that I had believed in what was hidden simply because it was hidden, and, hence, that I had all along somehow put more faith in the thing that I did not know (because it was hidden) than in the thing that was right before my eyes. Hell, I simply discounted what was before my eyes. I had fallen for the fallacy of interpre-tation; I had been living inside a poem. (Hence Plato's famous distrust of poets—Bove was fond of quoting Plato, whom he considered a superior sort of public relations flack for what was then the new technology of writing.)

It was 3 P.M. The markets would be open another hour; eTrans.com had gone through the roof, as they say. I had been watching CNN the last fifteen minutes, giggling softly to myself. A voluptuous young woman with a sensual overbite and eyes darting behind too much mascara spoke from the floor of the New York Stock Exchange. Rumour of Asian takeover interest in eTrans.com ("Meetings are being held as I speak," she said) had sparked a feverish rally during an otherwise sleepy trading day. Surging vol-ume had twice tripped the New York Stock Exchange circuit breakers, creating artificial stoppages which only seemed to in-crease demand. Institutional buying was strong; fund managers, usually imperturbable in a crisis, were frantically scrambling to turn cash reserves into equity; the eTrans.com rocket was drag-ging the whole market upwards. Three times the announcer men-tioned that Indonesia was a vast country made up of many is-lands, the third most populous nation in the world. Once or twice, I thought the phrase "shadow puppets" was on the tip of her tongue.

Harley was watching Nickelodeon on another screen. Elsewhere eight people boarded the elevator on the first floor, Bove spoke into his wireless phone. Phones rang in every corner of the office, message lights blinked. At my own network terminal, the little arm on the mailbox was up. Was Bove trying to reach us? The stock ticker whirled about our heads like a giant halo, now largely ignored because CNN was transmitting real-time eTrans.com quotes in an on-screen box.

Janet worried me. She seemed somehow vacant, if not quite mad. I had wrapped her in a bath towel retrieved from the executive spa and sauna off Bove's office. The towel was imperial purple with the eTrans.com logo in gold thread. Janet knelt at my feet, shivering or shuddering, her body wracked by desire or unspoken terrors, cuddling her pig, talking to herself. From time to time, I caught the words, "Piggy needs to get out of here. It's not safe. Something terrible is going to happen. Piggy needs to get out." The sound of her voice, the nagging little you-have-mail icon, the ringing phones, the thought of the missing Indonesian client and the equally absent Bove triggered a wave of paranoia in me that warred against the redemptive digital read-out in the CNN box. "We're rich," I kept repeating, the words consoling me like a mantra.

A sober-minded commentator came on in a network cutaway to remind us of eTrans.com's record losses in the last quarter and read a company warning (which I did not recall writing) of increased losses in the current quarter. But then he went on to say (yes, with a messianic gleam in his insane eyes) that there was no arguing with the market, which had clearly shaken off conventional worries about eTrans.com's balance sheet. "The market is never wrong," he said. "What we are witnessing is history in the making, nothing short of the birth of a new economy, a mechanism we will only come to understand in retrospect. Money is being sucked into the market like air into a tornado. Any man, woman or child who can beg, borrow or steal a buck is putting it into eTrans.com this afternoon."

I could almost hear the pneumatic sound of money, money everywhere being sucked into the vacuum of desire. I felt a chill. The hair on my neck would have stood if I'd had any. And I realized the eerie unreality of it all, the suck and whoosh of money being hoovered out of pension funds, retirement plans, endowments, charity trusts, college funds, rainy day accounts, nest eggs, mattresses, cookie jars, piggy banks, all of that cold, hard cash transforming into electrons and digital readouts.

Suddenly I wanted to get out, too. Janet's words had somehow seeped beneath my conscious thoughts and re-emerged as my own. I needed to get out. Of what? I asked myself. The market? Surely I could sell my stock in an instant and retire fabulously wealthy, even with the losses I had sustained to Harley during our bridge game earlier in the afternoon. But the thought sickened me. Somewhere inside I could sense an electronic buzz of desire searing my brain. I wanted to turn it off completely. Merely succeeding, merely being wealthy, I realized, would never quiet the buzz. I had ceased, you realize, to think; my mind was a clutter of strobe-like images: the digital spiral of eTrans.com's stock price, Janet's naked, shuddering flesh, Dad's face in the moon-glow of the television so long ago. I realized it was the stock quote box, steadily clicking upward like an odometer, that was driving out thought. Replacing thought, I felt a painful, balloon-like burgeoning of what at first I took to be hope but which I suddenly realized was desire itself, an open-ended, ever more voracious need dragging me into the future. That little box on the screen looked like nothing less than the grave itself.

At 3:18 P.M., again suddenly (everything was moving forward with a jerky immediacy, as if time itself had been digitized), the CNN picture changed, and there was Bove himself, not ill at all, but looking relaxed, fat and avuncular in an open-necked shirt and suit jacket. Wind blew through his wispy white-blond hair.

Behind him, the sea stretched into a sunlit distance. His face wore an attentive, amused expression as he listened to the commentator's gushing introduction: how in a single hour Bove's personal wealth had exceeded that of all the great computer entrepreneurs of the eighties and nineties, how the Gateses and the Allens and the Cases were nothing but forerunners and footnotes, how it had been his gift to see the next great technological wave and catch its crest.

Then Bove began to speak. "I cannot comment at this time on the rumours involving our Indonesian client, but I can say that Indonesia, the third largest nation in the world in terms of population, is extremely important to our growth strategy. We are a small company, just coming back after the recent takeover and restructuring. But we have been blessed with an impressive product development team and a future-oriented marketing philosophy. We are entering the post-technology, post-Internet era, when all the rules that were broken in the past five years will simply be broken again, only more quickly. Since the invention of the personal computer, there has been a geometric trend: products have become better and cheaper at an ever-increasing rate. The time lag between one revolutionary change and the next has decreased with a regularity that has stunned many of the pundits. But one only need accept these new assumptions, say, as a new kind of natural law, and the future becomes radiantly clear."

As Bove spoke, the eTrans.com stock price clicked relentlessly higher. The Dow and the S&P 500 were nosing down, first tentatively then more steeply.

"My God," said Janet, shivering in her eTrans.com bath towel, "they're dumping blue chips to buy eTrans."

"Are you all right?" I asked, relieved and actually surprised to hear something like a normal voice coming from Janet's lips.

This calm new voice had a comforting, down-to-earth timbre. You could hear the quiet, muddy waters of the North Saskatchewan River in that voice. She reached and took my hand in hers, a gesture which brought tears to my eyes.

I squeezed her cold fingers almost violently in a reciprocal gesture of affection. And it suddenly occurred to me that love is an impure emotion, that it somehow takes into account all the failures, betrayals and inconsistencies in the lover, that it is not love if it does not accept and forgive the humanity of the other. Precisely what this meant I was not sure, but it produced in me a mixed feeling of sadness, generosity and warmth. I knew that something flowed between Janet and me at that moment that canceled the images of latex sex with Bove and bathroom sex with Naylor and countless other flagrant spasms of delight with nameless partners.

On the screen, Bove had stopped talking while the interviewer posed another question. But the network had lost the interviewer's sound feed, and Bove seemed to be listening to something else altogether, the sound of light moving, or that mystical wind stirred up by the billions of electronic dollars swirling around the Earth toward the New York Stock Exchange, or the rustling background noise of the universe, the great Om of God talking.

Abruptly, the network cut away and the CNN stock floor bimbo came on the screen, weeping like a child, mascara streaming down her cheeks. "Something's wrong," she moaned. "I'm scared. I'm so scared. It's not supposed to be like this." Then she grasped her microphone in both hands, shut her eyes and began to recite in the squeaky voice of a terrified eight-year-old, "Now I lay me down to sleep. I pray the Lord my soul to keep."

Behind her the stock exchange floor turned strangely quiet; traders, superseded by electronic trading programs, stood in awe, watching the numbers swirl around them like flames, watching their doom. And I recalled Bove waxing philosophical about the great bull market of the 1990s, how, he said, the stock boom was a direct result of Nietzsche's dictum "God is dead," which had also led to surrealism, postmodernism, MTV and the abandonment of the gold standard. "When Nietzsche unlinked God from the Word, he began a process of divergence: ideas which had once seemed connected began to drift apart. Signs separated from meaning, and money, which always had a syntax of its own, separated from value. And it became easier and easier to sense the inscrutable forces which drive existence, the backdrop of our illusions."

I shuddered now to think what he meant: the infinite, endless, oceanic desire of which each of us was but an expression, a minute incarnation—yes, the self as an ephemeral concretization of the World Greed, which Bove had understood so well. It was 3:33 P.M., and the New York Stock Exchange circuit breakers had tripped a third time. The numbers in the little eTrans.com box stopped rising. A well-known CNN anchorwoman came on with a series of news briefs: rioting had broken out in a number of American cities, a dozen states had mobilized National Guard units, right-wing militia groups across the country had notified members to arm themselves and proceed to collection points, politicians everywhere were telling people to calm themselves, which naturally had the effect of increasing hysteria. Yet the anchorwoman's words momentarily lulled me. Yes, I thought, words still did work, still described reality, still knit up the dangling threads of cosmic despair.

And then, inexorably, the numbers began to rise again. Fifteen minutes remained in the trading day, but one had the distinct impression that, on this day like no other, trading would not stop. Mechanisms put in place to ensure the easy flow of capital around the world would somehow keep the stock in play. As the New York Stock Exchange closed, another market somewhere else would open, and another, and another, following the movement of the sun, the flow of time itself.

What was the product? I asked myself. What was it Montag, Naylor and Straith had slaved so secretly to invent? What was it the eight production lines ran night and day with invariant efficiency to build? What mystery did the falsified engineering specs, those runic glyphs, conceal?

"We should leave," I said. The office, the whirling stock ticker, the flickering screens signalled a reality that suddenly seemed toxic.

"Where are we going, boss?" asked Harley, the perfect image of my black other, dusky, obedient and trusting. I had not even meant to include him, but now I knew I must—the world was teaching me.

"Yes, where?" asked Janet, whose desire I had desired as crudely and insanely as any Bove or Naylor. When would I see my friends as anything but a projection of my own dysfunctional dreams? When would my stories bloom with real people? And was there a reality beyond the digitized images of my fantasies?

"Baffin Island," I said, "as far north as we can get, way up in Canada."

I knew it was essential to remain focused and decisive. Even as I said the words, my eyes caught the upward-clicking numbers on the eTrans.com box, and, briefly, I wondered if I was doing the right thing, or if the market would redeem me. My God, the riches we were leaving behind. And yet they seemed inconsequential as dust. The Earth turned, the continents shifted, the vast currents of ocean and air churned as endlessly and meaninglessly as desire itself. I no longer wished to be redeemed into that nothingness of pure motion and greed. I wanted love and work and friendship—old things. I didn't even know if they existed.

Would we survive? I didn't care. I claimed that necessity for my own. Janet tottered back to the ladies' room to retrieve her clothes. She left the latex suit in the trash like an old self. Harley went to telephone his mother and find his tool belt, which he thought might come in handy on Baffing Island, as he called it. I reached to turn off the security array before the market closed. Just as I did so, a strange little man with dark skin, large glasses and a round brimless hat something like a Turkish fez appeared to enter the elevator on the ground floor. He nervously checked his watch as the screen went dead.

The stock ticker still swirled about my head, but I ignored it, putting my desk in order one last time (old habits die hard). I thought of leaving a message for Bove, something like "Pull the plug—save yourself!" but decided not to. He would understand, he was the master of absences and knew their manifold meanings. Perhaps, I thought, he never intended to return anyway.

Janet came back from the ladies' room, looking girlish and fresh, which I didn't understand until I realized she had taken off her makeup as well. She looked cured of her addiction, though I knew human nature well enough not to trust this perception and forgave her just the same.

Harley had abandoned his orange maintenance uniform and was wearing neat khaki cargo pants, a polo shirt, a golf jacket and a look of ironic amusement which made him seem, suddenly, intelligent.

What was I going to leave behind? I wondered. I took out my wallet, bulging with IDs, licenses, credit cards, debit cards, ATM cards, even cash, and set it atop my computer monitor. I placed my Rolex next to it in an afflatus of television-style romanticism.

We passed Mr. Wahid on the way to the elevator. He was struggling within the arbour of security sensors, answering computer-generated questions designed to establish identity and purpose of visit. When we cracked the weather doors to the outside, the air felt suddenly like air. Janet, looking buxom and good-hearted—that is to say, beautiful—linked her arm in mine and took Harley by the hand. Vast distances beckoned us. Harley thought the walk would do us good. At our backs, I still heard the ghostly hiss of money like the beating of a billion unseen wings, but Harley insisted it was just the wind in the pines. Maybe it was.

La Corriveau

I

I WAKE UP THE NEXT MORNING in my little rented tourist flat on rue des Ramparts with a really terrible headache and a strange dead man in bed next to me.

First, let me tell you that nothing like this has ever happened to me before.

In bed with a dead man—never.

Often they may have seemed dead. You know—limp, moribund, unimaginative, sleepy or just drunk to the point of oblivion. But until now I have avoided actual morbidity in my lovers.

I resist an initial impulse to interpret his sudden and surprising fatality as an implicit critique of our lovemaking the night before.

To tell the truth I don't remember our lovemaking, but the man and I are naked and the sheets are in wild disarray and I am a bit sore here and there, which leads me to draw certain embarrassing conclusions.

Embarrassing because I don't remember any of this and especially his name or anything else about him.

He is clearly dead and naked. And a man. Beyond this I know nothing (although, with his sinewy slimness, protuberant eyes and thick lips, he bears a strong resemblance to Mick Jagger, the man of my dreams).

To tell the truth, it makes me a little panicky being in bed with a corpse (however handsome) and feeling that I might be held responsible for him at some point, when in all honesty I can't say that I have ever seen him before in my life, though our having had intimate relations before, and quite possibly after, his demise seems indubitable.

Briefly, I entertain the sanguine fantasy that this is a joke, that my lover possesses a sick sense of humour which lends itself to overly prolonged impersonations of dead people. Perhaps this is some sort of weird sex game. I laugh lightheartedly and pinch his earlobe as hard as I can. It is cold as ice and stiffish to the touch.

Dead.

I jump out of bed with a shiver of disgust.

At least, I think, he didn't get up and leave in the middle of the night the way most men do.

On the other hand, our breakfast conversation is going to be a little one-sided.

In the bathroom, I pee and splash cold water on my cheeks to promote circulation. I look everywhere for some aspirin but find none. My hair is a nest of tangles on top of my head, and there is something, possibly chewing gum, stuck in the back. (What *did* we do last night?) My breasts look bruised and tiny—androgynous is one word for my chest. I am so tall I have to stoop to see my face in the mirror above the sink. Once a man told me I had the figure of a Yugoslavian volleyball star. I don't think it was the man in the bed, but it might have been.

When I return to the bedroom, he is still there (I had had hopes he would disappear, that I had been dreaming or hallucinating).

I think, a girl comes to Quebec for a little winter carnival fun and the next thing she knows a dead man gets into bed with her and ruins her vacation. I should complain to the Ministry of Tourism—anonymously, of course, and from home when I get there.

His eyes are open, little brown gelid globes. I have a weakness for brown eyes and men with accents. I realize now he must be French and am briefly fearful of the constitutional implications, I being English-speaking and from Toronto; I can see the headlines: ANGLO TOURIST SLAYS INNOCENT QUÉBECOIS FAMILY MAN IN FATAL SEX ORGY.

The French are so sensitive these days.

I recall his name suddenly—Robert. Not actually recall, but there is a work shirt draped over the chair, one of the kind garage mechanics and delivery men wear, with their first names stitched above the breast pocket, and the name over the pocket is Robert.

Poor Robert.

Dead for love. Heart attack, I think, or anaphylactic shock brought on by eating shellfish. (Had we eaten shellfish before making love? I make a mental note to look in the kitchen trash.)

But then I notice the dark stain on the sheet beneath him, the spillage on the fire-resistant carpet next to the bed and the Swiss Army pocket knife (mine, I am forced to admit—a gift from a former lover obsessed with outdoor pursuits) protruding from his ribs just beneath his shoulder blade.

My headache is suddenly worse, possibly the penumbral overture to a full-blown migraine. Also, I am extremely irritated with Robert for inflicting his personal problems on me like this, first thing in the morning before my shower and a cup of coffee. I make up my mind then and there not to let this spoil the rest of my time in Quebec (a mere three-day weekend, a third of which is already gone).

Briskly, I form a plan and put it into action, grasping Robert by his ankles (slim, handsome ankles, unlike my unfeminine tree trunks) and dragging him out to the tiny balcony overlooking the river and Lévis, on the far shore, shrouded in a brilliant icy mist.

I recall reading in a tourist brochure how drovers once herded cattle across the frozen river to the abattoirs of Quebec and how, if you see a man's severed head upon the ice, it is a sign you will shortly die. Had Robert seen a head upon the ice? If so, I don't believe he mentioned it to me.

(On the whole, I find it disturbing that the people who write these brochures seem to think that tourists will be interested in such bloody and lugubrious bits of information. How strange, dark and tortured the Québecois mind seems when you begin to examine it closely, how obsessed with death, separation, the loss of memory—they have that motto *Je me souviens,* which I translate loosely as "I remember myself"—and hydroelectric power. I leave you with this thought free of charge for what it's worth.)

I arrange my silent lover in a plastic patio chair, his arms crossed on the balcony railing, his chin nestled against his forearms, and drape his shoulders with a blanket, so he looks like a man enjoying the view.

Then I strip the soiled sheets and replace them with fresh ones and bathe and dress in jeans and mukluks and an oversized duffel coat, which must have been Robert's, for I neglected myself to bring anything so eminently suited to the climate.

I trudge through the fresh accumulation of snow along rue Port-Dauphin past many stately and historic buildings made of grey stone, thinking apropos of nothing that the tourist's lot is a lonely one, and also about Hélène Boullé (also lonely, also a sort of tourist) who married Samuel de Champlain, founder of Quebec, in 1610 when he was forty and she was twelve. How jolly for him, I think, somewhat acerbically.

She came to Canada in 1620 but had a difficult time adjusting to life in the New World and returned to France four years later. When her husband died in 1635, she entered a convent under the name of Sister Hélène de Saint-Augustin.

This is a sad little story which reminds me of my own. Like Hélène Boullé, I have had a difficult time adjusting to life in Canada, though, unlike her, I have nowhere else to go.

This present contretemps—Robert, clearly a victim of murder, showing up indiscreetly in my bed—is merely another instance of a bizarre and insidious synchronicity that has dogged me from the beginning.

I am thirty-seven years old (Hélène Boullé-Champlain's age when she entered the convent), a poet and office temp, unmarried (unless you count my twelve-year affair with an already-attached CBC radio producer named Edward, now aging and paunchy) and desperate. Also prone to fainting, blackouts, syncopes and blinding migraines—I have been advised to take stress-management instruction.

Oh yes, I have given everything for my art, just as Robert has given everything, including his jacket, for love, just as Hélène Champlain-de Saint Augustin, née Boullé, gave everything for God. (Or have I missed something?)

We are people of extremes, a nation within a nation, without language or identity.

At a bookstore called Librairie Garneau in Place d'Armes, I buy a book of Quebec military history (more death and defeat—whatever you say about them, they are a people of poetry) and two newspapers (in French—unreadable). Then I slip through an alley to a café overlooking Parc des Gouverneurs, where I sit next to a window and order a croissant and a cappuccino.

It occurs to me that someone ought to be alerted to Robert's condition, that an investigation should take place. But then I think of the bother, the questions, the searching interrogations, which might reveal—what?—more than I care to say about myself. For example, my dismal poetry career, my love for Mick Jagger, certain bizarre sexual preferences that point to childhood abuse (of which I have no memory).

I have surprisingly little curiosity about the actual events of the previous night, suspecting, perhaps with reason, that it was all too, too humiliating for words.

Across from me, in the little park, there are snow and ice sculptures representing mythological and folkloric figures, figures of dream or nightmare. But no severed heads or death-driven cattle. No statue to Hélène Boullé, perhaps the first woman to speak her mind in Canadian history.

(One can imagine the scene: Dead of winter, wind howling through the chinks in the log walls, a miserly fire glowing on the hearth, Hélène wrapped in coarse wool and animal skins, sneezing and coughing between sentences.

Hélène: M. Champlain, I don't like it here.

Samuel: But it's lovely. And the savages are really nice once you get to know them. And why do you keep calling me M. Champlain?

Hélène: I hate it. No one ever asked me if I wanted to come. I was playing with my dolly, Jehan, and they told me I was to be married. And then I was married and you went away for ten years. And now look, you're very old and I'm not having fun.)

I feel suddenly claustrophobic, as if I have wakened to find myself immured behind the stone walls of a convent. (Do I hear police sirens in the distance, trailing along the walls of this medieval city, founded first for greed and then for God—poor Jacques Cartier, when he got back to France and discovered his diamonds were quartz?) My mind is wandering. My headache . . . well.

Suddenly, I recall horses and a carriage and a nighttime ride with a man who seemed, with his horsewhip, duffel coat and French accent, the very image of romance, a boreal Mick Jagger.

But what did we do with the horse? (Now I do detect a distinctive equine odour on my coat.)

I believe things are coming back to me.

This leads me to rush off, leaving my coffee cold (as Robert), my croissant untouched, my newspapers unread (what could possibly be new?). Movement seems imperative to ward off the flood of memories which just might possibly prove unpleasant if not actually inculpatory.

There are still few people about on account of the extremely low temperature and the generally threatening nature of the weather. The place is as hospitable to human habitation as Mars. (Oh, Canada, our home and alien land.)

No wonder Hélène Boullé hated it.

Then I have a jarring thought. What if history is a male lie? What if she actually loved Canada, and Samuel sent her back because he was envious? What if she was having too good a time, the Indians loved her, she found the savage religions appealing, she was beginning to take their side in beaver trade disputes?

Perhaps she never got to speak her mind, do what she wanted to do.

And when Samuel died and she went meekly like a lamb into the convent, did she even know what she thought?

Did she remember?

Je me souviens is a difficult motto to live up to; I myself remember nothing.

I circle back past the funicular, following the city walls again, till I stand just opposite my darling little flat (with kitchenette and sitting room and Sacred Heart bleeding above the bedstead, all for an extremely reasonable price). Robert, a.k.a. Mick, is still peering out at the steaming river and the ice-rimmed, smoking buildings of Lévis on the far shore, though the snow is beginning to drift a little behind him and he has an odd-looking triangular cap upon his head.

What do his dead eyes see? I ask myself. Figures of ice and floating heads?

Does he hear the lurid song of La Corriveau, the Siren of Quebec (see those tourist brochures), who murdered her husband and was hanged and exposed in an iron cage above a crossroads till her body rotted? (Later the cage became a minor exhibit in Mr. Barnum's circus—you can make whatever you want of this outré fact.)

Did I dream this, or did Robert? A naked woman running, slipping in the snow. La Corriveau, to be sure. Calling for help, calling the men of the city to their deaths.

(This is the legend, at any rate, that she returns from time to time, attracts men with her pitiable lamentations, then slaughters them. To my mind, she is just crabby, just a little premenstrual, if you know what I mean, because the whole thing was such a mess, what with the cage being built too short and she having to crouch even after they hanged her, a victim of incompetent male technocrats. Ugh!)

I think of the great and saintly Bishop Laval who died here three hundred years ago after suffering frostbite on his bare feet while doing penance in the snow.

Oh, Quebec (as a poet, I am an aficionado of the rhetorical device called apostrophe), death-driven, poetical, and strange. (The obsession with hydroelectric power, dams and rivers seems symptomatic of a mother complex—in the throes of passion, did not dear Robert call out for his church and for his mother, or possibly his horse? Am I making this up? Or am I merely, like all English Canadians, obsessed with dissecting my French other—my mother calls them Kew-beckers?)

2

I AM WRITING my confession down—I might as well let you know—under the grey stare of a police detective who tells me his name is Gilbert and who has once or twice interrupted my narrative to tell me amusing anecdotes about his children and his wife, whom he insists on calling "ma blonde."

He resembles Mick Jagger somewhat, though perhaps it is only the black leather bomber jacket he wears that gives me this impression.

Gilbert particularly wants me to explain the presence of my Swiss Army knife in the interstices of Robert's ribs. He calls this knife "the cause of death," a summary designation which I find reductive and unpoetical.

If Robert had not been born, he surely would not have died, I say, remembering (as usual) nothing, feeling the iron bars of the cage squeezing inward on my brain. Yes, my headache has not abated.

The police found the horse, it seems, wandering in the streets before dawn, dragging its empty carriage, suffering frostbite and loneliness.

From time to time, she would lift her head and whinny plain-tively for Robert to take her home.

Her name is Nellie, and she is now in police custody.

When Gilbert tells me this story, I break down and weep.

I have seduced a man into betraying his horse.

(With this, I remember again my solitary midnight ride among the ice sculptures, the fantastic, contorted shapes, all lit up and glowing. I recall Robert, duffel-coated and masterful, wrapping me in blankets and guiding the horse with clucks of his tongue.)

Gilbert peers over my shoulder and clucks his tongue sympa-thetically. Perhaps I would like a cup of coffee, he says. Perhaps some other refreshment, a change of air.

His English is only adequate, I think. But charming. His eyes are brown. When we stand, his head reaches to my shoulder, but I feel certain he has enough self-esteem not to be bothered by the physical discrepancy.

Even so I crouch a little as we walk.

He takes me to a café a block from the police station and orders a cappuccino and a brioche.

I tell him of my memory lapses (a common Anglo-Canadian complaint), my language problems, my blackouts and my in-ability to find a publisher for my poetry.

Somewhat irritatingly, he keeps trying to steer the conversa-tion back to Robert, who is a dead letter as far as I am concerned, a character to be written out of the story.

I tell Gilbert he reminds me of Mick Jagger.

He smiles and lights a cigarette and tells me I too remind him of someone, a woman he saw in a dream.

Uh-oh, I think.

I say, I suppose you assume I'm the sort of girl who travels around preying on French-Canadian calèche drivers named Robert.

He gives a throaty, Mick Jaggerish chuckle, and I can see right away that we have established a relationship that goes beyond the purely professional, that he sees me as someone other than the run-of-the-mill murderess, someone who perhaps needs a protecting arm.

A tiny muscle in my neck begins to pulse like a second heart.

There are snow-covered statues at either end of the street, resembling the icy sculptures in the Old Town, tortured, demonic creatures, visions of some frigid Hell.

My headache is worse, a virtual blazing light of pain, as though my skull were caught in the bars of a cage.

I realize suddenly that my infatuation with Mick Jagger is merely an extension of English Canada's pernicious anglophilia—substitute the Queen for Mick and I am like anyone else from Saskatoon or Victoria.

To cover my discomfiture, I tell Gilbert the story (culled from inane and ubiquitous tourist brochures) of Marie de l'Incarnation, an early religious pioneer in New France, who (like me) had visions and was married twice and who, in 1631, entered the Ursuline convent at Tours despite the pleadings of her only son, who stood outside the doors screaming, "Give me back my mother."

On the whole, I think, French-Canadian history is littered with dysfunctional families. It is difficult to know what to make of this fact.

Gilbert has a tear in his eye. I have touched him with my little tale. He understands, as any member of his race would, that all life is either metonymic or synecdochic. The policeman in him is at war with the poet. It is refreshing to see such passion in a public servant.

We warm to each other in the humid little café, despite the cold front descending on the city beyond the windows. People walking in the streets take on the aspect of ice statues. Ice statues begin to resemble ordinary tourists, shoppers and dead calèche drivers.

Night is falling, despite my impression that day just dawned moments ago.

Gilbert says that at first they thought Robert had frozen to death. Only after he thawed out did they discover the knife wound.

I remember nothing, I say.

They found me at the city zoo, which specializes in native species now extinct in southern Ontario where I live. (There are, for example, cages full of Native Americans, Anglo Poets, Entirely Free Women, Liberated Men and Innocent Children.)

I think, how I long for the time when the black bear and moose will return to the tepid streets of Toronto.

Gilbert leans forward, his face pregnant with pity and empathy, and touches my wrist with the tips of his fingers. He wishes to tell me that he is not a projection of my dreams, that he is himself, separate and whole, and that he will help me if I let him.

I remember nothing, I say.

But his gentleness disarms me. All at once, I begin to weep. It is clear that I have gotten off on the wrong foot with this man, that there is still gum in my hair, that when I left the flat this morning I put on the same clothes I wore the day before, that killing Robert was a monumental faux pas. (My constant reference to loss of memory in the foregoing is clearly a case of reaction formation; we all try to put our worst crimes in the best light possible.)

All I can say in my defence is that homicide is totally out of character for me, most days.

Gilbert suggests a calèche ride. Perhaps we might attempt to recapitulate the events of the evening before so as to jog my memory.

Meekly, I assent.

(I think, soon now my lifelong fantasy of being hung above a crossroads to rot, in full public view, will become a reality.)

Through the testimony of witnesses who saw me in Robert's carriage, the police have been able to reconstruct much of our route.

The driver is a non-French-speaking Irish exchange student named Reilly.

The horse's name is Retribution. (I mention this, though quite possibly it is an unimportant detail.)

In moments we emerge from the Porte Saint-Louis and turn down Avenue George VI into the former battlefield (now rolling parkland). A gusty wind drives swirls of ice particles round the lampposts and into our faces. Gilbert and I huddle together, wrapped in a five-point Hudson Bay trading blanket.

Here, as everywhere else, city officials have erected myriad ice statues commemorating significant events in the nation's history. Behind us, the city walls are illuminated, shrieks from revellers and bobsled riders pierce the night air, the funicular rises and falls like breath. But here, Iroquois warriors stalk unwary habitants, Jacques Cartier is mining diamonds along the river shore, Abraham is herding his cows and planting cabbages, and a sickly Wolfe is climbing a narrow path, surrounded by his intrepid, kilted soldiers, with death in his heart.

At the centre of the park, we reach the place of memory (where I believe Robert kissed me for the first time).

I can see by the horrified look on Gilbert's face that he can see what I see—the ice statues come alive, wounded soldiers piled in heaps, dying generals, weeping savages, fatherless children, widows touching themselves in ecstasies of loneliness.

I say to him, I am guilty. Of everything. I wanted to sleep with my father. I poured boiling water into the goldfish bowl when I was eight. I began to masturbate at twelve. I killed Robert the calèche driver (though I fully believe that, after an evening with me, he wanted to die).

I do not say that any of this is trivial, but I shall plead extenuating circumstances. I shall blame history, lurid tourist brochures and love gone wrong.

This time I'll get off, I say. You'll see.

I do not think he hears me.

Why I Decide to Kill Myself and Other Jokes

THE PLAN BEGINS TO FALL APART the instant Professor Rainbolt, Hugo's graduate adviser, spots me slipping out of the lab at 11 P.M. on a Sunday. Right away he is suspicious. I am not a student; the lab is supposed to be locked. But, like a gentleman, he doesn't raise a stink. He just nods and watches me lug my bulging (incriminating) purse through the fire doors at the end of the corridor.

Problems. Problems. Professor Rainbolt knows I'm Hugo's girl. He's seen us around together. Now he's observed me sneaking out of the lab at 11 P.M. (on a Sunday). He's probably already checked to see if, by chance, Hugo has come in to do some late night catch-up work on his research project. Hugo will not be there, the lights will be out, and Hugo will be in shit for letting me have his lab key (I stole it).

Now, I didn't plan this to get Hugo into trouble. At least, not this kind of trouble. Other kinds of trouble, maybe. Guilt, for example. But now, when they find my corpse and detect the distinctive almond odour of cyanide, they will know exactly where the stuff came from, whose lab key I used, and Hugo will lose his fellowship, not to mention his career, such as it is. Let me tell you, Hugo is not going to lay this trip on me after I am dead.

Also, the whole Rainbolt thing raises the question of timing. Let us say that a person wants, in general, to kill herself. She has a nice little supply of cyanide, obtained illegally from a university research lab (plants, not animals), which she intends to hoard for use when the occasion arises.

She might, for example, prefer to check out on a particularly nice day, after a walk with her dogs along the River Speed. Perhaps after sex with Hugo—and a bottle of Beaujolais. In bed, by herself. (Hugo exiting the picture; forget where he goes. Probably a bar somewhere, with his guitar, flicking his long hair—grow up, Hugo—to attract the attention of coeds.) Her Victorian lace nightie fanning out from her legs and a rose, symbol of solidarity with the plant world, in her hand.

But now she has to factor in Professor Rainbolt and the thought that her little escapade into the realm of break, enter and theft will soon be common knowledge on the faculty grapevine, the campus police alerted, the town police on the lookout (*slender blond, five-ten, twenty-six years old, with blue eyes and no scars—outside—answers to the name Willa),* and that Hugo will be, well, livid and break something (once he broke his own finger, ha ha).

A girl decides to kill herself and life suddenly becomes a cesspit of complications. Isn't that the way it always is? I think. And suddenly I am reminded of my father who, coincidentally, was waylaid and disarmed on his way to the garden with the family twelve-gauge one afternoon, after kissing Mom with unusual and suspicious fervour because, he claimed, of her spectacular pot roast (why he kissed her, not why he was going out the door with the gun—target practice, he said).

He was already far gone with cancer, in his brain and other places. Trying to sneak into the garden was the last sane thing he did. Can you guess that it was me who wrestled that gun from his pathetically weakened hands? That I spent the next six months lifting him from room to room, feeding him mush, wiping his ass? That in my wallet I still carry, along with other photographic memorabilia, a Polaroid of Dad in his coffin?

Let me pause to point out certain similarities, parallels or spiritual ratios. Gardens play a role in both these stories. That lab is really an experimental garden full of flats choked with green shoots. Hugo breeds them, harvests them, pulverizes them, whirls them, refrigerates them, distils them, micro-inspects them—in short, he is a plant vivisectionist. It is a question of certain enzymes, I am told, their presence or absence being absolutely crucial to something . . . something—I forget. We have made love here amongst the plants, me bent over a centrifuge with my ass in the air and my pants around my ankles, which did not seem seriously outré at the time. (On one such occasion, I noticed the cyanide on the shelf above, clearly marked with a skull-and-crossbones insignia.)

Gardens and suicide run in the family. Failed suicides, I am now forced to conjecture. Clearly, one did not foresee the myriad difficulties, or that fate would place Professor Rainbolt at the door as I left the lab/garden, feeling sorry for the plants—I have heard that African violets scream—thinking, why, why can't they just leave well enough alone?

The time factor is crucial. I do not relish being rushed. But when will I have another chance? Also, quite suddenly, I realize I have forgotten to find out if cyanide poisoning is painful. I have a brief, blinding vision of blue me writhing in the Victorian nightie, frothing vomit and beshitting myself. Someone would have to wipe my butt, and I, like my father, never wanted that. Never, never, never.

I see I have reached my car, our car, Hugo's and mine, a wine-coloured Pinto with an exploding gas tank. We both like to live cheaply and dangerously. Bismarck, the Doberman, and Jake, the mutt, greet me with preens, wriggles and barks of delight. It is nice to be among friends.

The dogs sniff at my purse where I often carry treats—rawhide bones or doggy biscuits or rubber balls. This time we have cyanide, which I ponder while the car warms up. The winter outside corresponds to the winter of my spirit, which is a dry, cold wind, or the snow crystals on the windshield remind me of the poison crystals in the jar.

I will be the first to admit that I have made mistakes. Once I was crossing Bloor Street at Varsity Stadium, being a cool, sexy lady without any underpants, when the wind lifted my skirt and showed my pussy to eighty-five strange men. And once I confessed to Hugo's mother about my affair with a lead guitarist named Chuck Madalone.

Hugo called this fling with Chuck an affair on a technicality. In my opinion, Hugo and I were not: a) officially going together, b) in love. I was in love; Hugo was in doubt, which is an entirely different thing. In my opinion, my date, tryst, rendezvous or whatever with Chuck (the innocent in all this) was pre-Hugo. Hugo said we (he and I) had had sex. These are his words. Hugo, like many men, appears to believe that ejaculation is a form of territorial marking, like dogs peeing on hydrants. I say, it washes off.

How was I to know, as Hugo claims, that he was in love, though in a kind of doubtful, non-verbal way, or that he would follow us home that night and spy through the window in a hideous state of guilt, rage and titillation? Hugo says "affair." I say, meanings migrate like lemmings and words kill.

Here we have, I think to myself, a jar of cyanide, which, as we who live with guitar-playing scientists know, is a simple compound of cyanogen with a metal or organic radical, as in potassium cyanide (KCN). Cyanogen is a dark-blue mineral named for its entering into the composition of Prussian blue, which I think is rather nice, giving my death an aesthetic dimension. The cyanide (in this case KCN) will also turn me blue, as in cyanosis, a lividness of the skin owing to the circulation of imperfectly oxygenated blood. Something like drowning—inward shudder.

The time factor, as I say, is crucial. I do not wish to die in this Pinto with my dogs looking on. Life will be sad enough for them afterward. With dogs, as with women, Hugo displays a certain winning enthusiasm, which is charming at the outset, though it soon wears off as he develops new interests.

I must use guile and cunning; I must be Penelope weaving and unravelling. The trick will be to secrete enough of this snowy, crystalline substance, which turns people blue, in, say, yes, a plastic cassette box, which when filed in Hugo's cassette tray will resemble in external particulars every other non-lethal cassette box. Then I can surrender the jar to Hugo for return to Professor Rainbolt with beaucoup d'apologies. I will look like an ass, but this is not new.

I carefully pour out what I consider to be the minimum fatal dose, then double it. (Oops, we spill a little—I flick it off the seatcovers with a glove.)

I dread facing Hugo, but without actually using the cyanide, in unseemly and undignified haste, there seems no way out. We are going to have a scene, no doubt about it. Hugo loves production numbers. He invariably assumes an air of righteous indignation, believing himself to be a morally superior being. This has something to do with his being a vegetarian (though a smoker—consistency is the hobgoblin of other minds) and my "affair." Which reminds me about his mother, that particular production.

How we arrived there for my first visit in the midst of a vicious quarrel over Chuck, with Hugo threatening to leave me after each fresh accusation. Now he was in love with me though doubtful if I were worth keeping. I was in tears, or in and out of them. We separated on gender lines. I went upstairs to his bedroom with his mother trailing me, all feminine concern and sisterliness; Hugo stayed with his father in the living room. His mother soothed and comforted me. She said she understood Hugo was a difficult boy (he is twenty-nine), but that we have to keep smiling, put a bright face on things.

Gullible Willa fell for this and confessed all, thinking his mother would understand and perhaps explain to Hugo that a tryst, before we were together officially, should not be regarded as high treason. You could tell that the mention of sex before Hugo upset her. Right away I sensed I had made the biggest mistake of my life (next to taking the gun from Dad's shaking fingers—that look of helpless appeal). She continued to stroke and console, but we did not pursue the conversation.

Presently Hugo, having had an argument with his father, came bounding up the stairs. "Are you two talking about me?" he shouted (hysterical). "Are you two talking about me?" His mother was frightened, or (this is my opinion) pretended to be frightened, and hurried downstairs. Thus goaded, Hugo fell to raving about his parents, treating me as a friend, a co-conspirator against the older generation. He did his usual fist-smashing and book-throwing routine. (At the peak of his performance, he will even try to destroy himself, beating his chest or thighs or temples with clenched fists. It is amazing to see and clear evidence of simian genes in that family.)

Downstairs his mother was busy telling his father everything I had revealed to her in confidence, woman to woman, about my sordid and nymphomaniacal sex life. (Chuck and I did it once, though I suppose it seemed worse because Hugo actually watched us. I did not tell his mother this.) Next morning, when we appeared for breakfast, his father said one word, in a low but distinct voice, then left the table. "Slut."

Clearly, Hugo had ruined any chance of my being accepted into this family as his wife. Or I had ruined it. Living with Hugo, one begins to suspect one's own motives, actions and inactions in a vertiginous and infinite regress of second guesses.

Perhaps I had engineered the whole thing. I confessed, and I confess I was too trusting. Or is trust just another moment of aggression? Very early in our relationship, Hugo said, "I don't want to feel responsible." His theory of psychology goes like this: behind the mind, there is another mind which is "out to get you." Sometimes it is clear to me that I wanted Dad to live those extra six painful, humiliating, semiconscious months. My soul is shot with evil.

The dogs cavort and make peepee as I climb the icy steps to our apartment, lugging my suicidal burden, now ever so slightly lightened. I compose my face into an expression of shock and remorse. "What have I done? What have I done?" I keep asking myself. Though I don't particularly feel any of this, Hugo will expect it.

I walk into the kitchen where he studies (the table strewn with graphs, print-outs and used tea bags) and place my jar of KCN before him like an offering.

"Hugo," I say, "I wanted to kill myself. I stole this from the lab. I would have gone through with it, but Professor Rainbolt saw me. I didn't want to get you in trouble."

His handsome face wears an expression of irritation. I have disturbed his concentration; I have created a situation with which he will have to deal; a situation to be dealt with is a crisis; his world implodes, crumples, disintegrates.

He says, "It's my fault, isn't it? It's all my fault."

I am ready for this. When we were first together, I found it endearing the way Hugo thought everything was his fault—his willingness to take blame, to confess his failings. Now, after some years of experience, I realize that this is a ploy to diffuse, not defuse, the issue. By taking the blame for everything, Hugo takes the blame for nothing. Also he expects you to console him for being such a fuck-up. And sometimes you do, if he catches you on the wrong foot.

This time he doesn't catch me on the wrong foot, mainly because I have a secret agenda and cannot be bothered.

I say, "Okay, well, as I said, Professor Rainbolt saw me, so you'd better take it back. If you take it back, then he won't find anything missing. You can just say you sent me to pick up a book."

"I can't lie about a thing like this," he says.

Of course, he can't. If he tells the truth, it puts me further in the wrong. I've stolen his key, broken into the university lab and burgled chemicals with which I intend to kill myself. Not since he watched me "having sex" with Chuck has Hugo possessed such damning evidence of my inadequacy as a human being (and this time without the embarrassing question of what he was doing outside my bedroom window).

The phone rings. Rainbolt or Mama Hugo.

"Mom," says Hugo, excitedly. "I can't talk. I'm in a jam. Willa tried to kill herself. She's all right now, but she stole some cyanide from the lab. I have to put it back somehow, before she's charged!"

Charged! Now, this is interesting. Hugo intends to bring the full weight of the law to bear in his incessant battle to prove that he's right and I am wrong.

I have often wondered what he would do if he ever proved it, if he ever actually satisfied himself that it was true, because I think he needs this war of words to keep his energy up, this dialogue with me, with a woman—that's what I believe. He gets his élan, his charm with other people, from the struggle to prove himself.

But it doesn't really matter, and I drift down the hall to the bathroom, run water in the tub and pour bath salts (resembling cyanide), depressed and indolent. The problem is if I love Hugo, he slays me, and if I don't love him, it proves what he's been saying all along (just as I cannot bring back Dad, or the moment when I wrestled him for the shotgun), that I never mean what I say, that I loved Chuck to humiliate him. It's a battle of words (dialogue, duet, duel) to the death.

Presently, as I soak and pretend that I am already dead, reminiscing light-heartedly about my little stash of KCN, Hugo pushes through the bathroom door, urgent, worried and self-important. He is somewhat disappointed to find me taking a bath. Hanging from the shower head with my wrists slashed would have been better.

He says, "Rainbolt called." (I had heard the phone ring a second time.) He kneels on the floor beside the tub. "I told him what happened. It's amazing. He understands completely. His wife has been trying to kill herself for years. She's been hospitalized three times."

This is an intriguing turn of events, I think to myself, recalling a wan but gaily (bravely) dressed individual evanescing through one or two student-faculty get-togethers. Now I feel I should have paid more attention to her (me with my punk hair and skin-tight jeans and silk blouses open to my breasts), for we have something in common (and in common with Dad).

"Does Professor Rainbolt play the guitar, too?" I ask, watching my nipples float above the iridescent, soapy water like twin island paradises. Swim to my little island homes, Hugo. He is looking at them, but they do not distract him; rather, he seems to be thinking he has seen them too often.

I shut my eyes and slide beneath the surface of the bath water, feel my hair wave gently like water weeds, sense a bubble tickling the end of my nose, and relax. Everything is dark and warm, and a sensuous pressure enfolds my body (except for my knees, which are above the water and feel a little chilly). I have rather hoped that death will be like this but suspect I am mistaken. And if I were dead, I wouldn't be able to hear Hugo's voice hectoring me in the distance, echoing through the tub and the aqueous elements.

It is pleasant, and there is a sense in which I even nod off. Which gives me time to tell you that I am a photographer whom no one recognizes as such. That Polaroid snapshot of Dad in his coffin was my first inspiration and the ideal of compositional clarity toward which I have been striving ever since. For money I wait on tables at a chicken restaurant. Because I can't get anyone to look at my photographs and I work in a chicken restaurant patronized by undergraduates, Hugo often slips into the error of believing I want to be a chicken waitress and not an artist.

". . . therapy," he says, plunging his arm into the bath water and hooking me up by the shoulders. I am mildly irritated at the interruption but truthfully cannot tell how long I have been under the water, years maybe. He looks exasperated, yet faintly self-righteous; he has just saved a chicken waitress from possible drowning.

"For heaven's sake," I say. "I don't need therapy. I don't want to turn into Mrs. Rainbolt. Evanescence is not my preferred mode of existence."

Hugo pounds the lip of the tub with his palm, a preliminary to chest-thumping. He doesn't like it when I carry on conversations like this, jumping ahead, bringing in thoughts I have had on my own. He will never understand my intuition about Mrs. Rainbolt. I have only seen her briefly and, at the most, once or twice; and perhaps I am thinking of an entirely different woman, though that has nothing to do with what I know I know about her.

Hugo lives in a world of progressive rock, vegetables and plant molecules. He loves rules. Every riff, every experiment, is controlled and conventionalized, though clearly he believes he is, and the world sees him as, a person on the cutting edge of—choose one and fill in the blank: chaos, nature, knowledge, genius, protein deficiency.

Bismarck runs into the bathroom, making a dog face when he tries to drink from the tub. For a dog with such a killer reputation, he is timid and a clown. I giggle and splash him a little, and he slides on the tile floor trying to escape. Hugo loses his temper and rips his shirt open, popping buttons into the bath.

Then we adjourn, after I pause for drying, to the bedroom where Hugo lies on the bed staring at the ceiling. He says nothing while I dress, won't even look at my body (too familiar, functional). Only grunts as we throw on our coats, collect the jar of cyanide and head outdoors to the car with a warm avalanche of dog on the stairs behind us.

Hugo drives. He usually drives when we're together. It's all the same to me, and now especially he feels it's his prerogative. A woman who commits crimes and tries to kill herself automatically loses her ability, ever shaky at the best of times, to perform simple everyday tasks like, say, driving a car. The dogs, now sensing a fight, cower in the rear, pretending to sleep. I try to remember the exact shade of blue Prussian blue is and wonder if I would look good in that colour. Perhaps I should dye my hair.

We are about half-way to the university when Hugo suddenly pulls into a Wendy's parking lot and stops the car. For a while he stares over the steering wheel into the snow which is beginning to pile up and melt on the warm metal above the engine. Clearly, he has thought of something to say, and I wait patiently as I know I am supposed to.

"Is this all of it?" he asks, enunciating carefully, without looking at me.

"Sure," I say. "I may like the stuff once in a while, but I'm not an addict."

Hugo smashes his fist down on the dash and a cassette ejects from the player. This kind of humour is subversive and he doesn't like it. Male humour is based on the stupidity of women. I have to grab my ribs beneath my coat to keep from laughing as Bismarck sniffs the cassette between the seats.

Actually I don't feel like laughing, but my nerves are frayed and I am tired. My bath has not been a success. And, though I affect stoicism vis-à-vis Hugo's temper, his violence, his imprecations, I am quivering inside. I have failed at the simplest of human activities, dying. It seems proof of a deeply engrained and amazing incompetence on my part, an incompetence reinforced by my lack of artistic success and the chicken-waitressing, all emblems, signs or icons of my earlier lack of shrewdness and foresight when I stopped Dad from killing himself.

I am not surprised that Hugo suspects me of hiding a portion of the KCN for future use. He is used to sifting possibilities in a rational (some would say irrational) manner, used to making lists of might-have-beens. What might we have become if four things had gone right: if I hadn't prevented Dad from killing himself, if I hadn't misunderstood Hugo's doubt, if I hadn't slept with Chuck, if I hadn't told Hugo's mother? And he thinks I am devious (right from the start—sneaking off with Chuck—though we didn't sneak, it was a date).

The worst thing is that I am wondering if I am doing this all myself, manipulating Hugo into a position that is an analogue of my own ten years earlier. Or, have I simply become my father in order to punish myself? I seem to be drifting into a phantasmagoria of analogies or substitutions (or myth or psychology) where only the verbs remain constant and the nouns and modifiers are interchangeable. For Hugo, I am clearly often his mother, or previous girlfriends; we fall in love, I think sometimes, in order to get even.

My sense of guilt increases as I recall how much I love Hugo, when I remember the gentle, loving man he wishes to be, when I think of his multiple talents and his struggle to be a musician (the scientist/musician thing induces a kind of schizophrenia in Hugo, a doubleness with its own hierarchy of substitutions). There are times when, in confusion, he lets you see this. Then you want to rush up and hold him and let your pity wash over him. When we are at our best, Hugo and I, we share this sense of dismemberment or dis(re)memberment, a sense that the beauty and magic are gone. (This is my explanation of Original Sin. Men have invented whole religions to divert themselves from this germ of self-doubt. They are an amazingly industrious sex.)

Just then Hugo makes one of those intuitive connections he is so good at but which he distrusts in me. He's been eyeing the cassette that has just popped out of the player, thinking. Suddenly he looks at me, surprised that he knows what he knows. Then he begins rifling through the cassette boxes till he finds one that doesn't rattle when he shakes it.

"No," I shout, but it is too late.

The cyanide (KCN—stands for twelve-gauge shotgun) scatters in the air like snowflakes. It is as if we are inside one of those glass globe shake-ups, a winter scene, couple with dogs, but the snow smells like almonds.

This is funny and scary at the same time. The cyanide rattles against the seatcovers like tiny balls of sleet or spilled salt. I hold my breath, shout "Get out!" and scream at the dogs as they lift their noses to test the air. Hugo, startled, watches the falling KCN with his mouth wide open, a somewhat suicidal expression, I think to myself.

Suddenly we are both fumbling for door handles, heaving ourselves into the open air. I am a split-second ahead of Hugo because I know what is going on. I race to the hatchback to release the dogs, screaming at them to jump out. This dramatic and violent behaviour on my part intimidates Bismarck who refuses to leave the car until I grab his collar and drag him out, whimpering and choking.

Hugo stands at the open driver's door, staring into the Pinto with disbelief. Snow sifts through the open doors and mixes with the white crystals, starting to melt almost as soon as it touches the vinyl. Perhaps he is thinking of possible headlines (AREA COUPLE KILLS DOGS IN BIZARRE DEATH PACT) or of his own near brush with extinction.

The Wendy's parking lot is silent. Though light blazes from the restaurant interior and there is a constant shushing sound of cars along the street, these seem not to impinge upon our little world. The dogs sit and shiver nervously, plainly confused and frightened.

"Are you all right?" asks Hugo. "Do you feel okay?"

He looks straight at me, into my eyes, as if to read me. I am a book he usually doesn't care to take off the shelf. Unaccountably and somewhat infuriatingly, I begin to cry.

"No, I'm not all right. No, I don't feel okay. Okay?"

I turn away, and the dogs follow me.

"Where are you going?"

"Home. I'm tired of this."

And I am tired. In the past few hours, I have broken several laws, had a fight with Hugo and failed to kill myself, not to mention thinking many desperate and ingenious thoughts to pass the time. Now, for all I know, we will never be able to drive the Pinto again. How will I get to work? How will Hugo drive to Toronto for rehearsals? What is the resale value of a cyanide-filled Pinto with an exploding gas tank? They probably won't even take it for junk. My life is a sorry and pathetic mess, and all I want to do is go home, crawl into bed and pull a pillow over my face.

Hugo runs after me and takes me in his arms. Either he thinks a hug will improve my outlook or near-death has made him horny. His cheek is cold and stubbly, rubbing against mine. Bismarck whines thinly. My nose begins to drip. I begin to lose my balance. I wish Hugo would let go because we are making a scene for people coming out of the restaurant. Suddenly I am aware that he is crying; Hugo wants *me* to comfort *him*. Who just tried to kill herself? I think, a little nonplussed. Jake chases Bismarck in a tight circle around the parking lot.

I pull away and walk back to the Pinto. With my gloves I begin to dust the snow and cyanide off the seats and out the door. I keep my scarf over my mouth and nose. Listen, I definitely don't want to die in a Wendy's parking lot. After watching for a while, Hugo walks into the restaurant, returning with paper towels which we damp in the melting snow and use to wash down the inside of the car.

It is cold, dirty work, and my hands and lips turn blue (as do Hugo's—not an effect of cyanide; this is because the body directs the blood to the major organs, the heart and brain, for example, to keep the warm). We are all cold and wet and miserable.

At length, we get back into the car and drive with the windows open to the lab (basement rec room) where I wait with the dogs while Hugo (Willa) returns the jar of cyanide (shotgun) to its glass-doored shelf (deer-antler rack). He seems to take an exceptionally long time, and I imagine him (we are creatures of each other's imagination) lost in thought, surprised and troubled, amongst the whispering plants, arrested, as it were, by the thunderous echoing whispers of things which, daily, he compels with his thoughts. Momentarily, he understands, as my father and I did, what it means to finish the sentence.

Home again, we shake our clothes outside and wash the dogs in the tub (the evening has turned into a complete horror show for Bismarck), and then take turns holding the shower attachment over each other. I keep my eyes and mouth shut while Hugo gently and carefully hoses my face, my neck and ears and hair. I do the same for him and have to bite my lip, seeing him with his eyes closed, naked, blind and trusting.

It is after 2 A.M. when we finally go to bed. We're both exhausted. Hugo curls up with his back to me and begins to snore. Bismarck's nails click nervously up and down the hallway outside our door, then he goes and curls up beside his friend under the kitchen table.

I lie awake thinking, thinking about what happened to Hugo back there by the car, what made him run after me, embrace me and weep—some inkling, I think, some intuition of the truth, that I am leaving, a truth that only now begins to spread like imperfectly oxygenated blood through my arteries and capillaries, turning my limbs leaden and my skin blue.

Bad News of the Heart

REC'D DISCHARGE FROM BELLEVUE. Discharge nurse, named Iris McVity, escorted me to a public entrance and said I would be a hunk if I had a brain more than a minute and kept off the sauce. So naturally I hung around till she got off work, and we went for a drink in an Irish karaoke bar around the corner. I could see right away we were a match from the way she smiled when she saw me, a little exasperated but flattered nonetheless, with a sad, knowing glint in her eye.

She was a big girl, maybe forty-five years old, slow yet graceful of movement, with hams like oaks and breasts like small hills, and maybe she hadn't been lucky in the men she had met till now. Something made her think it worthwhile taking a chance on a former patient, fresh from the ward where my friends called me Freud on account of my reading up on the subject at every opportunity. (They also called me Dutch or the Cleaner for other reasons later to be explained.)

We drank three beers and I sang her "The Rose of Tralee" in my uneducated baritone, reading the words from the screen, and she invited me home for bacon and eggs if I promised not to exhibit any symptoms, and I said yes and hefted my book duffel onto my shoulder. There was romance in the air, it was a tonic to both of us. And I thought also that I might, after all, be able to get by without my medication, which I casually sold to a bar patron in the men's room on my way to the street.

It was cold in the night outside, moonless and black like someone had shut the refrigerator door, but we walked arm in arm to the bus stop and hung on straps, nudging each other pleasantly as the bus slithered through the streets. Only one or two strangers seemed suspicious to me, possible android impostors, agents of a foreign power or Central American refugees. I was about to accost a tow-headed waif with the sniffles and a metal ring coming out of her nose (primitive receiving device), when Iris caught my eye with one of her disapproving looks.

She's read my file, I thought. Thinks she knows me through and through, all my secrets. I smiled and, with but a glance in the direction of the waif, demonstrated that I had as much self-control and judgment as the next man.

It had not yet occurred to me that Iris McVity herself might be a cunningly devised machine or a Russian spy. I had started calling her Doschka in the bar, a pet-name she affected to despise. She was large. Many Slavic women are large, great mountainous women with faces like pumpkins and noses like buttons. It should have been a clue, along with the way she had followed me from the hospital and insinuated herself into the fabric of my life.

Doschka, Doschka, I whispered.

Don't call me that, she said. It's not my name.

She lived in a one-room efficiency decorated with a vast collection of paint-by-number horse pictures she had executed herself in her spare time. Stacks of romance novels huddled next to the unmade bed, with drink and dust rings on the topmost covers. Curled, unframed photographs of her parents dangled from bits of tape along the walls. There were no curtains on the single window overlooking a back court where a lone dog rummaged in upturned garbage pails and dirty snow.

Everywhere there was an air of disuse, decay, decrepitude and dust, as if she barely lived there or as if words beginning with the letter *d* had taken over her life. But she smiled as she bustled about, turning on lamps, unplugging the carpet sweeper and stowing it with some difficulty under the bed. She was still wearing her long coat and seemed breathless from the exertion. Then she disappeared into the bathroom, and I listened to her pee voluminously as I dropped my coat and duffel in a closet full of empty paint-by-number boxes and dirty laundry.

I was just going through the top drawer of her dresser when she emerged, blowing her bangs up with a hearty sigh, her face fresh and damp after a wash, her coat looking like a body crouched behind the toilet.

Doschka, I said.

The doorbell rang. Another young woman tottered in—energetic, irritable, trailing a cloud of cigarette smoke. She had a pale, liverish complexion and hip-to-ankle braces on both legs. She stopped when she saw me, aimed her cigarette, and said, Who's he? Jesus, where do you find these guys?

I said nothing. She was not addressing me. My sweet Slavic princess, my precious dumpling, seemed suddenly deflated, seemed far too small for her clothes. She blushed. His name is Hugo, she said.

The radiators were tapping up a thunder, heat rising, steam dripping off the windows, winter outside looking more and more inimical to human life. I was a bit tense. I could manage a simple two-person dialogue most of the time, provided there was adequate medical support at hand in case of trouble. But with a third added to the mix, not to mention my sudden suspicion that, besides me, unnumbered other men crowded Doschka's life (which made the situation positively claustrophobic), I felt my hold on reality beginning to falter.

What I had gathered, reading my way through the hospital library, was that the structure of human experience is essentially paranoid. The opposition between self and other which defines so-called normal life also defines the paranoid. It's not us against them, it's me against them, and them is everyone else. The self is an oppositional construct, created in a *krieg* (war) with others—everyone else, women, small dogs, illegal aliens. The essence of becoming is that someone is out to get you. I remembered trying to explain this—oh, on dozens of occasions—to Dr. Gutfreund, who told me my attempts to apply reason and system to human relations were evidence of a deep psychosis.

Doschka was explaining to Vi (this was her name, short for Vidalia, Vitality or Vibrator, I was not sure which) who I was in words and syntax which recalled the insidious bureaucratic efficiency of an intake sheet. Name: Hugo Tangent; Age: 62; Place of Birth: Netherlands; Nationality: Dutch/Resident Alien; Marital Status: Separated; Next of Kin: Jack Vance, son-in-law; Occupation: Cleaner; Diagnosis: Mild Schizophrenia, Obsessive Compulsive Disorder, Post Traumatic Stress Syndrome, Cranial Bumps, Irritable Bladder, Nail Biting, Drug and Alcohol Dependency. Upon my admission, she said, someone had signed a Do Not Resuscitate order, which was always kept at the top of my file, though no one could make out the signature.

I listened, with some ambivalence, as she went through my particulars. None of this seemed familiar to me—even my name—though I began right away to feel like I had to pee, and I started to fidget, picking lint off my pants, straightening the pictures I could reach. Doschka glanced at me reprovingly, as if to remind me of my promise, and I stopped. I regretted now selling my medication in the bar, for it occurred to me that I might actually like the medication.

I looked at my hands. Did these look like the hands of a sixty-two-year-old? Yes. Who was I? What was I doing there? Besides the everyday, garden-variety human desires for the love of a large woman and a cheap roof overhead. Who had signed the Do Not Resuscitate order (commonly referred to by those in the medical profession as DNR)? If I had a son-in-law (a prime suspect in the DNR mystery), then I must have a daughter. And a wife! I felt the clammy hand of fate or history upon my shoulder, suddenly felt the whole authoritative weight of selfhood (as defined by a large set of relationships I didn't know I had with people I had never heard of who plainly hated me and wanted me dead).

Vi eyed me suspiciously. I gathered from internal evidence that she was also a nurse, also lived in the building, collected Hummel figurines and glass globe shake-ups, had a brother named Beldon, a mother named Phonita, an ex-lover named Gary, wanted to have a baby by artificial insemination but was afraid she was too old, liked to fantasize about black men, went to Bingo every Friday night with Doschka (whom she insisted on calling Iris), and it was Friday night.

Trying to be friendly, I said I knew Vi's brother Beldon. I'd met him in 'Nam when he was a gunnery sergeant in a little place called Nop Lop outside of Da Nang where I went to refit after a long range reconnaissance patrol over the DMZ in '63. I sold him eight of the little VC heads I'd brought back in my grenade pouch. Had Vi ever seen any of those heads? I asked.

No, she said, frostily. Beldon was never in Vietnam.
I'd check on that if I were you, I said.

What about the bacon and eggs? I said to Doschka.

Things were not going well. It was the eternal triangle: recently released mental patient, woman and other woman from
down the hall. I didn't know what exactly I'd fallen into, maybe
one of those lesbian hookups, or maybe just lonely single ladies
with a Bingo lust. But I was in the way. Doschka clearly wanted
me there, though she was embarrassed a) by me and b) by having
her desires exposed like this in front of her friend. Vi didn't want
me there, was jealous of Doschka and didn't like the look of me,
though she was also secretly attracted—I have the bad-boy look
women love. I felt whipsawed in the violent crosscurrents of their
desires, a situation bound to make me crazy if I wasn't already
and a reminder of why, in the past, my passions had tended to
the inanimate.

In session with Dr. Gutfreund, I had once let slip (possibly
under the influence of sodium pentothal injections adminis-
tered surreptitiously) details of my youthful fascination with
"lifelike" mechanical toys. What did I mean by lifelike?
Gutfreund had demanded. He was always trying to get me to
explain myself to myself, which I understand is standard thera-
peutic technique.

What did I mean by lifelike? I meant moving about, performing complex and repetitive actions up to and including
making simple speeches. I loved my little tin drummer boy, a
barking dog that turned somersaults when wound up and a frog
that hopped. I also loved automated bank tellers, self-serve gas
stations and vending machines (there was one in the hospital caf-
eteria which I took to calling Mother).

Somehow, I told Gutfreund, these machines managed to essentialize all that was good in life while subtracting the emotional confusion and darkness. You never saw a vending machine beat an old woman to death for her handbag, I said. With a machine you know where you stand.

Which was what I was thinking as we sat down to eat the bacon and eggs. Vi was shaking pepper and cigarette ashes over her eggs. I had my hand on Doschka's knee under the table.

She said, Get your hand off my knee. You said you'd behave.

Doschka, Doschka, I whispered.

She frowned.

I can cook a mean ox tail soup, I said, if you have some spare chicken stock, a bay leaf and an ox.

Vi started to laugh. I liked her laugh. Hell, I was in love with her leg braces (for obvious reasons). My recent sojourn in the ward had taught me that pathology is real. Sometimes it's the only thing you can put your finger on.

We were drinking vodka and powdered fruit juice Vi had brought from her apartment. I'd found some pills in Doschka's top drawer, one of those generic drugs. The name started with "anti"—the rest I couldn't understand—but I thought I'd take some prophylactically.

Vi had warmed to me—her initial defensiveness was typical of women with low self-esteem and physical deformity (all women believe they have low self-esteem and suffer a physical deformity). Once you crack the shell, the real personality starts to come out. Vi was a clown and a flirt, but she was on a clock—no matter how pleasant she got, she had to say something waspish or mean-spirited every five minutes. Doschka was sentimental, romantic and given to witty double entendres. When Vi threw back her head to laugh, Doschka's face would melt into the faintest trace of a smile, enigmatic and lost. The talk turned to sex. Vi told jokes with a hard glitter in her eye; Doschka told stories about former lovers.

It was going as easy as pie, the mood had changed, but for some reason I suddenly grew thoughtful. I looked at the two of them chattering away, glad to have a man to watch them, acting up like schoolgirls, lighting their cigarettes in the candles. Their voices went away from me, the table seemed to lengthen—a hallucinatory sensation not uncommon when I went off the drugs.

I had a moment of peacefulness, when I didn't feel the need to speak, when I could just listen to their cheerful voices. I was the perfect listener. But then just outside that silence I could hear the noisy, hectoring sound of my own voice talking up a storm, trying to make Doschka like me. I hated that voice and I hated Doschka for liking me. I started to speak. I started a story, an old story that came out of the silence of the perfect listener, but as soon as I spoke the first words they became a bribe, and I got disgusted with myself.

I told them about my sister Luna, the one we always said was the most tangential of the Tangents, how when she was thirteen she began to sleep with German soldiers to help feed our family, how one night she went home with an SS officer who showed her photographs he'd taken in the death camps, how they made love that night in a bed littered with pictures of dead Jews, how sweetly and insanely they made love, and how, in the night, the SS officer shot himself to death while Luna held him.

She came home a week later, after being detained for questioning by the authorities. There was an irresistible light in her eyes. She wanted to talk, she told me the whole story—I was a little boy. When she told me how sweetly and insanely they had made love, I didn't know what lovemaking was. She showed me one of the photographs. I started to laugh at the funny naked bodies. She embraced me. Yes, yes, little Hugo, she said. Laugh at the dead. Don't stop laughing. That was my reaction. Then she went out the door and was gone.

After the war, my father searched the DP camps and Red Cross registries, even the cemeteries. In truth, I don't think he looked very hard, though he seemed to be hunting constantly. He felt guilty that his daughter had become a prostitute, that she had slept with Germans. Part of my father didn't want to find Luna, part of him couldn't live without her. Later he hung himself.

I've been looking for her all my life, I told Vi and Doschka.

Is that why you're crazy? asked Vi, refusing to be won over. Doschka wept silently. I put my hand on her knee, she left it there.

It's just a story, I said. I may have made it up.

I had their attention. Love's entry. But it was a mess. The story had calmed me down, but my machine dreams hovered just off stage. I wanted Doschka to love me. But I'd told her a story instead, a story about my sister who disappeared. The subterfuges of love always end up making love impossible. By telling the story I'd seduced Doschka, just as the SS officer used his death camp pictures to seduce Luna. But I'd pushed her farther away as well, she was disappearing, fading from sight, just at the moment I pressed my fingers to her knee.

(I had tried to explain this to Dr. Gutfreund one day during session. The vertigo of experience, or our daily experience of vertigo. I told him love and the self were like two dogs chasing each other around a tree. If they ever connected, they'd try to kill one another. He said, But people manage, Hugo. That's the point. People fall in love, get married, have children, muddle along. I loved Dr. Gutfreund just then for his sweet naïveté, his belief that soul-management could keep the wolves out of the kitchen, the forest out of the heart.)

Then Doschka started to speak, to tell a story. She was staring into the candle flame, tears sliding down her face. The first time she had sex, she said, was with her brother Teddy. Vi gasped and nearly swallowed her cigarette. They became lovers when she was fourteen, secretly, though innocently, without guilt. They were in love, she said. In bed, they pleased each other, doing things she'd never had the courage to do with another man. This lasted four years, until Teddy left for college. That Thanksgiving he borrowed a friend's car to drive home to see Doschka, slammed into a concrete abutment in a rain storm and died. She knew it wouldn't have worked, that they were heading for a guilt-ridden and uncomfortable future—or worse, some sordid disaster. But the way it happened she never got to say goodbye.

Now she tried to find Teddy in every man she met. She gazed at me in the candlelight, measuring me against the ideal Teddy. And I knew, for the time being, I looked just like him.

I was in love with her, though unnerved. I don't normally fall in love except when I skip my medication. Her story made me fall in love just as my story had earned me the right to rest my hand upon her knee. Her horse pictures, her dingy apartment, her size, the fact that she was a nurse and hence a maternal figure (yes, even I can admit she was more maternal than a vending machine)—all these made me want to love her. But her story seduced me.

Why? And what is love? An erotic accident prolonged to disaster. Can I say that? Her story was like a dream. The best stories are like dreams, or are dreams, come out of the silence or out of the page like a dream of words. She was lawless and educated in loss. Just the sort of woman I am always looking for to redeem me, to stand by me when my relationship with reality falters.

Dr. Gutfreund said I looked for women like this because I had failed to acquire a good inner object. Maybe my mother dropped me on my head when I was wee. Or I bit her nipple while nursing and she whacked me on the face with a rolled up newspaper. (Don't do this, ladies. It only makes the baby desperate. I learned to bite very hard.)

I glared at Vi (short for Viper, Vicious or Vicuna?), suddenly finding her presence at best a distraction, at worst a pit of evil. I wanted to get a screwdriver and take her apart bolt by bolt. I glanced at Doschka, she was eyeing Vi nervously. Perhaps she was nervous about her friend's reaction to her confession, but it could easily have been a look of love. You can't tell with looks.

Once upon a time, I said—and they both turned to me, slightly irritated—once upon a time, there was a girl named Ghislaine and a boy named Adhemar. They fell in love one day when Ghislaine happened to spy Adhemar and some other boys swimming in a canal naked. Adhemar happened to look up just as Ghislaine saw him, poised for a dive from the towpath. Ghislaine's eyes met Adhemar's. She blushed and turned coquettishly away, then ran home laughing. Her look, her blush and her flight—the ancient signature of Eros—kindled passion in Adhemar's heart. He slipped on his clothes and followed her to her house, watched her disappear behind the blue door with just one glance back to make sure that he was there.

Who could resist the drama of love and pursuit? Ghislaine and Adhemar were married. But almost as soon as they married, they began to grow bored with one another. Ghislaine invented erotic games to excite them—she flirted with other men, she demanded more money and beautiful things from the already pressed Adhemar. The mood of their marriage developed drastic swings, from lust to contempt. In short order, because they were also dutiful souls, they had two children: a girl, Luna, and a boy named Hugo. This made things worse because Ghislaine no longer felt as if she could run away, and Adhemar, seeing that she was trapped, began to disregard her. For both, this was a tragedy because they could still remember the sweetness of their early love.

The war came, their circumstances grew more difficult. Life for Adhemar and Ghislaine was a treadmill of drudgery and despair. Sometimes Adhemar would try to smile and put his arm around his wife—for the sake of comradeship, for old love. But she had grown spiteful and bitter. And when their daughter disappeared, Ghislaine used the awful event as an excuse to slip away herself into madness.

Exhausted by life, Adhemar yet forced himself to resurrect a ghastly parody of the old game of desire and pursuit, hunting his daughter ceaselessly after the war, though he never found her, perhaps never really wanted to find her because he was afraid of what he would find. At length, having given too much of himself for love, he hung what was left from a beam in the attic where the boy Hugo found him at peace at last.

Vi (short for Viable, Vitamin or Virus?) sighed. She had her hand over her mouth, her eyes were shiny, sad and wide. Doschka looked the same. They could have been twins or a metaphor.

This is what madmen, poets and lovers have in common, the gift of metaphor, the knack of seeing the same in difference. It's what makes life so confusing—you think you're talking to a genius and he turns out to be a dustbin schizophrenic. Or that luminous woman you fell in love with for her wit turns out to have boundary problems. She can't tell the difference between herself and the rest of the world. Metaphor. I had a dream once, that I'd found Luna and died. What does that mean?

There was weeping and gnashing of teeth in the room. I'd taken the girls to a place, very low. We had intensity, often mistaken for love, maybe it was love. The candles were burning low. With a sniff and a scrape at her nose, Doschka got up and began foraging in drawers for more candles. Vi disappeared down the hall for cigarettes and music. I took Doschka in my arms. Her eyes were closed. She kissed me tenderly. What was she seeing? Whose face?

She'll be back, she said. It made it more exciting. She kissed me again. Are you really crazy? she asked. A little voice. Not the nurse who would know the answer, but the lonely dreamer, the metaphorist, who wanted a different answer.

I was, briefly, sane and said yes. I felt good about myself. I'd told the truth. But it didn't help. Doschka had gone crazy herself.

She said, Well, I don't believe you. I don't want to believe you. I want this to go on and on.

It is my belief that we were very drunk. Vi came limping back with another bottle of vodka and more of that powdered juice. She had found a package of drink umbrellas to liven up the party. She had a CD player, put on something bluesy and surprising. The woman had hidden depths, obscure tastes. She began dancing dreamily with her eyes closed, smiling to herself, oddly graceful despite the stringiness of her figure and those leg braces. Doschka was having a candle fugue, maybe twenty glowed around the darkened efficiency, on plates, saucers, upturned coffee mugs. If you squinted, it looked like you were in a church.

I felt sane, though it crossed my mind that I only felt sane because everything around me was intense and somehow reflected what was in my mind. But I wasn't afraid just then. Not at all. Thoughts of androids and double agents seemed far away (yet still there, hovering in mid-distance—once I slept with three women in a row who turned out to be holographic images of women and not real women at all).

Vi beckoned me with a lit cigarette and a worldly look. We began to dance, our bodies aligned, folded together from knee to temple. She blew smoke in my ear. I caught sight of Doschka, half in shadow like the moon, watching us with a forlorn expression on her face. Keep this up, I said to myself, and you'll be back in the jug in a week.

Vi stroked the nape of my neck and said, Shh. I hadn't been speaking, but I knew what she meant. I had stuck two of the drink umbrellas behind my ears—she lifted them out and dropped them on the floor. She whispered, I'm in love with Iris. That's my story. Look at her. She knows that I'm telling you. We've been together for ages, but it's always like this. When I make love to her, she shuts her eyes. She says, yes, yes, and lets herself go but never looks at me. She pretends it's not happening. But while she's pretending it's not happening, she can do anything.

That's not all. Once, when we were just together, she had an affair. She's like that. She gets sad and men notice and take advantage. When she's sad she thinks she needs them. When she told me, the bottom fell out. I cried and cried as if the world had ended. Iris was kind. She held me, let me rage, fed me orange slices and sips of vodka in an egg cup, read me a love letter I'd written her, her soft voice saying my words of love in the darkness.

I should have left her. Instead my desire changed. Instead of wanting to make love to Iris, I wanted Iris to make love with men while I watched or listened in the next room or waited outside. I wanted her to come to me after, soaked with sweat, smelling of man, blowsy and relaxed from pleasure, and hold me and tell me what she had done and whisper that she loved me. In the moment when she betrayed me, I had lost Iris forever. But she taught me to love the pain, and when I make love now it is not to a woman named Iris but to a woman who is never there, who is always betraying me. My desire has become impure. I'm a sick fuck. All for love. Even if she were to leave me, I would still want love like that. The only way I can get out of this is to kill myself.

Her voice had gone gravelly and strained. The hair went up the back of my neck at her final words. Poor Vi. One thing to lose a lover, another to lose the ability to love. Never such loneliness in a voice (other than my own sometimes). I tried to push away, but she held me fiercely.

Despite myself, I was getting aroused. First Doschka, now this. It's not my name, I heard her say. Yes, I thought, with a sickening drop in my gut, you're always mistaking this one or that one for someone else. Reality is tangled. They tell you there's a path, but all of a sudden there are eighty-nine paths or none at all. In any situation, you think you're in charge, only to find out the situation is in charge of you.

I have tried to explain this sensation to Dr. Gutfreund—the moment when you'd rather be a chair or a rock or dead because you're tired of tap dancing in the strobe light. Gutfreund always said, somewhat impenetrably, You feel like that, Hugo, because you're crazy. Take your pills. He said this in a kind way. I always liked talking to him, though I tended to exaggerate, put him on, give him the juice. Sometimes he would get it and laugh.

I was trapped between Vi and Doschka (all right, Iris—even I was beginning to see past my own pathology to her pathology— Iris was its name, and she looked Dutch, not Slavic). I was no longer myself but a figure in their erotic tableau, the necessary accelerant for the firestorm (metaphor) of their love. As the evening wore on, I had been feeling distinctly seedy. Low self-esteem and all that. As if I were disappearing inside my clothes. And as I disappeared I became more and more anxious, fidgety, full of desire—for what? Call it love, but it could have been any-thing intense, explosive. Fill me up, I thought, just fill me up with light. Then turn out the light.

But even I could see there was something the teensiest bit unhealthy about this. I needed a delay, time to think.

Candles all around, the two werewolf women, melancholy with their desires, giving me the eye, horses everywhere I looked, some of them with the little numbers showing through the paint; it seemed utterly dark and human, a story of love, bad news of the heart. And I knew I was going to be the one to go back to the ward for this because inside the machine called Hugo Tangent there was an ON/OFF switch which went click when things got too painful or confusing. I wasn't worried about this. I was just waiting for the click.

But I started to speak, nothing fancy, just another story.

Once upon a time there was a boy named Hugo who liked to clean. After he found his father like that, he cleaned the house, then he went out and began to clean the street. He went into the neighbours' houses and cleaned them. He used small brushes, buffing cloths and little pans of soapy water because he was very thorough.

This was in Holland, which is a very clean country. At first people didn't mind, especially after the war when things were such a mess. The country was having a national cleaning frenzy anyway. But soon the neighbours began to get nervous. One day he almost cleaned Mrs. Eindorp's cat Millie to death. Mr. Oostijen, two doors down, nearly ran over Hugo with his Renault when he didn't notice the boy beneath the car cleaning the undercarriage. The boy cleaned all the blossoms off Mrs. Henke's prize-winning tulips. One morning Hugo was found at the canal at the foot of the street cleaning the water. He wasn't eating, no one was taking care of him. He talked only to a collection of wind-up toys he carried in his crazy mother's net grocery bag. So Hugo was packed off to a hospital for children who cleaned too much and had no family. The hospital was crowded already. It was a very clean hospital.

A few years later, one of the hospital nurses (hefty Dutch girl, big thighs) told Hugo that he ought to go to America to look for his sister. Lots of DPs went to America, she said, to escape the past and start fresh. When she told him this, the nurse and Hugo were making love in a broom closet where Hugo kept his cleaning supplies and wind-up toys.

The nurse was in love with Hugo. Hugo couldn't tell if the nurse was a wind-up toy or a Russian spy. But he listened to her and soon after found his way to New York where he took a day job in a laundry and a night job cleaning offices on Wall Street. Later he opened a string of dry-cleaning stores in the boroughs. Got rich.

Hugo never found Luna, though he took out ads in newspapers and hounded the immigration authorities. Nights, he would walk the streets accosting women, repeating her name. Often, when he was making love to a woman, he would be stricken with the thought that it might be Luna herself (and not a wind-up toy).

He was a glutton for sadness and stories. He saw her in the streets a dozen times a night. She would be standing just off the curb in the moonlight, skinny, waifish and blond, with eyes like bruises, with her thumb up or just waiting for whatever darkness came in a car. Scared to death or stoned or strung out. He fell in love with them. He would speak to them softly in Dutch.

He would try to save them, though hardly any of them wanted to be saved and most mistook his motives.

They broke his heart over and over, always leaving in the night, going off with his money, coming round with their boyfriends or pimps for more money, telephoning into his sleep from distant call boxes, whispering words of hate and desperate need or love, which was the same thing. It didn't matter. It was what Hugo expected. That kind of love.

One he married—Louella from Tennessee. He met her outside a cemetery one night, turning tricks in a crypt. She had white-blond hair in spikes, cheeks like a skull. She was already pregnant. It made her want to be good. She was certain she loved him. She had Luna's eyes. She was certain it wouldn't work. He tried to protect her, make her feel safe. She got bored, she hated him. After the baby came, she left, telephoning from call boxes in a dozen states, getting fainter and fainter. How's my baby? Tell her I love her. He called the baby Moon.

When Moon was five, Louella swept back like a malign wind out of the west. She had gone to prison, found Jesus, hated men. She came to the door with two cops, a social worker and a court order to rescue Moon. I have to put my life back together, she told Hugo.

She looked twenty years older. The muscles in her cheeks jumped with rage. Moon was screaming, Daddy! Daddy! The only thing he could think to do was lie and tell her he would follow shortly, that they would never be apart again. He packed her an overnight bag with her favourite dolls and wind-up toys. It was like packing a tiny coffin with the belongings of the dead. He did not know what Hell she was going to. He kissed her goodbye on the forehead, on her lips, on her fingers. She was sobbing quietly in the social worker's arms. She believed him.

Hugo thought, What a strange little wind-up toy that woman is carrying. It seems so lifelike, with eyes just like my sister's. And then he thought, We are being destroyed by love.

Hugo woke up in a hospital with a mop in his hand, speaking to a water fountain. He still remembers the water fountain fondly, though they are no longer in touch. Then he was in and out of hospitals. When he was out, Louella appeared asking for support for Moon, asking for money for psychiatrists to repair the damage he'd done to their daughter. She said, You'll never get rid of me. Hugo thought, This is funny. I can't find my sister. I've lost my daughter. But I've got an alien for a wife who's sunk a tether into my heart.

Once Louella had him arrested for molesting Moon. Hugo was hopeful. He thought he might get to see Moon if she testified in court. But then he was in a hospital again, the charges dropped. Louella kept saying Jack this and Jack that. Hugo thought Jack was her boyfriend, but then Jack married Moon back in Memphis. She was fifteen. Louella asked Hugo to pay for the wedding. You can't come, she said. She hates you. Jack wants to kill you after what you did.

Louella looked like death, looked exactly how Hugo thought Luna would look, given the life she led. She was on something, cranked up, every time he saw her, breathless with the excitement of confrontation. She made him want to kill himself. When it got intense like that, he would think, This is love. This is what love is all about.

Once, in remission from his lunacy, he was staring out his apartment window. He heard muffled thuds, the crash of glass breaking somewhere above. Then a shape flashed in front of him, pink and white with handles in the back. Wheelbarrow, he thought. Or a doll. After, as he watched the crowd gather below, he realized it had been a woman jumping to her death. What sadness had driven her to this desperate act Hugo could not tell. Though he read in the papers how she had run away from a husband who beat her, lived in shelters and halfway houses and lost her child to the Department of Social Services.

Sometimes, now, the skies seemed full of falling women, thin blond Dutch girls with their eyes wide open, mouths gaping in voiceless screams, legs out like the handles of a wheelbarrow.

Vi and Iris were holding hands across the table, their eyes fixed on a candle flame. They seemed still to be listening like lost children to the words of an old story. I could feel the click coming like a blessing, like the hand of God or like the doctor's hand closing the eyes of the dead, which, though unseeing, seem to stare greedily, to be unwilling to let go the terrible, fleeting incandescence of the world.

Fill me up with light, I thought again. I prayed. And turn out the light.

I remembered Mama in her madness reading from the Book of Revelation, the sombre, awful, insistent repetitions of the call: Come, come, Lord Jesus. Even so, Come.

Yes, yes, I thought. Come save me. Save us from this gorgeous world of love. I could feel the click coming. This might be the record, I thought. Out of the ward and back inside in about six hours. Long enough to remember what I was always trying not to remember, that the world is a Hell of tortured souls and demons—not machines or aliens or wind-up toys.

I pictured Iris (not Doschka) gently leading me to the taxi, giving the address, then taking me by the hand at the hospital entrance, just as the electric eye picks us up, recognizes me and opens the door in welcome. Perhaps she'll envy me my sweet confusion, that envy being an aberration of the sane who otherwise hold themselves steadfastly to the flame even as they yearn for it to end.

Briefly I was myself, someone I hardly knew, only visited from time to time and barely recognized. With a sudden clarity, I thought how clarity itself is a species of redemption, and how this melancholy moment just before the click, when I saw my story and everyone else's—whole and unendurable, was a moment of equilibrium tinged ever so slightly with meaning. It was nothing I could hold on to.

The click was coming, I wanted it. Come, come, Lord Jesus. Even so, Come.

Vi and Iris were in that moment, too, part of the universal tragedy. We were companions in arms, which is the most you can hope for. A nod of recognition across the broken ground in the flash of shellfire. Before we go back to killing each other. An extension of the *krieg* (war) metaphor—something to tell Dr. Gutfreund next session. The self not created in strife but dismantled, shivered, exploded, until the moment when there is no self, when the not-self shimmers like a mirage, like pure yearning, and disappears.

Iris turned to me with gentle eyes, her hospital eyes. She had always been a good nurse, schooled in sadness. I was eating one of Vi's drink umbrellas, beginning to make circular, scrubbing motions with my hand upon the tabletop. Even so, Come, I thought. I felt like a bug with a pin in my back.

She took me by the hand, Vi took my other hand. Nurses' hands. Kindly and efficient, not so warm, slightly distanced. They led me to the bed and pushed me down. I felt their bodies on either side. I felt a cool hand on my forehead, like Mama's hand, though Mama had never been much of a mother. I felt someone ruffle my hair with her fingers, begin to scratch my scalp ever so gently. It was almost too hot between them, but the heat made me drowsy. I wanted to sleep. I wanted the hand to go on rubbing my head.

I'm going now, I said out loud.

Shh, someone said.

My Romance

OUR BOY NEDDY DIED when he was three months old. I hardly remember any of this except for the brief hours following his birth when we were a normal, happy couple and then afterwards when Annie would wake in the night, choked with sobs, her milk seeping through the cloth of her nightgown. "The baby's hungry. He needs to eat," she would whisper, then curl into a tight, convulsive ball, a spasm of despair.

When I heard her weeping, I wondered how anyone could live through such sadness. The look in her wild eyes pleaded with me to save her, to wake her from the nightmare, but all I could think of was holding him those first moments, dancing him a little in the delivery room, peering into his dark blue eyes, crooning, "Neddy, Neddy, Neddy."

Afterwards I stopped sleeping. I forced myself to sit in his nursery with the dinosaur wallpaper, the crib with the delicate white spindles, the Babar poster and the panda bear mobile that played "Twinkle, twinkle, little star" when you wound it up.

I drank neat bourbon, knocked back Valium my doctor had prescribed and smoked cigarettes. Sometimes I would pass out, but I never slept. "My baby is hungry," I heard her whisper. I couldn't go back into our bedroom. The grief drove us apart. We were drowning in separate wells. Neddy had never actually slept in the nursery. The nursery was all future. He slept in our bed, tucked between us. Without saying a word, we both believed we could save him with the power of our love. That's when I stopped sleeping.

Afterwards, in the nursery, I couldn't feel anything; I wondered if feeling would ever come back.

"What are you doing, sweetheart?" she cried once.

I couldn't say. I was surprised she even noticed. I was playing "Twinkle, twinkle, little star," watching the bears and stars circle above the place where Ned would have slept.

She said, "I came to get the baby. I heard him crying. You know I can hear him quite well from the bedroom. He needs me. He needs to be fed."

She smelled sour from the old milk on her nightgown. Her breasts were huge and bountiful and useless. "You shouldn't smoke in here," she said sternly.

"He's dead," I said, sobbing so hard I couldn't catch my breath.

I was so lonely. At the same time, I was envious of her. She had slipped right out of herself into some fantasy. I remembered the afternoon we made Ned, the orange indicator on the ovulation test kit, our single-minded love, the sex without fear, the exhilaration of leaping into the future together. We looked into each other's eyes until I came and my eyelids slid shut and I sank onto her shoulder and she held me. Now, even when we were in the same room talking, we were never together.

Part of me knew we were play-acting, cheering ourselves up. I understood we were performing ancient rituals of grief. At the edge of the abyss you dance or you fall in. I didn't really believe Annie thought she heard Neddy's cries in the night. This was her way of creating drama out of her heartsickness just as drinking bourbon and playing "Twinkle, twinkle, little star" was my way of passing time that was otherwise utterly empty. Neither of us could abide the chilly emptiness we had fallen into, yet neither of us had the least idea how to climb out.

I remembered everything: the first intimations of disaster, the falling weight, Neddy's constant whimpering cry, his bluish pallor, the blue haloes around his eyes, his lassitude, his clammy skin. The doctor had a phrase for this—failure to thrive. She didn't choose the words, they were all she had.

She was young and tall. I had never met anyone I could call willowy before I knew Dr. Tithonous. In better times, in her examining room, she had charmed us with a little dance she did, miming with her hands the finger-like fimbriae harvesting eggs, her undulating body representing the Fallopian tubes. The fimbria dance. When she told us the bad news about Ned, she broke down herself, her long, pale hair fanning out over the cluttered desk as her head went down on her hands.

Annie and I were a little shocked at this show of emotion in a comparative stranger. After all, Annie was holding Neddy on her lap, and he was still alive, if somewhat blue, and we couldn't quite credit the words of this overwrought woman across the desk. She said they called it failure to thrive. But I remembered reading in old books other phrases—mysterious wasting sickness, for example—which seemed more apt, more in tune with the inexplicable nature of things.

It was as if Neddy, having ventured into the world, never quite managed to get a firm grip on existence. His whole short life was an inexorable slipping back. It made you think: What is life and what is death? Is there such a thing as being half-alive, tentatively alive? The darkness spewed him out, then sucked him back as if canceling an error. I don't think he felt joy—he had a wry, flickering smile that would play across his face from time to time. And his whimpering signalled discomfort, not grief. I sometimes thought it might not have been so bad if he had lived a little, lived in the metaphorical sense—suffered joy and pain, raged and laughed. But he only lingered.

Oddly, the night Neddy died Annie and I both managed to sleep. We cradled his cool body between us on the bed, mashed our hot faces together and wept and wept and then slept. Nature is merciful, I think. They say that small animals go into an anaesthetic shock as predators tear them to pieces. We didn't believe it was over, but something in us knew what had happened and yet briefly allowed us more than the usual fantasy of hope. We were momentarily together in a travesty of the togetherness we had felt a year before, making love, making Neddy.

There was some terrible irony in this which neither of us understood. We could not put names or explanations to the contradictory emotions we felt. With a feeling that was sometimes uncomfortably close to embarrassment, we had lost all sense of who we really were. Everything was tasteless, colourless. Words were meaningless. We told each other "I love you" because we both had a vestigial, somewhat dutiful impulse to comfort one another. We remembered, as if in a dream, that other time when we were really together. But we both also knew these were empty words.

Language is a machine of desire. It works along an axis defined by hope and future. When there is no hope, no imaginable future, the mysterious bonds of syntax, the wires that convey the energy of meaning from word to word, disintegrate. Words become the snarls, shrieks and gurgles of despair or they become rituals, motions you go through to pass the time, to keep your spirits up. If I say "I love you" enough times, perhaps I will remember what that felt like, what the words mean. But the truth is all I remember is how cold Neddy was, lying between us that morning when we woke up and I reached for the telephone to call Dr. Tithonous.

Of course, at that time of day, I only got her service. My voice was breaking. I could barely croak out the words. I said, "Please tell Barbara"—I had never used her first name before—"please tell her Neddy died in the night, that we're here with him in the bed, that we can't leave him, that we don't know what to do now and could she please help us?"

You expect answering service operators to be distant and bu nesslike at best. But this one seemed, through some miracle of wire and electrons, to understand every nuance of what I was saying. Her voice came back to me full of sorrow and reassurance. "Sir, I want you to know I will call Dr. Tithonous as soon as you hang up. I'll call her till I find her. I don't want you to worry about this. I'll get someone there right away."

She knew she couldn't help me much, but she wanted me to be sure she would do everything she could. And she didn't offer to do more. She didn't say goodbye.

Almost as soon as I hung up, the phone rang and it was Dr. Tithonous. "I am just calling to let you know I am driving right over myself. I wanted you not to worry."

It broke my heart a second time to have these people trying to take care of us. All the protocols and stereotypes were breaking down. Out of all the wretchedness came the distant mutterings of the human heart. I did not think this then, only later. At the time I simply felt an unreasonable relief and turned to try to cuddle little Neddy one last time, to try to pretend he was alive. And then, moments later, it seemed, I heard the doorbell and stumbled out into the living room in my pajamas.

Dr. Tithonous embraced me at the door, just held me, for an eternity, it seemed. I felt her dry sobs catch on my ear. Then she let me go and strode quickly into the bedroom. She was wearing faded jeans and a man's shirt not tucked in properly, evidence of her haste in coming. Her hair was still in disarray from sleep. She knelt beside Annie, stroked her hair and whispered to her. I don't know what she said.

Annie had the baby at her breast. Her breasts were bare, distended, ready to burst. Milk had spurted out over the sheets, pooled on her belly. Dr. Tithonous cradled her head and whispered. She touched my wife's breasts, she kissed her temples, she felt the baby's cheek with the back of her hand. At that moment, she seemed to shudder, and she buried her eyes briefly against Annie's shoulder.

ιt of myself in Annie's full-length mirror against
. Eyes like dark stones, mouth hanging open. I
, I suddenly noticed. The wild incongruity of this
ne to my knees. And I could not think about it
ιght about it later in my bourbon and Valium stu-
por, when I could only wonder at the paradoxical messages ripping through my heart, as if I were somehow completely separate from those things called "body" and "self," as if the self I
was, or wasn't, was more utterly alien and mysterious than anything I had ever experienced.

At length I crawled into bed with my wife and dead baby,
with my erection, in a gross and humiliating parody of the moment of conception, when, yes, we were all together, too. And
Dr. Tithonous stayed with us in the death room, in this state of
barbaric intimacy.

Weeks later it is like this: I tell Annie I am going to play golf. I
don't even bother to put my clubs in the trunk. They sit there in
the garage behind the infant car seat neither of us can bear to
move or give away. If Annie looked, she would know that I am
not playing golf. I don't know if she looks, she never says a word.
I just tell her. The Canada geese have come and gone, snow flur-
ries fall—still I head out to play golf with obsessive regularity.
What is Annie thinking?

I drive out Route 9 to a little motel called the Royal which
climbs up a shattered limestone ridge and hangs in a state of in-
stability and tension with the scrub pine, sumac and poison ivy
tumbling down the steep slopes. Dr. Tithonous meets me there
when she can break away from her patients. I wait for her in one
of the guest cottages, sipping Old Crow. Sometimes I fall asleep.
The guest cottages at the Royal are the only place I can sleep
these days. Often I waken to find Barbara tucked up beside me

wearing nothing but her bra and underpants, her cell phone and beeper placed neatly upon the bedside table next to the lamp.

What happens next is difficult to relate. One's deepest desires are always paradoxical and humiliating. You go there as into some dark vortex at the bottom of which is death, which seems, in this aspect, breathtakingly sweet. Or put it this way: sex is inextricably entwined with desire, with wanting, but what we want is not always sex. Sometimes we desire pure desire, the endless wanting whose only end is the extinction of itself, that point of voluptuous rest from wanting. Or we crave some replica of the utter desperation of life, the way it eats itself up, the self-destructiveness of it all. So it is with all desperate, whispered entreaties, whimpered protests, grunts, moans and cries in the dark. I can guess why I am there, but what secret sadness drives Barbara to the Royal Motel I cannot tell. I cannot connect the dancer who showed us with her body the ancient processes of conception with the lover who begs me to perform the most unseemly acts, who only cries out for rest so that she can reach some stranger ecstasy.

Once she told me the story of her life, how she had married another doctor named East, how he left her the year he did eight ultrasounds on a pregnant woman and missed the fact that her baby had no brain, how the year Dr. East left Barbara's twin sister Miranda died of leukemia. Near the end, Barbara came often to sit by her bedside, spelling their exhausted, heartsick parents. One night Miranda woke, vomiting, from a drugged slumber. Unable to quell the spasms, even to catch her breath, she threw herself off the bed in agony and crouched trembling on the floor like an animal, horrid blasts of air and fluid shooting up her esophagus and out her anus, tears, sweat and spit spattering the carpet. She cried, over and over, "I'm dying, Barbie. I'm dying."

"She wanted me to leave. She was terrified. Her voice sounded like a little girl's. But it was all her own, the dying consumed her, she wanted to be alone. Her body was ripping itself apart, but she didn't want help or comfort. She wanted me to leave so I wouldn't distract her from the dying. She was tired of caring for people. What does that mean? I'm a doctor, but I don't know what it means. That year everyone abandoned me."

"The trouble with modern medicine," I tell her, "is that it has simply extended human life expectancy twenty or thirty years into the limbo of anticlimax—not something Neddy had to worry about, either."

We both flinch at the sound of Neddy's name, though we both also know that if I didn't just keep talking like this I'd have no recourse but to slash my wrists, eat rat poison, run a hose from my car exhaust or just beat my brains out with one of the white-washed rocks lining the parking pad outside the cottage.

She says, "What modern medicine has taught me is that experience is suffering, and most of the time we have drugs for that."

Beyond the limestone ridge lies a tract of wild country called the Devil's Den. Bobcats haunt the tangled undergrowth, maybe a bear, plenty of deer, the motel owner tells me. The motel owner's name is Ben. He lives with his wife Marge, who hacks around the diminutive owner's suite with a tank of oxygen on a little cart and a mask over her face. Ben smokes in the breezeway by the neon sign that says OFFICE. He wears his long white hair pulled back in a ponytail so tight it seems to drag the skin of his bony face into a mask.

Ben and Marge have a son named Mike, who lives in exile in one of the guest cottages. Ben says Mike's a loner, which is short for a divorced part-time woodcutter who spends most of his time gambling at the harness track or riding around the Devil's Den on his four-wheel ATV, getting drunk. They also have a Brazilian grey monkey named Michael, which they keep caged in Mike's former bedroom in the owner's suite. Ben and Marge think this thin domestic joke is hilarious.

We are all accomplices, it seems. We will do almost anything, enact any cruelty, to keep from thinking about what we are not thinking about. And this strange antithesis of a romance, which Dr. Tithonous and I prosecute in the little housekeeping cabin beneath the Devil's Den, is nothing but a trick and a sign of what it is not. It would be a mistake to think that we are sad, precisely. It is closer to the truth to imagine Barbara, Annie and me (and Ben and Marge and Mike) pursuing our dark ecstasies with a certain ruefill zest—after all, we are not dead yet. Having watched Neddy slip out of the mist and then drift quietly back into the mist—always the mystery of the sweet half-smile—we lurch backward from the edge with a sharpened sense of self. The sounds Dr. Tithonous makes during sex are almost indescribable (as were the sounds her sister made grappling with her death). They haunt me still.

I tell you this mainly because it makes me feel better. It's not worth speaking otherwise. Language is eighty percent consolation, twenty percent aphrodisiac. Communication is an outmoded enterprise, honesty a fake, love a conservative political agenda. Sex is a form of prayer, a baroque topological assault upon the envelope of the soul. All the orifices are good because they get you closer to God. The only sense of self left to us is the sense of the self as actor, that is, when we are pretending to be someone else—hence our ruinous cult of Hollywood celebrity. It is as if we have all been inoculated with that same mysterious wasting sickness, contaminated with death.

One day when Barbara and I are in the throes of something or other, her beeper sounds. She shrugs her shirt and leans over her pale, bruised body. Her lips are bleeding, her breasts are palimpsests of bruises fading from black to gold. She seems faintly noble, if not heroic, buttoning herself, tossing her long hair over her shoulders, staggering out past the shuttered windows into the blazing sunlight. Her lips wear a thin, rueful smile, the twin of Neddy's.

Left alone, I smoke a cigarette. But almost at once I fall prey to remembering, to my ineluctable past, to visions of empty nurseries, abandoned infant car seats, my wife's seeping breasts, her night cries, memories which inevitably drive me out in search of distraction. How can you sit alone after you've heard those words: "My baby is hungry. He needs to eat"?

Outside Mike is packing cans of beer into saddlebags in preparation for his version of a nature hike, a jaunt through the Devil's Den on his ATV. I watch him in silence, but the silence only compels me to engage him in conversation, to make some claim on existence through the sound of my own voice.

I tell Mike this thing with Neddy has put me in a state. I ask him if he thinks Annie has the moral edge on me because she just sits in the nursery weeping, zonked on Zoloft and Restoril she gets from Dr. Tithonous. I tell him I can't stand to be with her, that I am scared to death of really feeling as bad as I feel, that she only reminds me of that. When I'm in that room with her, I say, I think I might have to kill her to get through this, kill her and then call in an air strike and nuke the nursery, the house, the yard (with that swing set I bought as kit and spent a weekend putting together), the whole damn city, and let loose a cloud of radiation that circumnavigates the globe, exterminating everything else.

Mike says, "Right."

He says very little at the best of times but generally knows exactly how to calm me down. I know he has his own family issues. Ben is always looking at Marge's breathing apparatus and saying things like, "Can't wait till we get that shit out of the house." And Marge has told me with some enthusiasm that Ben has an aneurysm, that he'll probably die the next time he sneezes. They both tell me they made a will giving the motel to the Brazilian grey monkey instead of Mike, though they made Mike the executor. They despise Mike for some obscure failure, some purely human thing, I suspect.

Mike himself traces it back to when he was six and his guinea pig Pinky died and he cried too much. He says Ben felt so bad that he couldn't fix things that he decided to blame Mike. "He decided I was a wimp and a crybaby," says Mike. "I've been a flop ever since."

I tell him it's a fundamental human trait to be inhuman to other humans. And then I say, "Maybe it's a kind of love, you know, not wanting to disrupt your father's view of things."

Mike says, "Right."

And then he says, "You want to go into the Den and raise Hell?"

And I say, "I'm in the mood to drive all the way to the bottom and kick Beelzebub in the nuts."

We climb past the deer lick where Mike puts out corn and salt through the winter, through a narrow gorge along an old logging road as far as a row of water-filled caves cut into the side of a hill, a former graphite mine abandoned at the turn of the last century. A cold wind blows steadily out of those caves. The soft rock above the gaping entries seems ready to fall at any moment. They could be the gates of Hell. Mike says a hunter disappeared into those caves once going after a dog that fell through the ice early one spring.

We drink beer, sitting back to back against a young oak growing up from the top of a ridge of mine tailings.

"We're sitting on history," Mike says. I have never known him to wax philosophical, and I take it as a sign of advanced drunkenness. I myself can't stop thinking about our earlier conversation.

I say, "I don't think there is any such thing as love, or love is just humouring the other person, not wanting to disrupt her vision of things."

"Two people humouring each other?" Mike asks.

"No," I say, "I don't think it works like that. One or the other." And then I add, "I think people can't stand to be in love, that it makes them nervous, that they try to wreck it because the memory of love is everlasting whereas love itself is always fleeting. I read in the paper about this new condition called reactive attachment disorder, where people keep themselves in constant physical pain to ward off the larger emotional pain of the loss of love. Now no one said they were going to lose love, but they might. It's the terrible thought that love might end that pushes people to destroy love and themselves."

"That's probably what I've got," says Mike. "I had it before they invented it," he says.

He pulls a .357 handgun from his saddlebag, and we take turns potting the trees. I am a terrible shot, but Mike can nip the twigs off branches. We shoot and shoot, and when we run out of bullets, a litter of fresh-fallen twigs and leaves lies about us.

We pack up and head back down to the Royal. Mike fetches a fresh clip from his cabin, and, for no reason at all except that it seems like a good idea, we head over to the owner's suite. Ben is away. Marge is sleeping, snoring into her oxygen mask. We sneak into his old bedroom, where Michael, the Brazilian grey monkey, darts up at the sound of visitors. The sweet smell of pine chips and rotting fruit mixed with the acidic tang of monkey piss rises from the floor of his cage. A pennant from Niagara Falls, a KISS poster and a plastic dream-catcher, remnants of Mike's boyhood, adorn the otherwise Spartan walls. A plastic ME-109, built from a kit, swings on a length of fishing line. But there is no furniture, just the cage.

For some reason, I think the room is an image of the inside of my mind, or Mike's mind. I am almost too drunk to know which is which. Mike holds the pistol to Michael's head. The monkey, after his initial enthusiasm, has lapsed into apathetic torpor. He squats on the floor of the cage, flipping his flaccid, worm-like penis back and forth with the back of his hand. He peers at the gun without interest and then, as if understanding what's to come, places his other hand over his eyes, the long fingers seeming to stretch almost halfway around his head. His long, skinny limbs make him look insect-like, but the overall effect—the steel bars, the flapping penis, the awkward crouch— is of pathos, of things not in their right place, of interminable anxiety.

I feel a thrill of dread, an almost delicious anticipation of some terrible climax toward which the day or my whole life has been tending. The smell from the cage or the vision of monkey brains soaking into the pine chips makes me gag. But I cannot tear myself away. I am already worried that this will end too soon, that Mike and I will run out of interesting things to do for the rest of the afternoon. I am dying, Annie, I think. I am dying.

But then, as if the whole thing had been a whim, Mike lowers the barrel of the gun, feels with his fingertips above the door lintel for a key, unlocks the cage and grabs Michael by the scruff of his neck. One-handed, he slides open a window which looks out upon the trail to the Devil's Den. I can just see the deer lick two hundred yards into the woods and the lime-stone walls of the gorge poking out of the pines. Mike kicks the screen out of the window and heaves the monkey into the yard. Michael falls in a dusty heap, then resumes his apathetic squat.

But it is cold out there, the chill wind (it seems to come down from those caves, seems to be following us) ruffles his fur. The monkey peers about, then squints at us watching him from the window. You can see questions beginning to form, warring with years of habit, boredom and loneliness. He dabs at the dry pine needles with his fingertips, watches a handful fly away in the breeze. He faces the wind coming over the Devil's Den, and sud-denly the shadows within his eyes deepen as if opening into a long-locked room.

The wind in his fur gives him an ancient warrior look. (What this really means I don't know. And I was drunk. Perhaps all meaning is context, or perhaps I was simply prey to sentiments which no longer had a natural outlet after Neddy's death, but I saw him so.) Mike's reaction is to drop to his knees, cradle his shooting arm against the window sill and take aim. A ball of terror collects in my stomach.

Mike aims, fires. But the bullet flies wide. The monkey's head snaps around, his suspicious eyes absorbing the picture of the two men and the gun, none of which he understands. But some intuition, some reserve of instinct warns him—the air seems suddenly to thicken around us. And he begins an easy four-legged lope up the hillside.

Mike blasts away till his clip is empty. His face glows crimson above his collar, his gun-hand trembles crazily as though some invisible being were struggling to wrest the gun away from him. He looks beaten, defeated, or like a man about to have a stroke. He shouldn't have missed. I wonder why he did. The monkey pauses at the deer lick, squats again, cranes his neck to look first up the trail and then back at us. He is clearly uncertain about the future, about bobcats and the cold. But uncertainty holds him only a moment, and he bravely resumes his upward journey in the direction of who knows what bloody future hurtling toward him.

"He'll be dead in a week," says Mike, breathing heavily, watching the wispy grey fur of the monkey's back disappear into the trees. "If the cats don't get him, he'll starve to death."

Mike starts to laugh, starts, then pauses to see what it feels like to laugh at this juncture, then continues, the volume rising in waves. I can't tell if this is an act or not. Perhaps the whole thing has been an act. Or perhaps there are good reasons for Marge and Ben to keep their son in one of the farther cottages. His face looks like the head of a match bursting into flame.

I can only think how heroic the monkey looks in contrast to his human brother, how satisfying a prospect his night of freedom and violent death seems. And I ponder the mystery of that judgment. This is the old romantic trap, I think. In what sense can it be true that the monkey's brief, sweet sojourn in the Den can be more real, more authentic, than a life in a warm cage?

I am sick in bed for three days after this bout of drunkenness (what my father used to call a toot), but it wakes me up, wakes up my moral being. I once thought you could get through anything by striking attitudes and spouting a little philosophy. But that's not true. I am not going to get through this, and what I am doing with Dr. Tithonous is wrong. I mean I am going to get through it. I am alive, after all. But my life has changed irrevocably. The person I am now and the person I was before Neddy died are discontinuous, though related, like second cousins once removed.

On top of everything else, I decide my marriage is coming apart. Little indications of seismic upheaval abound: the way Annie drifts out of rooms as I enter, the sound of uncontrollable sobbing behind locked doors, her perfect composure when she finally does appear, her sudden interest in therapy and her reconnection with an old girlfriend named Rosellen who recently moved back to town. There is nothing definite, only an incremental decline, a mysterious wasting.

Annie knows nothing of my affair with Dr. Tithonous, but she accuses me with her eyes when she thinks I am not looking. These silent accusations are troubling in their implication. What betrayal am I being charged with? Did I wish Neddy dead? Am I taking it all too lightly with my endless golf-playing? What can she think? To me, her anger seems gratuitous, its own species of betrayal. Does she think I actually want to act the way I am acting, that I have any control? I stopped getting what I wanted the moment Neddy died. Everything since then can only be described as fate or gesture. Am I really to be blamed because I am no less capable than she of bridging the silence between us?

Not that there weren't signs of trouble before Neddy was born. Annie and I were both ambivalent, but we were both also tired of our dithering. So we went ahead and made the baby, and briefly the act of taking a risk restored to us our sense of adventure, brought us together as nothing had since the very beginning of our relationship, when, likewise impelled by panache and a willingness to gamble, we threw ourselves together. Character is action, action is fate. You are someone when you do something. The rest of the time you wallow. Life becomes this endless tension between wallowing and little abortive attempts to compose a self through action. The polar modes of existence: wallowing and a desperate, mindless darting. Annie and I are just two normal, modern people caught in the soup—but she blames me for this.

Annie and I met one summer between college terms in a little café around the corner from the Rodin Museum in Paris. I was travelling alone. She was with her brother and his fiancée, a buxom Californian who resented having to drag Annie along wherever they went. I had watched them wander through the museum. The brother and his fiancée were clearly bored—they kissed in front of *The Kiss,* they held hands in front of the hands, they leaned on each other in front of *The Burghers of Calais.* Annie looked forlorn, miserable, her face pale, as though she hadn't slept. You actually had to look twice to see her beauty.

I followed them to the café, then made myself a nuisance, asking directions, folding my map out onto their table. I asked Annie to come with me for the afternoon. She said no. The fiancée urged her to have an adventure. You could see relief flooding all three faces. "You saved me from my version of a wicked stepmother," she said afterward, laughing. But, equally, she had saved me from a terrible loneliness and self-perpetuating insecurity. And her laughter had a forced quality, as if she were trying to put the best face on things.

How this sense of uneasy relief and gratitude turned into love is a caution and a mystery. Perhaps it was only that we did not know what love was and mistook whatever it was we were feeling for love. Or that, both of us being unable to bear disappointment in the other, we manufactured an enthusiasm that was otherwise lacking in order to feast on the delight in the other's eyes. Hence the eerie emptiness, the silence which seemed always to surround our love, the sense that if we did not keep upping the ante, risking more, our love would disappear. This, it seems to me, is the essence of romantic love, love founded upon its own impossibility, love which paradoxically feeds upon itself in order to grow. In time, Annie and I both grew to feel left out of our marriage. Who were those two people fornicating so energetically, so joylessly, upon the counterpane? Not she, not I. Would Neddy have made us real again?

My new moral self, discovered after bottoming out and conspiring to murder a Brazilian grey monkey at the Royal Motel, decides to make a clean breast of things. Perhaps this is not a new moral self, perhaps it is only the old pathological self that just has to keep stirring things up in order to feel alive. It's difficult to tell. I meet Dr. Tithonous at the Royal and tell her I can't see her anymore. She tells me she isn't wearing any underwear, that there is dampness trickling down the insides of her thighs, that she has longed for this moment, the moment of rejection. Weeping, she falls to her knees and, fumbling with my belt, begs me desperately to make love to her, a locution she has never used in the past. She has become a glutton for humiliation. Why do I feel, once again, that we are acting out some universal drama? Our obsession with one another is about to transform itself into shame and loathing on her side and mild distaste and irritation on mine. A week ago we were at each other like dogs in heat, and a week from now we'll both be wishing it had never happened. It's a wonder to me that the so-called experts haven't realized that we're all going around in a state of chronic low-grade schizophrenia, that identity is a fiction.

My new moral self drives home with a certain self-righteous precision and discovers Annie in the nursery, rocking almost imperceptibly in the little rocking chair she meant to use for nursing Neddy, listening to the panda bear mobile playing "Twinkle, twinkle, little star." She's in there communing with our son, I think. But then again maybe she is in there communing with me—for this is now my favourite room in the house, the place where I spend my lonely hours. I smell of sex with Dr. Tithonous (my new moral self winces at this admission). Annie looks sad, pensive and suddenly more beautiful than I have ever seen her, as if after all the undignified suffering she has achieved some deeper knowledge of the meaning of things.

I had marched into the house full of hatred for myself and my wife, ready to slay her with my revelations, ready to demolish her with honesty for all that pathetic flailing about I hate in myself (so much for the new moral self—whenever you feel the moral self waking within, you can bet an act of injustice and inhumanity is about to follow). But she only glances up at me with a bemused, slightly embarrassed smile on her face which reminds me of nothing so much as Neddy, oh, these eons ago. For it was her smile I was seeing on his face, only I'd forgotten.

And all at once I feel a welling up of love for Annie, love and passion and desire. My limbs tremble as contrary emotions surge through me. My eyes grow hot, heavy-lidded with tears. I remember the splendour of making Neddy. I recall the terrible hope in our hearts. I want just to touch her and go on touching her for the rest of my life, to catch her hand and put my cheek against hers so that I might feel the warmth of her flesh and smell the sweetness of her breath as it goes in and out and remember, oh, remember what hope was like. There has never been anything else I ever wanted and nothing more I will ever want. I am completely undone, unstrung, helpless.

She says, "Hey, you." She touches my foot with hers and holds up her arms to pull me in. Her eyes are full of mischief, a weary merriment, irresistible eyes.

I hesitate because now I have a terrible truth to tell, something unforgivable that will come slamming down on us like a steel door, crushing this sudden afflatus of love.

I call it love, for want of a better word—I don't know what it is, really. Beyond us there is a void, and inside us there is a void. At the centre, the self is inscrutable. We ride the dark, lunar surfaces of unknown objects our whole lives long; we are receivers of messages the provenance of which is as obscure as death itself. It seems to test us, to drown us, grow us, betray us, destroy us. Before it, we are alone. And yet between this void and the shallow dogmas of psychotherapeutics there remains some residue, some faint sediment of—what? The thing you can't see for looking at it, the thing disappearing at the corner of your eye, the thing not conceived in any of your philosophies, the thing that is not the void and not the half-crazy, shambling beast of desire that dogs our lives (what the Buddhists call "the little self"). This is the place where love resides, if love resides.

I lay my head upon her lap. The rocking chair is still. Annie strokes my temples, the nape of my neck, and, sobbing because my heart is broken, I tell her that our boy is dead, that this is the only real thing that's happened, that getting so close to reality is like putting your head in a giant wall socket, that every certainty has been upended, the linchpin knocked out of my life, the keystone dropped from the arch. I can't figure out how to take another step, but I wander on, embarrassed by my own seeming indestructibility. I can't say who is telling my feet to move. It's not me giving the orders. "I tried so hard," I sob. I don't know why my heart seems suddenly to break again when I say the words. "I tried so hard." But the tears are gushing out of me, my body is wracked with sadness.

The rhythm of Annie's caresses never falters. She says nothing. I feel the gentle insistence of the flesh of her thigh against my cheek, reminding me of her sexual presence, of our consequential passions. I think how my present prostration is the only correct response to the world, that if we could see the world the way it really is, there would be nothing but this weeping and biting of hands. I think, now I am where I belong.

But presently, without looking into her face, I begin to tell Annie about my afternoons at the Royal Motel with Dr. Tithonous. (How many times, in the grip of some outré perversity, did I recall the vision of the doctor crouched beside the bed, whispering into Annie's ear, the soiled nightgown, the streaming breasts, both women mysteriously out of themselves, forgetful of me? How many times did I pity the doctor for her subterranean hungers? It seemed, yes, that she was the most tragic of us all, the one to whom science had revealed all secrets but who had drifted farthest from the truth. What is the truth? Once I told her, "Modern medicine is a crutch we should throw away." Impossible to know what I meant.)

I can barely get the words out, but each sound I utter increases my confidence in the story. Somehow, I suppose, I'd thought language would prove incapable of conveying the monstrous details, that I wouldn't be able to tell her. But the very miracle of turning my assignations into sentences and paragraphs has the odd effect of domesticating them, making them feel reasonable, part of the known world (another function of language: it renders everything it touches trivial and slightly seedy). I hadn't gone beyond the moon—I had met our doctor at a motel because I was upset about what happened to Neddy, who died at three months of a mysterious wasting disease. This sounds so plausible, and Annie's response—silence—seems so benign that I almost stop feeling guilty, though moments later my heart races with anxiety over the obvious discrepancies between my words and the facts, language's inadequacy as a device for communicating, signalled here by Annie's first words when she does begin to speak—something about a monkey, as if I have somehow mixed up the story about the monkey with the story about Dr. Tithonous.

Fresh reasons for despair—I can't even confess to my wife without inspiring a misunderstanding, without the words somehow being misconstrued. The thing is absolutely impossible—she can't see into my heart. Or have I simply been lying again without knowing it? I repeat here that the only real thing that's happened is that Neddy died. All the rest—Annie crying, "My baby's hungry, I have to feed my baby," my affair with Dr. Tithonous, the attempted murder of the monkey—all the rest is true, too, but in the manner of a code or a substitute for the real thing. The sad truth is that part of me already no longer believes Neddy lived and died. The New Agers call this the healing process. Mourning has its rhythms and stages, and pretty soon it is as if the thing itself didn't happen, just the mourning and the healing. The aftermath becomes the thing—like the intergalactic radiation that remains our only evidence for the Big Bang at the beginning of Time. By substitution, by the metaphoric process of language, we move incrementally away from the edge of reality, back into the everyday zone of safety and lies—we ought to put a stop to healing, I think.

Annie gently asks again about the monkey. This time I have to look at her face to see if indeed she might not have gone completely insane (always a distinct possibility with human beings), but there is only that curious smile, Neddy's smile, about which now I see I was mistaken. It's not uncertain, wan and etiolate, as I had thought. Rather it is a smile of affection, only slightly uncertain of response, waiting for a response. It occurs to me suddenly, blindingly, that Neddy loved us—that was the message of the smile—and that he knew he was loved.

This realization unleashes fresh grief. I am a boy again, sobbing inconsolably over the unfairness of life. I have never felt such pain and, simultaneously, such release—an access of fatigue and self-pity. Annie cradles my face against her breasts and begins to rock again ever so slightly.

All at once I am kissing her, struggling to undo the buttons of her shirt. She releases me slightly from our embrace to help. Her breasts are large, slightly under-inflated, as it were, as they begin to shrink to their normal size. Flawed like this, they have never seemed more desirable. They tell me a story, something about the life of women. I suck them, tasting the bittersweet taste of her milk. She rocks me, croons one of those children's songs she had been memorizing through her pregnancy. And soon we are making love on the floor, very carefully, very tenderly, without thinking about birth control, just the way we did when we made Neddy.

It is a strange sort of excitement, full of history and sadness, calm somehow, without the usual agitation of sexual desire. We look into each other's eyes and feel our bodies rising, but we are distant from that. The thing that is empty inside me is pouring itself into Annie and into the minatory and morbid future.

Nothing makes sense. And it has stopped being a story. I have to fight to keep my anxiety for sense and explanations from corrupting the moment. The moment is already corrupt when I think that it doesn't make sense, for there is no perception without words. And there is no such thing as the things we call by the words "love" and "human being" and "soul." I can only hope that, by some backwards logic, the moment that makes no sense somehow makes the most sense, that the truth is true because it is unrecognizable. In this moment, I also do not recognize myself or my wife. But I feel a surge of forgiveness and generosity flowing from her, out of the mysterious and alien emptiness that is all I can know of her. It has none of the conventional passion or even coziness of the thing we normally call love. All that has burned off with the loss of Neddy.

As we come back to ourselves, we are like tired, wounded soldiers, strangers to one another, supporting each other out of the battle. We cannot save each other, we cannot escape, but there is some human dignity to be claimed in the comradeship of the doomed. We hold each other, a little abashed at what we have done. And I can see the old pieties and anxieties beginning to reassert themselves in Annie's eyes. There is some hurt there now, the beginnings of resentment (the feeling of the age), though I can also see that she is fighting this, clearly surprised and proud of her spiritual daring.

I myself am startled by a sudden perception of Annie's mysterious depths, how different she is from any expectation I have of her, how she is herself, astonishing and other. I cannot calculate the reasons for this, but where I could only think to touch her with my anger and violence, she has found a way to reach back with love and forgiveness. This gesture is transformative just as it is tentative and temporary. So much of what is good in life has this quality of fleetingness, a glimpse snatched through a closing door, an infant dying. But it makes me love her back, though I don't know what it means to say that.

Six months later they find Ben and Marge dead together in the bedroom, holding hands. There is a note that says they decided they could not live without each other and were afraid they would soon lose the chance to make that choice themselves. Suddenly Mike owns the Royal Motel. He stops drinking out of shock, not because his parents killed themselves but because of that note. "I thought they hated each other," he says. He thought they hated him, too, and now his whole universe has been turned upside down.

I myself am puzzled by the violent shifting of things, the lack of continuity between words and actions. Nothing in the way they presented themselves had prepared me for the couple's dramatic liebestod. I say, "Mike, sometimes it seems as if life is designed specifically to demolish every certainty, every categorical statement. Or else it's a novel being written by an inattentive author who cannot even bother to keep the characters straight."

Since that fateful afternoon, there has been no sign of the Brazilian grey monkey—no body, no telltale fur patches or crushed, half-eaten bones. It is as if he walked into the Devil's Den and vanished. Mike, who has had a complete change of heart about the monkey and searches for him constantly (leaving little caches of food among the rocks), believes the monkey just kept walking and somehow is on his way back to Brazil, home.

A Piece of the True Cross

I

MY SISTER, DARLA, was struck by lightning the summer we bought the house on Block Island.

She wasn't killed, and now, twenty years later, she is married to an investment banker named Tad and has two healthy sons. She complains of deafness in her left ear and a residual ache in her left elbow and shoulder. She is apprehensive when storms approach. She claims sometimes to see auras around peoples' heads. A lot of people claim to see auras, but I generally disbelieve them. Darla I believe.

I was thirteen that year, and the world seemed an ineffably sad and lonely place to me. Our father had founded a chemical company with plants in Georgia and Louisiana. He had come from the South, those were his roots, but he had never taken us back for so much as a visit. Summers we usually went to Nantucket or Provincetown, until we bought the old Waring place on Block Island. I spent my falls, winters and springs at a boarding school in the Berkshires.

I was standing at my bedroom window watching storm clouds advance over the sound when the lightning struck our house. More distant bolts were etching maps in the sky. I had just spotted one that looked so much like the Mississippi River I could pinpoint where the family fertilizer factory stood, down by the delta.

I imagined the delta heat and humidity; I imagined elderly black men with floppy-eared dogs sitting before ramshackle clapboard houses, spitting and nodding to me as I rode by on my bicycle; I imagined fishing for catfish in the bayous on long mosquito-filled evenings. But I failed to notice that the Mississippi of my imagination had struck dangerously close to the house. It hung there a moment, illuminating everything in a brilliant chiaroscuro, until the clap of thunder broke over my head.

Almost at once a second clap erupted through the ceiling of my room. A spark the size of a tennis ball hovered over the metal bedstead, then split in two and traveled along the frame and across the painted plank floor before climbing the pipes of my bedroom sink. With amazement and delight, I watched it recombine and spiral into the sink, disappearing down the drain hole. With a loud pop, the sink exploded away from the wall, dangling free on its pipes, a cloud of plaster dust mushrooming up from the floor.

From elsewhere in the house, there came the sounds of splintering glass and wood. On the floor below, Mother began to scream, filling me with irritation and dread.

I was so confused I could only turn again to the window to watch the play of light and dark on last year's dead leaves swirling above the broken stone walk, the skewed croquet hoops in the lawn and the dying elm tree next to the mysterious octagonal carriage house with the revolving floor and the garret apartment where St. John Waring's mistress had once lived in luxury and car fumes.

Just below, the gardener's elderly black Lab, Sukey, raced her sinister shadow past the juniper bushes, her tongue lolling in fright.

Then, hearing Father's grumpy, short-winded imprecations and his heavy feet on the stairs, I finally ran to the doorway and peered out. The house was dark, the electricity having failed when the storm began. Lightning struck again, bursting white from the hall-end window. The pungent odours of smoke and singed hair penetrated my nostrils.

I saw Mother standing at Darla's door, her face a pale mask of horror, her mouth open, everything white and black.

The old Waring place was to be our summer home from then on.

The Warings, who had once been very rich, built the house with the intention of establishing a permanent family seat on the model of the old English country home, a refuge and retreat for succeeding generations of Warings stretching into the millennia. But Grace Waring, the widow, had closed the house after St. John's death, mostly because of that mistress and her bitter memories.

When she died, a son sold the estate for taxes, and for a time it had served as a tuberculosis sanatorium, hence the metal bedsteads and the chipped enamel sinks in every room.

The basement and attic concealed more macabre vestiges of those sad years: kidney-shaped bed pans and spit dishes, musty cardboard crates of patient records, bales of blank admission forms, a pyramid of unexposed x-ray film, the frame of the old x-ray machine, and neatly stapled files of invoices (for fresh vegetables from the local farmers, a keg of nails and a dozen copper pipe elbows from the hardware store in the village, gas and per diems for a doctor's trip to a medical convention in New Haven—homely things oddly unconnected with death).

These parts of the house were considered closed off by my parents, who seemed to have gotten an idea from their real estate agent that doors had been nailed up or bricked over, that whole wings had been condemned (this is why, they congratulated themselves, they had been able to buy it so cheaply), though, in fact, Darla and I wandered in there for days on end, alternately chilled and fascinated by each grisly discovery.

The last owners before we moved in the summer the lightning struck Darla were a French-Canadian family called La Douceur, a madcap bunch, by all accounts, who, when they abandoned the place, left behind a large assortment of beach furniture, a roomful of fake Japanese screens bought at a sale when the 1967 World's Fair closed in Montreal, a fieldstone and concrete shrine on the front lawn with a statue of the Virgin Mary in a niche, and their grandmother's ashes.

We only learned about the ashes a week after our arrival, when Mr. La Douceur telephoned from Quebec City in a panic.

Mother sent me racing upstairs to a room marked LINEN, where, in a back corner of a wall cabinet, I found a copper urn about the size and shape of a bowling pin. The urn smelled vaguely medicinal, as did almost everything in that house. The ashes made the sound of sand shifting.

When I looked up there was a stranger, a gaunt young woman wrapped in a sheet, like a mummy, I thought, standing in the doorway watching me. She had black eyebrows like bits of charcoal and wide, feverish eyes that gazed at me with startled affection. When she saw that I saw her, she smiled slightly, wearily, it seemed, then turned and vanished down the hall. Clumsy with the weight of the La Douceur family ashes, I ran to the door, but the woman was nowhere to be seen.

Reluctantly, I returned to the wall cabinet, where, just as she appeared, I had noticed something hidden on the shelf behind the urn. I reached up and fished out a clear plastic plaque with a jagged splinter of wood embedded in it. On the plaque backing, behind the splinter, there was an illustration of the Sacred Heart. Turning the plaque over, I found a legend printed in Gothic script: A Piece of the True Cross.

Later, when I told Darla about the woman in the white sheet and showed her the relic, she seemed unsurprised.

Darla was two years older than me, and it was about this time that she tried to have sexual intercourse with me in one of the eight bathrooms distributed amongst the upstairs bedrooms. This was our one and only attempt at physical intimacy, and it was unsuccessful (to be precise, I did not attain complete erection, and my bladder sphincter relaxed out of nervousness just as I entered her vagina, causing us both a good deal of embarrassment).

Mr. La Douceur arrived a week later, alone in the family station wagon, to retrieve his mother's ashes, sweaty, self-important and evincing little embarrassment at forgetting such an important item. Though there were several Japanese screens in evidence (Mother having decided she liked them as an interior decoration for breaking up the vast spaces and sight lines of the living room), he did not mention them. And he drove away quickly without a nod to the Virgin Mary.

Once a year Father had the basal cell cancers removed from his nose and forehead, his face becoming a pattern of red skin and flesh-coloured bandages. ("Quite a sight," Darla would say.) The last time I saw him was at the opening of a show of my paintings at Verna Walter's gallery in Soho, when he came through the door with his face bandaged, wearing a dinner jacket and carpet slippers.

Offering him a glass of champagne, I whispered huffily, "You always have to make yourself the centre of attention."

He blinked but did not reply, though I believe he understood what I meant, the whole depth and breadth of my lifelong accusation.

He was nearly blind by then and chronically depressed. He wore thick spectacles and read with difficulty, with the aid of a magnifying glass. This blindness contributed to his death three years ago, when he spilled something in a lab and the whole Louisiana factory went up. What was left of him could have fit easily in Madame La Douceur's urn.

I have his glasses, though.

Mother was mesmerizing, energetic, directionless and hysterical. When I was sad, Mother tore her clothes. When I was angry, Mother punished me. She was forever exhorting me to do things with the accent and enthusiasm of a girls' school field hockey coach (a tone Darla gradually acquired when it came to raising her own sons).

I would never have skied, played softball or ice hockey, sung in the St. John the Apostle choir (where I was fondled, pleasantly enough, by a lay brother named Peter McNab), gone out on dates or learned to paint if it hadn't been for Mother. I wouldn't have lived without her, Darla says, meaning "lived" figuratively.

Yet when my father died, she became a spent force.

Now, like me, she lives in the city. Once a week she telephones to ask what she should do, redecorate the living room or buy new china, go to Jamaica or take a tour of English pubs?

"Sell the old Waring place," I say.

But, like me, she never does anything.

Both my parents refused to see ghosts or anything else unusual about the summer house, or themselves for that matter (I was twenty-five before I realized there was nothing normal about my upbringing). They thought it was a sign when Darla did not die of lightning bolts. A miracle, Mother said, with her usual melodramatic flair.

I remember the three of us converging on Darla's door, the odours of singed hair, dry rot and ancient dust (since house dust is mainly sloughed off skin cells, Darla and I assumed we had been breathing dead TB patients the whole summer), and the sounds of glass breaking, clapboards tearing themselves from old square nails in agony and Mother's muffled shrieks.

Darla lay amidst her smouldering bedclothes, the hair on one side of her head burned down to the scalp, her window frame smashed in and dangling from the wall, shards of glass glittering on the floor and blankets every time the lightning flashed. Her left breast was bare, the nightdress torn or burned from her, and her nipple stood black and salient against the whiteness of her skin.

She looked like a queen of the dead, with her startled eyes, the black and white strobing of the lightning, the terrible music of the breaking glass.

Unable to see, Father stumbled forward with his arms outstretched (his magnified eyes peering everywhere, trying to identify who was a friend and what was dangerous).

Mother flung herself at his neck, crying inanely, "Oh, darling, I'll save you. I'll save you. Don't go near her."

Pushing past them, cutting my bare feet on the glass but feeling nothing, hypnotized by the beauty of the scene and the sense of strangeness, I touched Darla's forearm where it lay across her belly, half-expecting it to be cold in death, half-expecting it to jump with high voltage and drop me in my tracks. It was only then, in a flash of lightning, that I saw she was still breathing and that in her hand she clutched the La Douceur relic, the plasticized piece of the True Cross.

2

I AM THIRTY-THREE NOW. My private life is a disaster.

A year ago I gave Mother's Irish claddagh ring, the one my father gave her on their engagement (signifying love, friendship and loyalty), to a twenty-year-old leather boy who let me masturbate him in a peep show on 42nd Street. I did not know his name but believed, apparently without foundation, that we were in love.

For four years, I shared my loft and bed with an aspiring poet from Cleveland named Vicky Wonderlight, and though we kissed and cuddled and masturbated each other, we never made love (to be fair, this must reveal as much about Vicky's capacity for intimacy as mine).

I design and build museum exhibits for a living (growing up in my family, I had become accustomed to making old dead things the centre of my life), travelling around the country, sometimes sojourning for weeks in comfortingly anonymous motel rooms while I do my work.

Nights, I linger in my loft (now all my own) painting huge canvases that look, at first, almost preternaturally black. Yet, when held under a bright light, they come up in a dozen hues of electric blue-white and red.

The subjects are all the same, a naked man (self-portrait) falling in space. Around him swirl a number of objects, ash urns, thick wire-rimmed spectacles, croquet hoops, old Daimler automobiles (of the kind that St. John Waring used to park beneath his mistress's apartment), iron bedsteads and enamelled bedroom sinks, choirboy vestments and lightning bolts and tennis ball-sized globes of light that dance upon his fingertips.

Always half-hidden somewhere in the chaotic background there is an object that resembles a plaque of clear plastic containing a splinter of wood (like a lightning bolt) to signify the miraculous quality of life, our slim hope of redemption.

These naked male figures are like ghosts. You can see through them, and their faces wear hurt expressions of puzzlement and nostalgia.

Darla always claimed to remember nothing of her near brush with death by electrocution. A doctor examined her, gave her a sedative by injection, and closed her eyes with his fingers. She slept for three days, and when she awoke she was deaf.

The deafness lasted a month and then gradually abated— though for years Darla was haunted by mysterious pops, grindings, clangs and echoes. My mother and father never noticed, except insofar as they grew irritated with her inattentiveness. I managed to cover for her most of the time, answering their questions, giving her furtive hand signals and exaggerating my lip movements when I could get away with it. Alone, we seemed to communicate telepathically. By touching hands and pointing, or looking into each other's eyes, we knew at once each other's most complicated thoughts.

Mother cut Darla's hair so that the singed areas did not seem so obvious, though for several weeks, Darla drew stares when she ventured into town on grocery-buying trips.

Because of her deafness and the hair and a certain timidity caused by her fear of storms (at first she had only to look up at a clear sky to be overcome with terror), she grew to depend on me completely.

One day I found her in the bathroom next to my room, naked, stinking and moaning, covered with her own feces which she had retrieved from the toilet and rubbed on herself. I cleaned her up and helped her to bed, where she slept the afternoon away, only to appear for dinner, clean and fresh-smelling, silent and inattentive.

That summer I lost my virginity to the gardener's son, Billy Dedankalus, a pale, thin young man who was terrified of the ghosts (though he had never seen one). I think now that I was in love without really knowing it. Sometimes I think that this was the one great love of my life, the pattern for all the rest. For Billy quickly fell in love with Darla and left me with my memories.

In the days following Darla's accident, while she was still confined to her room, I began wandering in the gardens, sometimes following the aging Sukey on her rounds, or in the abandoned hothouses where old Dedankalus, the gardener, kept a few beds for starting vegetables and a collection of rare cacti, huge in red earthenware pots on the rough wood tables.

At first silently and at a distance, I watched him work, admiring the ritualistic precision with which he dug, planted, weeded and pruned. Soon I began to help, working alongside him with my sleeves rolled up and sweat rolling down my flushed cheeks.

He was a lean, sinewy man, with a sun-browned, cadaverous face and thin, white hair cropped close like a convict's. He carried a rifle wherever he worked to shoot stray cats, groundhogs and rabbits that threatened his plantings. His intensity and offhand cruelty both repelled and fascinated me.

He had first worked there as a boy, assisting a Japanese gardener the Warings imported from the city to lay out their estate. He had helped put in a pool where fat-cheeked goldfish swam and where the La Douceurs' Virgin Mary now stood contemplating her feet. Behind the house, where the shore dunes met the lawn, there were dwarf cedars Dedankalus had learned to trim and bind into agonized shapes, now mostly run wild or dead.

During the years the place had been used as a hospital, he had turned the ornamental flower beds into vegetable gardens. His greenhouses forced hothouse tomatoes and melons for the dying patients. Now he tended the place mostly out of love, or the memory of love.

Neither of my parents knew what a superb gardener he was; they only complained about the cost (though he charged for part-time work and supplemented his income doing odd jobs and caretaking for several other summer residents).

Darla joined us when she was out of bed, not because she loved gardening but to be close to me. She was pale and, with her singed and cropped hair, looked touched in the head. She would sit at the edge of a flower bed, pulling up tufts of grass and watching. Sometimes she would wander away a few yards and stare at the ocean or at one of the contorted cedars that separated the grounds from the dunes along the shore.

Dedankalus was kind to her because (this is what I believe) she reminded him of the patients who had once lived in the house and similarly spent their wan convalescence watching him garden.

It was on one of these hot working days, while Dedankalus and I sweated in the rock garden below the back patio, that Billy came home on leave from the army base in Georgia where he was stationed. He was twenty-two, fearful of ghosts, in awe of and hating his father. He wore jeans, a dirty T-shirt, a wallet on a chain and down-at-heel cowboy boots.

These memories are painful, let me tell you.

And I would not write them out this way except on the advice of my therapist who has come to understand that I cannot speak about what I feel but that I can hint at it in my art or in a diary that will be destroyed, in letters that will not be sent or in stories that will not be read.

The secret self is the real self, and I make my paintings difficult to understand because I am afraid that what I really have to say will be met with apathy and stony silence or a sigh and a quick change of subject. This would be devastating—so I make difficulty the subject of my paintings. The images adumbrate a soul whose unique activity is concealment. It is highly adept, it has made an art, a whole aesthetic out of concealment while yearning, aching, straining for some other connection.

"Why did you let them rob you?" asks Darla.

I don't know what she means.

I am the empty man. I have no feelings left because my habit of concealment has hidden me from myself

When I started therapy, she said, "This will do you good only if you don't turn it into another technique."

Remembering Billy makes me think of Vicky—the truth is I fell in love with both of them because they rejected me. In bed at night, Vicky would hiss at me in the dark, "Faggot! Queer! Shit-lover! Art-fraud! How many times did you take it up the ass today?" and I would spurt come on my pajamas, weeping and melting at the same time.

Then she would come by herself, shouting "Mama? Mama? Save them! Can't you save them?"

What she meant by this was a mystery.

That summer, working with Dedankalus, watching his rough hands delve in the soil and fondle the tender plants, watching him casually raise his rifle to kill small animals (so cold and stiff within minutes), observing him unzip his pants and urinate in the junipers, being aware of the ghosts or the sense that always there was someone watching and so much was hidden, I began to have sexual feelings that seemed unconnected with any particular person.

I began to masturbate out of doors, hidden in the dunes, or in the old sanatorium morgue, imagining someone tall and lank and beautiful coming upon me like that, stripping and joining me on the dune grass or the loose cool soil or on the padded gurney.

One day Billy did find me, or (and this is what I think) perhaps he had been watching me all along and only chose then to reveal himself. I pulled up my shorts and started to weep with embarrassment. When I tried to run away, he grabbed my shirt, tearing a button off, and laughed.

It was strange to see him laugh, a combined grimace and sneer. I could see the self-loathing in his face, the compulsion to do the worst thing, to seek danger, to put himself in jeopardy. His carelessness propelled him into some zone of freedom, and our sex became a composition of fear, violence and abandonment.

It was Billy who told us stories about the men and women who haunted the rooms of the old house, about the doomed patients, old and young, or the young nurses recruited with danger pay to care for them, who, as often as not, fell stricken with the same disease and died on the premises. About the babies born to patients lonely for love, babies born with the disease, who died almost at once, buried without names. About the doctors who lived in cottages in the village, their uproarious, drunken parties, their balls, their black-tie bridge tournaments.

It was Billy who told us about St. John Waring's mistress and her apartment over the garage, who showed us the machinery beneath the garage floor that turned the cars around.

Nights, Billy told us, his father had trundled the plain pine coffins from the morgue and buried them in the lonely, unmarked graves. It was the memory of this time, of all the anonymous dead, that had rendered him so inward, silent and cruel. The gardener had a recurring dream, that he awoke tied up, wrapped in a sheet, cradled in the frozen earth. A gaunt, skeletal man with red cheeks and shining eyes bends over and beckons him.

Old Dedankalus had finally married one of the patients, that was the romance of Billy's life. She was a fortyish, unmarried Italian woman from New York who had come to the island to die. No one had ever visited her, so Dedankalus had brought her fresh vegetables and flowers smuggled from his hothouses. When she was allowed outside, he would wheel her invalid chair to the row of contorted trees, explaining about the shapes and the Japanese gardener.

She had died a week after Billy was born, and Dedankalus had dug her grave.

Billy showed us her admission forms, her death certificate, and, most chillingly, her autopsy report. He even had a chest x-ray, showing the lesions and scars on her lungs, the enlarged heart, the tangle of arteries like the contorted limbs of her husband's trees.

His mother, Billy believed, haunted the house, and whenever I or Darla came across one of the ghosts (in time, it seemed, we saw them as often as real people—they grew to accept us and went about their business as though we weren't there), he would cross-examine us, hoping that we had spotted her.

I never told him about the woman in the linen closet the day I found the piece of the True Cross. With those eyebrows and the pale, gaunt cheeks, they could have been twins.

The worst is that this will go on and on without changing, that my father's heavy, depressive presence and Mother's melodrama will define me to eternity. I am happy only when I can lose myself in my paintings, which are really nothing more than elaborate messages, as Darla says, to the world outside.

It is as if the paintings are myself, and I am this oddly constructed and inept instrument for expressing them. Yet I also stand in the way of my paintings; yes, it is I who obstruct, inhibit, corrupt and deform them.

For me, the task was always to liberate myself from love.

3

DARLA TELEPHONED ME at my loft a week ago.

This was twenty years to the day (I checked the wall calendar next to the phone) since she and Billy tried to elope, stealing his father's car and driving as far as the ferry landing before my father and the gardener caught up with them.

"Why did you let them rob you?" she asked. Perhaps, I thought, she is only asking herself, though she seems to have everything any normal person could desire.

Hearing her voice, I remembered Father, Billy and Vicky and all the other losses and betrayals that seem to comprise my destiny.

One day Billy said to me, "The minute someone tells me he loves me, I start planning my escape as if he had taken me prisoner of war."

"I didn't say I loved you," I pleaded, but by then it was too late.

Sometimes out of loneliness I would crawl into bed with Darla in the mornings, and she would be fully dressed, the ankles of her jeans damp with sand and dew from the dunes.

Sand everywhere.

Darla had finally talked Mother into letting us sell the Waring place. She wanted me to drive up with her to meet the real estate agent, who was, it turned out, a cousin of Dedankalus.

She went on in a tone of voice I found surprising but also oddly familiar, a tone that was at once breathless and frightened.

Without pausing, she told me that Tad had gone into a corporate drug rehab clinic near Lake Placid, that Lonny, her youngest, her baby, was having nightmares, horrid dreams of dark men cutting off his genitals and throwing him off buildings, that her own life was falling apart. She had had two abnormal pap smears in a row and was scheduled for a biopsy. No one else knew.

After a moment's hesitation, I said yes, remembering the way she looked in the weeks after the lightning struck, her pale vacantness, her cropped hair and the outsized clothes she borrowed from me or Billy.

I said I would pick her up with the boys in the morning. We would make a family outing, complete with a picnic lunch and seafood dinner at Renaldo's on the ferry pier. I would pack the picnic, she should bring the wine from Tad's cellar.

"Don't pretend," she whispered. "You can't even take care of yourself. This terrifies you."

I hung up, wishing she did not know me quite so well.

I thought, these things that happen to us have no cause or reason. It is as though we are not real at all but being written by some ghostly hand. There is no presence, only a vast nostalgia and, on every page, just the shadow of something which never appears and is never named.

I could not paint any more, just stared and stared at my canvas, a black vortex of images, falling boys, a bloated face covered with moth-like twists of gauze, Japanese screens, bowling pins, a jagged crucifix of light, a girl with blazing hair, Billy Dedankalus slumped in his chair with his rifle propped against his forehead, the way we found him, and myself as a grown man, standing to one side, watching in horror.

That night the black dog visited, by which I mean that I dreamt of Sukey, the gardener's aged black Lab. Waking, I heard the distant rumble of a thunder storm, an occurrence which, for obvious reasons, always sets me on edge. Though it was 3 A.M., I tried to telephone Darla and kept getting a recorded message telling me to hang up and dial again.

We made the trip in silence.

I asked Darla once when Tad was coming back and then tried to remind her of Mr. La Douceur and his mother's ashes. But she was lost in thought, her fingers working nervously at her pocketbook. She was wearing jeans and one of her husband's checked work shirts. Her hair was done up at the back in a po-nytail—such informality has long been completely out of char-acter for her. The boys, in the back seat, seemed crabby and tired and fell asleep before we left the city.

Ray Dedankalus, the cousin, met us at the ferry dock and drove with us to the house, stopping for hamburgers along the way.

Darla maintained her reserved silence, staring out the pas-senger window. I could not help wondering if, somehow, she was reliving those long ago events. After all, she had driven this road with Billy the night they tried to escape, only to be dragged back from the pier in old Dedankalus's car. Billy had ridden just ahead of her in the back seat of Father's station wagon.

She remembered Father driving exceedingly slowly all the way back to the house, sometimes stopping for minutes at a time, then jerking forward again. She had had the feeling, she said, that something terrible, something truly evil, was taking place in that station wagon. And she strained her eyes in the dark for any sign of movement. But there was none. The car would stop and then creep forward.

In the morning, we found him dead.

"How did they know?" she wailed. "How did they know?"

I shrugged helplessly and burst into tears at the sight of Billy's body slumped over the rifle.

When we pulled into the drive of the Waring place finally, the boys leaped out and ran ahead, rested, excited to be out of the car, taking turns pretending to be accident victims needing an ambulance. We shook hands with Dedankalus and told him to give us a few hours to look around.

I went to switch on the lights and returned to find Darla gone, the boys shying rocks at the water just past the line of contorted cedars. When I was a boy, the place had seemed big enough to get lost in, much too big for us. Now it startled me how little had changed, with the smell of decay everywhere, the crumbling gatehouse, the dried-up lawn and peeling paint and the ivy growing across the windows so that the rooms were suffused with a dim, green glow.

I thought, if there are ghosts, this is somehow what they must feel, as though they inhabited a reality more vivid, familiar and substantial than themselves.

I called Darla's name and went hunting over the grounds, past the tennis courts and octagonal garage and through the greenhouses now open to the elements and littered with shattered glass. Old Dedankalus's cactus pots still crowded the wooden tables, but nothing grew in them. The earth was desiccated, cracked.

They had buried Billy in a regular graveyard, not on the grounds. We weren't allowed to attend the funeral. Darla stole a bottle of bourbon from Father's cabinet, and we drank it in her room till night came and we knew everything was finished.

"How did they know?" she asked again and again. Though I believe the truth had already begun to clarify itself like muddy water gradually becoming clear as the sediment settles.

I found Darla in the morgue, now used as a store room for years of accumulated summer furniture, boxes of Christmas ornaments abandoned when we no longer put up a tree, stacks of Father's business records in exploding file boxes, trunks bursting with childhood toys and old photographs—all the detritus of a family we no longer remembered, no longer felt part of. She was leafing through a photograph album, which she held up as I walked in.

"Do you remember the puppy you had when you were three?"

I shook my head, feeling the weight of all the things I did not remember. She jabbed a finger at a snapshot of a smiling toddler struggling to hold a miniature dachshund in his pale arms. The dog had a sharp, wet nose and charming little eyes fixed knowingly on the boy's face.

"You only had him a couple of months. Daddy couldn't stand the noise and the mess."

"I don't remember," I said. "I look happy, though."

"Mama called him Romeo. But you couldn't say that. When you said it, it came out Vemeo." Her face had gone dead, expressionless, yet there was a steely desperation underneath, a determination to assert the truth at any cost.

I handed her back the album and began rummaging, finding a torn Bloomingdale's bag with our remaining croquet mallets and, at the bottom, the plaque that once held a chip of wood from the True Cross. Someone had sawn through the plastic to remove the relic. There was only an empty space where it had been.

"You must remember the night Romeo shit on your bed and Daddy kicked him around the room till he couldn't walk and then said he was taking him to the vet. It was after midnight. We never saw him again."

"I don't remember much," I said.

But I did remember the morning Billy Dedankalus died.

It was in this very room, the place of the dead, that we found him, purely by chance, since no one yet knew he was missing, and we only came here to hide out. It was our secret place, which, of course, Billy knew.

He had shot himself with the gardener's rifle, nestling the muzzle in the soft V of flesh just beneath his chin and firing up through the back of his mouth into the brain.

Blood had drained from his throat and mouth, soaking his t-shirt and jeans and pooling beneath the chair. But his face was unmarked and bore, partly because of the wide-open eyes, an expression of mild astonishment.

Darla dropped to her knees in the blood and gagged and tried to embrace him, and he fell over onto the floor, awkwardly, like a marionette. The impact of his fall compressed his chest, forcing air suddenly out his lungs, so that he sighed, or seemed to sigh.

Or maybe this was my imagination.

Darla's teeth began to chatter, an inhuman rattle. And I noticed that she was staring into the shadows beyond the x-ray frame.

There seemed to be something there, a shadow within a shadow, a trace of movement.

I don't know now what I saw. But everything had taken on an air of seeming, and what was real was Billy and the blood and the details of the hole in his throat which I have never forgotten—the jagged line of skin, yellow fat, darkening clots of blood, that awful exhalation of breath, as though he had been waiting for us.

I was only thirteen.

I went down beside Darla and tried to touch her, not to comfort her but to try to stop that chattering, which I knew would drive me insane. She mistook my motive and grasped my hand and began to weep, smearing me with blood.

From where I knelt I could finally see what she saw, the gaunt face in the shadows, the pale dome of the woman's forehead above her charcoal eyebrows, her fevered eyes darting with anguish, tears glittering on her cheeks, her silent chest heaving.

As soon as I saw her, she began to fade, her eyes fixed on Billy. Love and pain fused in that look. I have never been able to separate them. There is no such thing as love without betrayal. You hold the thing that kills you as close as you can and watch it die, all the time whispering, Love me, love me, don't go.

Darla took my hand and pressed it.

But her voice was harsh, that tone of desperation. It rasped out the words.

I said nothing. I meant my silence as a confession. Her words were like a burst of light. I held the empty plaque in my hands. Her words went through me like blue fire. Choked with sadness, I remembered how she had looked with her smouldering hair and burned bedclothes.

But I quickly realized that whatever I had to confess was old news. Now she was going to die, and the story had taken on fresh meaning because, like Billy Dedankalus, her boys would always be alone.

We were in the morgue, and I suddenly felt like the only living creature in a room littered with corpses. I stumbled about among the corpses looking for signs of life.

I said nothing—more confession, it was pouring out of me, meaningless. I wanted to weep, but it came out a dry sob. For ages, I have been all dried up inside. I thought what I always think, How am I going to get through this? How am I going to endure such pain? It seems impossible that a human being could suffer this much and live. And just when you think you can't stand any more, it gets worse and you discover new possibilities of living.

This is the reason I have never owned a gun. There is only one person I would shoot and, like my father, I have always found it easy to kill.

Telling it, remembering the intensity, it seems impossible that we could get out of that room alive, that the ordinary world would let us back in. But Darla finally let go of my hand, and her voice began to return to normal. And the past receded until it was nothing but a presence and a dull ache, like a tumor.

I dropped the plaque to the floor. We had somehow agreed to take nothing, to leave everything for the next owner to deliver to the holocaust.

On the stairway, Darla paused. We were brother and sister again, leaving the intolerable splendour of the scene in the morgue for a lesser ecstasy.

She said, "I haven't seen them for years."

I nodded.

"But Lonny does. They're in his dreams."

I shuddered and glanced back, praying for a sight that would sear my eyelids shut forever, but the room was empty.

There was nothing there, nothing as terrible as the future.

LANNAN SELECTIONS

The Lannan Foundation, located in Santa Fe, New Mexico, is a family foundation whose funding focuses on special cultural projects and ideas which promote and protect cultural freedom, diversity, and creativity.

The literary aspect of Lannan's cultural program supports the creation and presentation of exceptional English-language literature and develops a wider audience for poetry, fiction, and nonfiction.

Since 1990, the Lannan Foundation has supported Dalkey Archive Press projects in a variety of ways, including monetary support for authors, audience development programs, and direct funding for the publication of the Press's books.

In the year 2000, the Lannan Selections Series was established to promote both organizations' commitment to the highest expressions of literary creativity. The Foundation supports the publication of this series of books each year, and works closely with the Press to ensure that these books will reach as many readers as possible and achieve a permanent place in literature. Authors whose works have been published as Lannan Selections include: Ishmael Reed, Stanley Elkin, Ann Quin, Nicholas Mosley, William Eastlake, and David Antin, among others.

SELECTED DALKEY ARCHIVE PAPERBACKS

PIERRE ALBERT-BIROT, *Grabinoulor.*
YUZ ALESHKOVSKY, *Kangaroo.*
FELIPE ALFAU, *Chromos.*
  Locos.
  Sentimental Songs.
ALAN ANSEN, *Contact Highs: Selected Poems 1957-1987.*
DAVID ANTIN, *Talking.*
DJUNA BARNES, *Ladies Almanack.*
  Ryder.
JOHN BARTH, *LETTERS.*
  Sabbatical.
ANDREI BITOV, *Pushkin House.*
LOUIS PAUL BOON, *Chapel Road.*
ROGER BOYLAN, *Killoyle.*
CHRISTINE BROOKE-ROSE, *Amalgamemnon.*
BRIGID BROPHY, *In Transit.*
GERALD L. BRUNS,
  Modern Poetry and the Idea of Language.
GABRIELLE BURTON, *Heartbreak Hotel.*
MICHEL BUTOR,
  Portrait of the Artist as a Young Ape.
JULIETA CAMPOS, *The Fear of Losing Eurydice.*
ANNE CARSON, *Eros the Bittersweet.*
CAMILO JOSÉ CELA, *The Hive.*
LOUIS-FERDINAND CÉLINE, *Castle to Castle.*
  London Bridge.
  North.
  Rigadoon.
HUGO CHARTERIS, *The Tide Is Right.*
JEROME CHARYN, *The Tar Baby.*
MARC CHOLODENKO, *Mordechai Schamz.*
EMILY HOLMES COLEMAN, *The Shutter of Snow.*
ROBERT COOVER, *A Night at the Movies.*
STANLEY CRAWFORD, *Some Instructions to My Wife.*
ROBERT CREELEY, *Collected Prose.*
RENÉ CREVEL, *Putting My Foot in It.*
RALPH CUSACK, *Cadenza.*
SUSAN DAITCH, *L.C.*
  Storytown.
NIGEL DENNIS, *Cards of Identity.*
PETER DIMOCK,
  A Short Rhetoric for Leaving the Family.
COLEMAN DOWELL, *The Houses of Children.*
  Island People.
  Too Much Flesh and Jabez.
RIKKI DUCORNET, *The Complete Butcher's Tales.*
  The Fountains of Neptune.
  The Jade Cabinet.
  Phosphor in Dreamland.
  The Stain.
WILLIAM EASTLAKE, *The Bamboo Bed.*
  Castle Keep.
  Lyric of the Circle Heart.
STANLEY ELKIN, *Boswell: A Modern Comedy.*
  Criers and Kibitzers, Kibitzers and Criers.

  The Dick Gibson Show.
  The Franchiser.
  The MacGuffin.
  The Magic Kingdom.
  Mrs. Ted Bliss.
  The Rabbi of Lud.
  Van Gogh's Room at Arles.
ANNIE ERNAUX, *Cleaned Out.*
LAUREN FAIRBANKS, *Muzzle Thyself.*
  Sister Carrie.
LESLIE A. FIEDLER,
  Love and Death in the American Novel.
FORD MADOX FORD, *The March of Literature.*
JANICE GALLOWAY, *Foreign Parts.*
  The Trick Is to Keep Breathing.
WILLIAM H. GASS, *The Tunnel.*
  Willie Masters' Lonesome Wife.
ETIENNE GILSON, *The Arts of the Beautiful.*
  Forms and Substances in the Arts.
C. S. GISCOMBE, *Giscome Road.*
  Here.
KAREN ELIZABETH GORDON, *The Red Shoes.*
PATRICK GRAINVILLE, *The Cave of Heaven.*
HENRY GREEN, *Blindness.*
  Concluding.
  Doting.
  Nothing.
JIŘÍ GRUŠA, *The Questionnaire.*
JOHN HAWKES, *Whistlejacket.*
AIDAN HIGGINS, *Flotsam and Jetsam.*
ALDOUS HUXLEY, *Antic Hay.*
  Crome Yellow.
  Point Counter Point.
  Those Barren Leaves.
  Time Must Have a Stop.
GERT JONKE, *Geometric Regional Novel.*
DANILO KIŠ, *A Tomb for Boris Davidovich.*
TADEUSZ KONWICKI, *A Minor Apocalypse.*
  The Polish Complex.
ELAINE KRAF, *The Princess of 72nd Street.*
JIM KRUSOE, *Iceland.*
EWA KURYLUK, *Century 21.*
DEBORAH LEVY, *Billy and Girl.*
JOSÉ LEZAMA LIMA, *Paradiso.*
OSMAN LINS, *Avalovara.*
  The Queen of the Prisons of Greece.
ALF MAC LOCHLAINN, *The Corpus in the Library.*
  Out of Focus.
RON LOEWINSOHN, *Magnetic Field(s).*
D. KEITH MANO, *Take Five.*
BEN MARCUS, *The Age of Wire and String.*
WALLACE MARKFIELD, *Teitelbaum's Window.*
  To an Early Grave.
DAVID MARKSON, *Reader's Block.*
  Springer's Progress.
  Wittgenstein's Mistress.

FOR A FULL LIST OF PUBLICATIONS, VISIT:
www.dalkeyarchive.com

SELECTED DALKEY ARCHIVE PAPERBACKS

FOR A FULL LIST OF PUBLICATIONS, VISIT:
www.dalkeyarchive.com